PRINCESS OF THE POMEGRANATE MOON

PRINCESS OF THE POMEGRANATE MOON

EMILY WYNNE

BALANCE OF SEVEN
Newport, VT

For information, contact:
Balance of Seven
www.balanceofseven.com
info@balanceofseven.com

Cover Design by Rue Sparks
www.ruesparks.com

Line Editing by Nyri A. Bakkalian

Formatting and Proofreading by TNT Editing
www.theodorentinker.com/TNTEditing

Publisher's Cataloging-in-Publication Data

Names: Wynne, Emily, 1983- . | Bruno, Emily Wynne, 1983- .
Title: Princess of the pomegranate moon / Emily Wynne.
Description: Newport, VT : Balance of Seven, 2023. | Summary: On a dying Earth marked by fear and uncertainty, a trans priestess and sorceress disregards ancient warnings to seek the truth of her identity. She endeavors to uncover what she needs to become whole, without losing herself to the Mountain.
Identifiers: LCCN 2023949773 | ISBN 9781947012264 (pbk.) | ISBN 9781947012271 (ebook) | ISBN 9780991083992 (itchio ebook)
Subjects: LCSH: Magic - Fiction. | Self-realization - Fiction. | Mythology - Fiction. | Fairies - Fiction. | Environmental degradation - Fiction. | Transgender women - Fiction. | Women priests - Fiction. | BISAC: FICTION / Fantasy / General. | FICTION / LGBTQ+ / Transgender. | FICTION / Fairy Tales, Folk Tales, Legends & Mythology.
Classification: LCC PS3623.Y55 P75 2023 (print) | PS3623.Y55 (ebook) | DDC 813 W–dc23
LC record available at https://lccn.loc.gov/2023949773

27 26 25 24 23   1 2 3 4 5

To my mother and father,
To my brother,
To Mom-Mom and Pop-Pop,
And to Vera:
Vivāmus, mea Lesbia, atque amemus.

CONTENTS

✳ | ✳

THE DANCER

The season was uncertain, as it always was, but the stars and the angle of the sun showed it was late in the year, and a cool wind blew over the earth and rustled the sparse grass in the lands beyond the forest. Shadows loomed over the treetops from the hills—long, crisscross shadows from things not quite like branches. Few now living had seen what cast the shadows up close, for of those from older generations brave or foolish enough to follow the witch lights through the woods, few had returned with the wits to describe what they saw. Those who were able had been unwilling to speak of it, nor even of whether their reluctance was out of fear or due to some occulted prohibition set upon them.

Though the shadows rose above the trees, they fell rarely upon the borderlands on the near side of the forest or the rooftops of the nearby town. The people disagreed whether this was a blessing or a more fearful omen, for the shadows were obscured by the greater shadow of the Mountain. It stood high above the valley and trees, above the hills and shadows, as tall as heaven and old as the earth, and it was called only the Mountain, for it knew no other name. From the town, at certain points of the year, the sun seemed to circle the Mountain in the sky, rising in the east to its left and setting in the west to its right.

In this late age of the world, only those skilled in sorcery and the hidden arts of subtle omens had a chance at telling the seasons rightly. Though the sun's yearly course was easy enough to follow, the winds and crops were fickle and prone to secret fates, and the moon itself was a mystery, its phases obscure and unreadable, the arcane crescents it traced in the night intelligible to only the most skilled astronomers.

Still, it had at last become clear enough that the Season of Shadows fell over the valley, a time when mists obscured the earth and clouds hung heavy in the air. The sun was weak and thin, too feeble to tell the time of year, but the whispers of the air were unmistakable to the learned, and the moon grew full enough for all to see. In the evening, the sky became a deep and crystal shade of violet, the stars glittered like gems in the night, and though the moon shone white, it was crowned all about with a ring of color, a rainbow prism through the mists that the people of the valley knew heralded the coming of Summer's End.

So the clouds gathered overhead and darkened wide swaths of the little village of Tudur, a quiet settlement in the fields bordering the forest. The people went abroad in the narrow stone streets only rarely as the Season of Shadows came, and then mostly during daylight. But on this day, as evening approached and the red tint of the setting sun cast long, fearsome shadows down the alleys, a crowd gathered in the square—an unfamiliar sight at this time of year. They encircled a dancer, straining above each other to see her, thoughts drawn for a moment away from their homes and their families, their labors and their fears, strung along like streamers in the wake of the dancer's grace. More than a few tossed coins, flowers, trinkets, and the occasional folded slip of paper bearing messages hastily scrawled in shame and hope, though most knew the dancer was little likely to give them a glance.

The dance drew on, and the performer—a woman of beauty unmatched by either the women or men of the town—showed little intention of stopping. Her skin was soft and smooth, her movements smoother still, and her brightly colored dress and rainbow shawls flowed and spun in her wake. Bangles and strings of beads rattled on her arms, and her nimble hands tapped gently but resonantly upon a small hand drum. With the tympanum, she kept a hypnotic beat that she followed in her dance and to which the people lost themselves. They nearly abandoned their reason, flowing along, clapping their hands, lost in the intricate labyrinth of sound the dancer conjured and weaved in the air with her drum.

The crowd grew larger the longer she danced, drawing in more folk who heard the rapidly spreading word of the performer in the square. Her costume was clearly meant to take advantage of this attention. Her dress was a bright, cutting purple of a rare dye, with a short skirt that spun around her knees. She waved turquoise and yellow sashes around her shoulders seductively, and her thick wild hair flew about her, unnaturally dyed the deep blue green of the pine trees.

Stuck in a patch of dirt between broken flagstones stood a short sword with a mirrored white blade and a silver crescent guard like the moon on the hilt. The sword marked the center of her dance, as the polestar in the tail of the Great Dragon above tethered the whirling planets that had begun to shine in the sky.

The dancer spun, and the crowd gasped with a clamorous mixture of amazement and fear as small fires bloomed in the air all around her. The floating, spinning flames cast an unnatural yellow-green light over the square, which reflected in the dancer's heavy-lidded eyes, making them flash in the growing dark of the evening. In this eerie cast, the ears that poked gently out of her hair seemed to come to slight, faunish points. The magic of the lights could be heard as well as seen; like strange, distant flutes, the lights bent the wind with an unearthly hum, accompanied by the beat of the tympanum.

Whispers hissed all around the crowd as the dancer whirled.

"She casts witch lights, like those in the woods."

"She's a mage."

"She's no traveler; she's a fairy," called a voice clear and sudden.

Perhaps she was a fae crept out of the forest on the eve of the Season of Shadows or a changeling left in the mortal world. Perhaps she was only a dancer, wandering into town for someplace to sleep warmly after days on the road.

No matter the truth, she laughed brightly and bowed theatrically, luxuriating in the impression she made.

As the dancer rose from her bow, a boy caught her eye. He stood right at the front of the crowd, head never turning from her as she danced, paying no attention to the rest of the audience. He smiled when she twirled with a particularly impressive spin, a growing expression of wonder on his face, his eyes lighting up whenever she cast a bright spell in the dark of the evening. She was used to such wonder from children and different expressions of attention from older boys and young men. But this enthralled youth looked to be about the dancer's own age, and the innocence and sincere joy that lit his face brought a smile to her own. She cast a light in the shape of a flower toward him, and he laughed and flinched back when it sparkled out where he stood.

Her dance drew to a close, the light and eerie music of her spells fading away as her body completed her improvised choreography almost automatically while betraying no sign of her thoughts. She graced the audience with a flourish as a few applauded, while others murmured lowly, wondering about the magic this woman brought to the town.

For her own part, the dancer cast kisses into the air, drew the sword from the earth, lifted it above her head, and—

Vanished. Not behind a curtain but into thin air.

Hushed murmurs turned to astonished gasps, and the thin applause rose to a clamor from those more delighted than afraid. Meanwhile, the dancer stepped silently and invisibly through ethereal mists to a corner of the square covered by trees.

The townsfolk lingered to talk and argue about the nature of this newcomer. Their voices carried far in the night, until one by two, they reluctantly retreated to their homes or the tavern.

Tonight, the moon grew huge and strange and drew around itself a cloak of clouds shimmering in a rainbow halo. It was the Pomegranate Moon, so common during this cloudy, rainy season—the same moon that had witnessed the tears that fell so long ago. Unseen by the villagers, the dancer looked up at the sky through the tree branches and the mists of her invisibility, and though the light shimmered and wavered through the fog between dimensions, it nonetheless emboldened her weary heart.

On the periphery of the square sat a high old house, whose overhanging second story nestled among the leafy branches of the surrounding trees. Inside, the atmosphere was warm and bright, the hearth and lanterns casting an orange glow that spilled out the windows into the evening. People flocked in out of the night, always leaving the door ajar, and they huddled in groups of friends around tables, their arguments lowered to a simmer or stirred to a heat by their ale.

So engaged were the tavern-goers in discussion of the uncanny girl in the square that few noticed the faint shimmer in a corner away from the lanterns or the slender figure in a dark wide-hooded jacket who slipped out of the shadows and made for the bar. In a hushed voice heeded by none but the barkeep, the figure procured a mug of ale and fell back to a corner booth away from the hearth and the light and the people. The figure sank into a seat and drank beneath the deep, shadowy hood.

"It isn't attractive to brood," said a quiet voice from beside the table.

The hooded figure looked up from the ale in her cup. Despite the shadow cloaking her face, gray eyes glinted clearly in the dim candlelight as a lock of blue-green hair fell across her forehead. "And if I'm trying not to attract attention to myself?"

A woman stood before her, leaning on the table, her smooth shoulders hunched within the drooping straps of her dress. Grinning, she sat uninvited beside the hooded girl. "Why shouldn't you? You're the dancer from the square, aren't you? You had half the town gasping at your every footfall earlier, and with good reason. You should be flattered."

"If I assure you I am, will you leave me alone? I'm not in the mood for company tonight."

"I respect that," the woman replied. "But I should warn you, if I leave, it'll surely only be a matter of time before a pack of rough young men notice you all alone and decide you would make welcome company. Your mood would be far worse then, I promise you. The men of Tudur aren't particularly . . . interesting."

"I'm more than capable of taking care of myself, but I appreciate your point."

"I'm sure you are," the woman said. "I'm Astra."

The dancer eyed her curiously, sighed, and pushed her hood back enough to reveal her face in the dim tavern light. "My name is Elsinore."

"And where do you come from, Elsinore?" Astra leaned in and playfully put her arms around her new friend's neck. "From somewhere else in the river valley? From the lands beyond?" Grinning slightly, she leaned in close to Elsinore's ear and whispered, "Or from somewhere . . . else?"

"Somewhere else?" Elsinore asked with a tangible lack of curiosity, almost to be polite.

Astra giggled. "Surely you know what they're saying about you? That you come from a place not far from here at all, but somehow, at the same time, farther than anywhere on earth."

"I don't understand what you mean at all," Elsinore responded quietly, looking only at the glass before her. She rotated her drink slowly on the tabletop with her fingertips, head down, her eyes only distantly considering the dark liquid within.

"From the forest," Astra said. "You must have passed it on your way into town. Unless that's where you came from to begin with. The forest and the strange place of mounds beyond the forest, at the base of the great mountain?"

Elsinore smiled at last, very slightly. "I'm sure you'd know if I came from that place. Don't your people here in Tudur do business with your neighbors beyond the forest?"

Astra laughed sharply, loud enough that Elsinore feared she would draw attention to their table in the corner. But as her eyes scanned the room, she saw that the others in the bar kept to their own conversations, still yelling their arguments or slamming their mugs on the tabletops; they paid a woman's laughter no mind, if they heard her at all.

"Your humor is very dry," Astra said. "I like that. Or at least, I presume you're joking and you're not truly ignorant of the forest and the place beyond."

"You're right on all counts," Elsinore said. "I'm not from around here at all, but I have heard a little. That there are creatures in the forest, dangers best left undisturbed. And that strange people live in the mounds, who follow laws the rest of us cannot fathom. People who aren't men or women at all but who townsfolk simply call the fae."

"The People of the Mounds," Astra said, clearly discomforted by the name Elsinore spoke. "No one sees them or speaks to them, but a few poor travelers hear their whispering voices if they approach too near the edge of the woods and come back claiming to have heard every manner of wild story. A few even say the voices speak of things that have yet to happen.

"Folks have also been saying that, more than just a fairy, you're a changeling—an unearthly creature left here years ago by the dwellers in the mounds in a mundane body, such as that of a simple country boy. But your true nature gradually revealed itself, shifting your body over time into that of an unearthly beautiful woman so you could prey on the boys in our good town and make them the same sort of creature as yourself."

Astra smiled and leaned in. "Is that the case? With your wild hair and dress and strange accent, what kind of woman are you?"

She looked deep into Elsinore's eyes, and both women breathed steadily and evenly. Neither spoke for a long moment that dragged on in its tension, before at last one of them laughed. It took Elsinore an awkward moment to realize the laughter had been her own.

"I'm the kind of woman who likes to dance and tell fortunes but to otherwise be left alone," Elsinore said quietly. "I came by the Northern Road and could only see the mountain in the distance. I'd been warned of the forest and the People beyond and didn't wish to risk tempting the fates by traveling so near the mysterious place alone."

Astra gestured at the short sword with the moon hilt that leaned against the traveler's bag. "You worry, even with a weapon like the one you carry?"

"I'd have thought someone who knows so much about the People of the Mounds would know the stories," Elsinore said. "About how the People are impervious to ordinary weapons. How stone and bronze pass through their bodies as if they were air. How wood grows from their heads like horns and leaves flutter from their arms like feathers, and gold accumulates on their skin and soaks into their bodies like water. They fear only wrought iron, whether spikes, bars, fences, or chains—even simple shovels and spades can cause them harm and drive them away."

Elsinore shook her head. "No, my mother gave me

the sword to protect myself from more earthly threats. I have a dagger, cold iron blessed on an altar to my Goddess, that I hope can protect me if the stories are true."

Astra smiled knowingly, and Elsinore felt her eyes scrape over her, from shoulder to fingertip. Astra's gaze lingered on the ring Elsinore wore on her middle finger, silver twisted decoratively around a tiny mirror. Elsinore smiled and looked into the ring.

When the light reflecting off the mirror dimmed, she looked up, afraid of being interrupted by yet more locals curious about her nature. It was the barkeep, a young man whose fat, muscular belly and broad arms gave the unmistakable impression of strength. He bore a tray with several mugs of ale and plates of food.

Laughing, Astra touched the startled woman's arm. "Elsinore, you've already met Rosario. My partner."

The young barkeep nodded pleasantly at the introduction. "You've barely touched your ale, so I didn't think you needed more. But I thought you could use something to eat." He set the tray down as he took a seat on the other side of the table. The plates all bore pieces of roasted chicken.

"Thank you, but I'm sorry. I don't eat meat." Elsinore self-consciously sipped from her glass of ale.

Astra narrowed her eyes teasingly. "It's ever less clear whether you're a woman or a fairy. Tell me, do you survive on flower petals and dew?"

"Bread," replied Elsinore, looking into her ale. "Root vegetables, fruit, bean curd. All manner of things, really, but animal flesh. Other creatures shouldn't have to die for me to eat."

Rosario shrugged. "Sorry, I didn't think. More for me, though."

"So, you're a priestess, then?" Astra asked. "A traveling mendicant maybe, dancing and telling fortunes in exchange for offerings to that goddess of yours?"

"Something like that." Elsinore rotated her glass on the table, running her finger along the rim.

"Do you see your goddess only through ecstatic dance and self-deprivation? Or do you ever use other methods?" Astra reached into a pocket in the folds of her skirt and drew out a pipe and a pouch tied tight with string. She packed the bowl tightly with weed from the pouch—which smelled pungently of cannabis—and then searched in the folds of her skirt with one hand, evidently for a match.

Grinning, Elsinore snapped the fingers of the hand on which she wore the mirrored ring. In the air just above her fingers flickered a tiny flame—the same she cast with the spell of colored lights that spun around her while she danced. It was only a simple cantrip, a little spell Elsinore could always remember, but Astra laughed quietly, eyes widening.

Leaning in, her lips on the mouthpiece of the pipe, Astra drew in smoke as she lit the cannabis with the magic flame. She exhaled thoughtfully, then smiled as Elsinore produced a pipe from the folds of her scarves. It was long and narrow, a straight stem of reed connecting a metal mouthpiece and a tiny bowl about the size of a fingertip.

Astra passed her the pouch of weed, and Elsinore prepared her pipe, lighting it with another witch flame. Taking a long drag, she blew a long, thin stream of smoke over the others' heads. Then she held the pouch out to Rosario, who paused in devouring his meal to hold up his hand in refusal.

"Keep it," Astra told her. "I didn't toss you any coins for your dance."

Smiling, Elsinore slipped it into her bag, which she shouldered, along with her sword, as she stood from the table and bowed. "Thank you for the company and for your hospitality, but I've decided I need to walk in the night air and think by myself in the quiet."

"And what if you run into any unappealing characters?" Astra asked. "Will your sword keep you out of trouble or lead you into it?"

Elsinore grinned. "I think all of that sort in this town are spending their night here in the bar." She indicated the tables, which had grown no less rowdy.

"Well, if you return, there will be a clean room ready for you," Rosario said. "You're welcome to stay as long as you're in town."

"That's very generous. Perhaps I'll return once the ale has quieted the company down. Or perhaps I'll find other accommodations."

Smirking deviously, Astra bowed her head, and Rosario waved good-naturedly before returning to his dish. Elsinore retreated out the door into the night, hood up, sword hilt over her shoulder, and pipe held delicately along her finger down at her side.

＊ 2 ＊

JHE BOY IN THE
LIBRARY

Outside, the air was clear and restless. Elsinore pulled her wide hood down from her face, letting it fall to her shoulders, and a breeze gently blew her hair over her eyes. Taking another drag of the cannabis, she inhaled more deeply than before and exhaled a cloud of smoke that shone sparkling and white in the strong light of the moon rising over the tree by the square. She watched the smoke drift in the wind and blow away in a spiral through the branches. She wandered along a cobblestone path that wound through the village, around buildings and down alleys. Finally, far from the square and tavern, she stopped and leaned against the trunk of a tree, her eyes on the moon and her mind reaching out.

She considered the sky, the earth, and this town. She considered her breath, white in the moonlight, mingling with the air and leaves. Her breathing, in and out, subconscious and continuous in its rhythm, was part of the deeper rhythm of the world around her: the halo of multicolored light around the moon, the pale leaves of the trees, the smoke from the pipe swirling up into the air.

When the weed had burned out, Elsinore became aware she had been meditating—or at the very least, she had been drifting away from herself. Whether she'd been meditating or dissociating, she felt calmer.

Of course, by now, she was probably a little high, which might have helped. Tapping out the ash from the bowl, she tucked the pipe in the scarves around her waist.

She'd been on the road for months; had it been so long since she'd met one of her sisters, a woman like herself? Priestesses of the Goddess were known throughout the valley, but she'd traveled far afield from the temple on the river. It had been a long journey to Tudur in the shadow of the Mountain. She'd grown lonely; while the aura of mystery she tried so hard to cultivate protected her, by the same token, it kept her more distant than ever from the people she met.

Taking stock of her surroundings, Elsinore realized how far she must have wandered from the square, as if her mind had been leading her in search of the secrets the town was keeping from her. The place she'd ended up in was clear in the moonlight, buildings and trees blue under the misty sky. Timber-built houses lined a cobblestone circle, which was dull and dry in the autumn wind. Two deciduous trees stood on either side of the circle, tall and old. Scattered throughout the village, these trees were striking, the only large trees Elsinore had seen growing in the region, outside the forest at the foot of the Mountain, which she had only seen from a distance.

She stood beneath one of the two trees, delighting in the dance of the leaves and clatter of hanging wooden signs in the night air. Beneath the branches of the tree opposite Elsinore was a sign she couldn't make out; it wouldn't hang still, and the leaves obscured it as it twisted in the wind.

She started across the circle, hair blowing in the breeze. As she walked out into the open moonlight, a voice echoed across the circle.

"That's her! The fairy girl!"

She stopped, a sharp heat burning in her chest. Two young men had emerged from an alley behind a dark house, rough-looking and lean.

"My friend missed your dance! Dance for him now, fairy girl!"

Elsinore's initial instinct was to run, to try to find her way back to the tavern, where Astra and Rosario at least might be willing to help her. But she didn't know how the rest of the crowd in the tavern would turn, and more than anything, she wanted to avoid a scene.

All she wanted was to vanish, but she wasn't prepared to cast the spell again so soon. She knew other spells, magic more potent, but she was reluctant to use any magic that would truly hurt anyone unless it was a necessity.

Closer now, the taller of the two men drew a long, curved knife as he stalked across the flagstones. The other man drew something from his pocket and whipped it at Elsinore; it missed without her having to duck and glanced off the trunk behind her. It glittered in the moonlight as it fell away, and she could see it was a coin.

"There, I paid you, didn't I? Dance for me!" The man with the coin purse began to mime a hideous drunken dance as the one with the knife drew nearer.

Elsinore's heart raced, even as her feet refused to. She stood her ground out of uncharacteristic confidence, misplaced or no, but she couldn't have denied that she was also more than a little frozen in fear.

As the attacker's knife waved threateningly, Elsinore hit upon a desperate hope to save herself. She drew her sword, its leaf-shaped blade flashing in the moonlight, brighter than the ruffian's worn dagger. It almost seemed to absorb the light and cast it back like drops of dew, though the man showed no sign of being put off by the short blade.

With her other hand, which bore the mirror ring, Elsinore snapped her fingers, and a fireball the size of a sunfruit erupted in the air above her palm. The attacker stopped, taken aback by what he had probably assumed would be easy prey, and his ale-borne courage flagged as she gazed deep into his eyes.

Appearing to steel himself, the man tightened his grip on his dagger and started forward again, but Elsinore was poised to react. Sword held at her side, she hurled the fireball at the man's feet, where it struck the earth and flashed brightly, burning a pile of old, dry leaves from the wide tree behind her. The man jumped back, dropped his dagger, and turned to run, trying and failing to catch up to his compatriot—who had started to back away at the first sight of the fire spell and was now far ahead and nearly out of sight.

Elsinore looked around hesitantly. She wasn't confident she had driven them off for good, and she feared the fireball and their voices would have drawn more out of the buildings to come look. She was no longer particularly well hidden, and she wasn't eager to run into any more locals.

The circle of houses she stood in was clear. Though many windows were lit, it seemed everyone had already taken shelter from the night in their homes or the tavern.

The wind had died down enough that Elsinore now had a clear view of the building by the tree on the other side of the square. Her heart sang a bright little note when she saw an artistic rendering of an open book, its pages flapping as if in the wind, under an inkwell and stylus. It was a library, and the lights were still warm in the windows, yellow and inviting against the darkness of the night and the silver-blue light of the moon.

Lifting her hood around her face again, she hurried to the door, desperate to get out of the open and someplace safe. Before entering, she looked around again, flying around the corner of the building and back, scanning the alleys and peering into the shadows, making certain neither the men or others like them were around. Once satisfied she was alone and as safe as possible in the circumstances, she turned to go in.

The door opened when she pushed it, and the scene inside was just as she had imagined it would be. Not as familiar as the library at home, or as urbane as the great archive of tall shelves bearing scrolls and codices in the temple where she had studied, it was homey, warm, and inviting—and most importantly, quiet and empty of people. Fires burned in the hearth and lanterns on the walls, pouring light out the windows into the street. All along the walls were books on shelves of worn, sturdy, ancient wood. Wide rectangular tables were piled with more volumes, whose order Elsinore couldn't guess, leaving only a few spots open for someone to sit and read. Comfortable-looking chairs hid in the corners, between shelves, and by the fire, ready and welcoming. A second level hung above on the next story, a balcony ringing the whole room, with yet more bookshelves, interrupted only by a few closed wooden doors.

Elsinore saw a stove and some cabinets through a door on the first floor—signs of a kitchen. Did the librarian live here? Looking around, she realized it wasn't only empty of noisy townsfolk and ruffians; she saw no one at all. Was the librarian even here tonight? Was this place even supposed to be open after all?

"You were the girl causing trouble outside?" creaked out the voice of a woman from somewhere in the stacks. Elsinore drew her hood from her face and looked around rapidly, surprised. "I wondered if you might come in."

An old woman—more than old enough to be Elsinore's mother, gray-haired and bent but moving with obvious vitality—crept around the corner of a freestanding bookshelf. She wore an apron stained with ink she wiped from her fingers, and a pair of glasses she adjusted once her hands were clean enough. The eyes that peered from behind the wire frames were strong and cutting, their black pupils focused and sharpened by the lenses, and they regarded the strange girl before her suspiciously.

"Oh! Are you closing?" Elsinore asked apologetically, ignoring the accusation for fear of being thrown out. "I can return tomorrow. I was just looking for someplace quiet, and there's just so much here . . . I would love to look around."

"I was just leaving, but we'll stay open as long as my apprentice keeps it open. And he'll keep it open as long as I tell him to." The old librarian leaned over a table. "Isn't that right, young man?"

This last part was said to a boy Elsinore hadn't noticed any more than she had the woman, squatting below a table to shelve books on a lower level. Only the shaggy hair of the back of his head was visible; he looked as if he were trying not to be noticed.

"Yes, ma'am, of course," he said timidly, neither turning his head from the shelves nor standing up.

"That'll make up for his running off this afternoon to see this—person—dance." The woman turned to Elsinore, and her hand darted up, gripping the girl's chin. "Awful, noisy, distracting business, exhibitions like that," she muttered, as if Elsinore were something she were commenting on and not the person she was talking to.

"You may close up when she leaves. So long as no one else stops by in the meantime." She wheeled about the end of the banister and started up the stairs. "And Vedon? Do try to keep it down."

"Yes, mother." Turning to the woman, the boy set the pile of books he was working through down on the floor and rested his arms on them.

Elsinore watched the woman ascend and withdraw into a hallway behind one of the doors between shelves, before turning to the youth. When her eyes met his, he quickly became flustered and turned back to the shelf, busily returning to organizing the books. It soon became clear to her, though, that the books needed no organizing. The apprentice librarian was occupying himself primarily in a futile attempt not to be seen.

"You were the boy at the front of the crowd today," Elsinore said, having recognized his face. As she broke the silence that had hung over the shelves since the lady retreated upstairs, Elsinore became self-conscious of her voice. The boy must have heard her speaking just now, talking to the older woman, but now that the two of them were alone, her mind insisted her voice was just a little too deep and breathy. She wasn't usually embarrassed to sing or speak in public, though she didn't have much use for songs during her performances. Why was she so self-conscious of her voice now?

The boy smiled, and Elsinore realized she remembered more of him than just his face from the crowd tonight. His name, Vedon, was familiar. She knew it from somewhere, didn't she?

"I thought your dancing was incredible." Standing, Vedon turned a little too quickly, almost tripping, and caught himself on the edge of the table. "I've never seen a performance like that. The way you move . . ."

He trailed off, mouth agape, eyes searching the air for a word to finish the sentence before giving up and settling again on the girl's face. She squinted at him and grinned.

"Thank you for the compliment," Elsinore said. "But I'm really very sorry for troubling the both of you. I'll go so you can close up for the night. I was only looking for someplace to be alone and think. I wasn't really looking for company."

"Wait!" the boy said. "Please? I'm sorry. I've given the wrong impression. After your dance, I had hoped you'd come here. Please take all the time you want if you wish to browse and read a bit." He looked around, gestured with his arms as if to tell her that yes, there are books here. "Or if there's something you're looking for? I can help you find it."

Elsinore considered for a moment. If she was honest with herself, she knew she came into the library not to idly browse but to look for something. Books of local history, of folktales, of surveys and stories and knowledge of this place. Books, she admitted to herself, about the forest and the Mountain.

But did she want to talk about that with him? She had only this moment found the strength to admit to herself that was what she was doing; the emotional energy to verbalize it was another thing.

"I don't know. Thank you. I might look around for a bit? If I need anything, I'll say so, and thank you for offering."

She turned away from the boy's look of—disappointment? Resignation? Hurrying behind one of the stacks, she began looking over the shelves and the piles on the tables. It wasn't that she was afraid—not of the boy, at least. Of something else—the past, perhaps.

Or herself.

There were novels, romances, and stories on one wall; a pile of recipe books by the kitchen; and songs and poems of distant lands on an ornate shelf in the next room. She grabbed a book with no title on the spine but then started to wonder if it would be better to just ask after all. Or perhaps she would rather call off the search for now and go back to the tavern and try to work up the courage to come back and ask the library apprentice later.

But then she risked running into the old librarian, and talking to her seemed worse. Elsinore wondered what she had meant with those last words she'd said before retreating to her room. She was not particularly pleasant to deal with, even if the boy was awkward and shy. And he was a little cute, after all . . .

"You know, I've been thinking all night."

The boy stepped into the room, startling Elsinore. She dropped the book she had taken absently off the shelf without even reading the title. *Love Poems and Songs of Intimacy*, it said clearly on the cover, face up on the floor at her feet. She quickly scooped it up and motioned to him to go on.

"You . . . when I saw you dance, I swore you reminded me of someone. Of some . . . time. But I couldn't place it till you came in here and I heard your voice. I know you. I'm sure. I don't know how I could ever have mistaken you."

Realization shone in the boy's eyes. Elsinore hadn't seen that look much—perhaps because there were so few who had known her when she was very young—but she recognized it: the look someone would give her the moment they remembered knowing her in a very different way than she now appeared.

Opening his mouth, the boy started to say her name as he remembered it, but she leaned forward and stayed his lips with her finger.

"Elsinore," she said. "My name is Elsinore Ningala. Or Elsie."

"Elsie," he said thoughtfully. "You're beautiful. You weren't as beautiful when we were boys."

It was Elsinore's turn to give a look; she rolled her eyes, sighed, and made a show of hunching her shoulders and slouching down into one of the chairs in the corner.

"When we were children, anyway," he said, suddenly ashamed. "My name is still the same."

"Vedon," Elsinore said. "I remember us playing together. I remember . . . I remember very little, but I remember running with you in the field behind my house, near the edge of town, tumbling down the hill, helping each other stand on our heads so we could see the grass in the sky and the clouds beneath our feet . . ."

Did she really remember? She looked down at the book of love poems she still held, forgetting what it was, her mind on something nearby but decades past.

Standing, she held out the book in both hands. "Here. This is for you." Vedon took the end of the book offered to him, also with two hands. They both held it for a minute, and the boy looked at the title, then blushed a bright, deep red.

"I mean, to reshelve it." Elsinore let go, and it fell to the floor from Vedon's grip.

Blushing deeper, he scrambled down to his knees to pick it up, while Elsinore stepped back, crossed her arms, and giggled as brightly as the boy blushed.

"You can borrow it!" Vedon said suddenly, jumping back to his feet.

"What?" Elsinore asked.

"The book, the poems." Vedon closed his eyes and shook his head. "You can borrow it to read and give it back when you've finished."

Elsinore smiled. "It's all right. You don't need to explain a library to me." She took the book and slipped it into her bag. "I'd love to look around more. Your place is small, nothing like the grand temple library in Sanisa, but still lovely. It's cozy and feels like home."

Vedon gave her a look that mixed wonder with curiosity—eyes wide, eyebrow raised, and mouth halfway between agog and smile.

"You've been to Sanisa? The great city, the Jewel of the River?" he asked, barely containing himself. "Even if I hadn't recognized you, that would have been enough to prove you're not a forest fairy after all."

"The rumors that spread in this town," Elsinore said with dejected thoughtfulness. "Surely everybody in the shadow of the Mountain now thinks I'm a fairy from out of the hollow hills."

"You said your surname is Ningala? So you're from Nin, then?"

"How in the world do you know of a little village like Nin?"

"It may not be a great city like Sanisa," Vedon said, not trying to hide his overgrown pride in his own knowledge, "but I've probably read all about every village and grove in the Great River Valley. I want to travel, see the world, and feel the wind from every corner and cave of the land."

Elsinore smiled. "I'll petition the Goddess to help you do so someday. But it's growing late, and I'm tired after my journey and my dance and the trouble I narrowly avoided. I'm going to ask about a room at the tavern, so long as I can sneak past any other miscreants wandering the streets so late."

The boy's face fell, visibly dejected. "Can I see you again?"

Elsinore left that unanswered as she gathered her hood over her head and turned to go. Hadn't she come to this town looking for something? Some source for her melancholy? Had she found it, a face from her past who could tell her . . . ?

"All right," she said finally. "Tomorrow night. Meet me at the tavern at the edge of the square in the middle of town. After my performance in the evening." She started to walk out, then called back over her shoulder, "You can watch me dance again. If you like."

She pulled the door open and set off into the night, not bothering to wait for a response.

* 3 *

REMINISCENCE

The next evening, Elsinore danced to a larger crowd. Word had spread quickly around town of her last performance, and it seemed that those who had seen her the first night each returned with several friends.

Elsinore scanned the audience when she had a moment, but she could not find Vedon. She didn't know what to think. Should she be glad if he didn't show? Disappointed? Would he be waiting for her after he finished working at the library? Or was he there after all, hidden in the crowd, watching her dance as eagerly as before? It was so hard to see faces in the fading light of the evening sun. It was so hard to make a connection.

Elsinore's worry always disappeared as she danced. It was perhaps her most important spell: vanquishing the worry. Her life was her dance; one of the only times her body felt totally right was when she was moving to the rhythm she decided, to the ethereal fluting hum of the light spell, and to the beat she set on her tympanum, which she drummed on her wrists as she spun across the square. Back and forth, ebb and flow, she flirted with an audience she could feel but not see beyond the lights of her sparkling cantrips.

In brief moments of clear sight, she picked a member of the audience, their sex making no difference to her, and played with them. She wrapped them in her scarves and pulled them close, danced with them, and made them shine with her for a moment, before letting them go with a wink, to the jealousy and delight of the rest of the crowd.

Finally, Elsinore leaped off a short stone wall like a bird and, alighting on the ground, drew from nowhere the exact flower a starstruck young woman was thinking of. She swooned, falling into Elsinore's arms, and the sorceress led her with feet flying lightly across the flagstones, while the audience laughed and clapped.

But Elsinore's mind wandered. She imagined how it would feel to dance with Vedon, to pull him in closer than other partners, to feel his hips and his shoulders and his breath. She surprised herself. She found him attractive, certainly, but hadn't he seemed too boyishly passive in their lone adult interaction? Or had he? Was she only dismissing what she saw of him and painting it over with the expectation of her memory from childhood? Was she drawn to him as a man, or was she drawn only to a piece of her past and what he might be able to tell her about herself? Did she appreciate even the chance of seeing her own reflection more than the craft of the mirror's frame?

Tired from her dance and anxious about meeting Vedon when the sun went down, Elsinore fled to the room she had rented above the tavern and shut the door. She considered the chamber pot in the corner and grimaced. It was a much less elegant method than she was used to, but at least there was also a bowl of clean water and a bar of soap for washing.

Once she was finished, she cast herself into bed. She wanted a few moments of quiet, all alone save for a beloved rooster doll she had carried with her on all her travels. She pulled the doll out of her bag and gazed into its eyes. She could see herself, faintly distorted, reflected in the solid black buttons, polished like glass. She gazed until her vision swam and the rainbow feathers of its wings blurred in her vision with the soft yellow cloth of its body. Falling dramatically back onto the pillows, she clutched the doll to her breast and kissed it.

When they met, it was very late, and the moon had risen high over a land clothed in the shadows of the dying year. The two of them walked slowly around the houses on the simple cobbled streets, taking their time.

Vedon showed Elsinore parts of the scenery other visitors might miss, and other residents might overlook out of familiarity, but that she knew meant the most to him. He showed her the tree at the outskirts of town where they'd played as children, climbing and falling and making swords out of branches. He took her to the stone steps that led up to the roof of the small shrine to the local gods, where they had examined the moss in the cistern to see if they could read how it grew and played at divining the messages they imagined the gods had sent.

At last, he took her to the stone bridge across the little stream at the edge of town. The bridge curved over the water, high and arched, its inverse reflected in the water below, bright in the full moonlight. As children, they would toss sticks off the side and into the water to see which drifted under the bridge first.

Elsinore remembered these things only dimly, as if

remembering a description someone had told her long ago. The whole town was like that in her mind: dimly visible, as if through a veil, and seen clearly now in a way that didn't match up—not quite.

She felt that way about Vedon as well.

They sat on the edge of the bridge, legs dangling, as Elsinore's eyes drifted across the town, trying to recognize whatever she could.

Vedon looked not at the town but at the young woman beside him. "It must have been a very different life in the city, away from here."

"Very different, yes. Different at the temple in Sanisa on the river, but even so in Nin, the village where I grew up." Elsinore's eyes lit up as she thought of her home. "I love it there, but there are fewer forests, sadly, so things are mostly built of river clay and stone. Oh, but the buildings are so grand! Temples and halls and houses. We don't live in cottages set apart, like here; we live communally in complexes, each in our own rooms and flats. And there are pillars and statues and parks and festivals—and steps up to balconies and terraces and down into cisterns and pools."

The longer she spoke, the more animated she became, gesturing and smiling as she described it to Vedon, who she suspected would have given her his full attention no matter her attitude.

"I was raised by women from Nin," she went on. "They were mothers better than any I could have been born to. Every year or so, the three of us travel, packing our supplies and visiting neighboring towns in the valley—one of my mothers is a healer, and she travels looking for people to help. The places I've been to, the forests, the countryside, the cities—that's been more real to me than this town, where I was born. More my life. I suppose it would have to be. Wherever I went with my mothers—that's where I've always felt safe, whether at home in Nin or on the road. This place, Tudur, is barely a memory."

Elsinore grew quieter and more thoughtful as she said this. She pulled her legs up onto the bridge and hugged them to her chest, hiding her mouth behind her knees.

"After I went to live with them, my mothers never traveled back here. I once thought it was only because of the vagaries of the seasons, but eventually, I think I realized that they deliberately avoided it. Perhaps it was to spare me the grief . . ."

Elsinore stared off into the distance for a moment, then shook her head and smiled at Vedon.

"I think it's wonderful, though, this town. There's something I like about your little home above the library, in particular."

Vedon laughed. "It's nice enough there, I suppose. It's simple and quiet, and folks come to read and talk. But it's the same folks, mostly. We don't get many travelers in town, and when someone new does come through, it's rare they stop in at the library, rather than the tavern. Or sometimes they'll stop at the shrine to pay respects. Our shelves have books of local history, but I prefer the romances of people who journey far afield, going on fantastic adventures in places of mystery. I always wonder if they'd be so mysterious if I made it there, after all. My mother says it's only that the neighboring valley always looks clearer and sunnier than the one you're in, but I don't know if that's true."

"I disagree with the premise," Elsinore said, "I think the sky is nicer when it's cloudy during the day, as it is in the rainy season. I think you can be happy wherever you are, if it's what you like to begin with."

"Maybe so. I think my mother would approve of that attitude." Vedon smiled, and Elsinore stuck her tongue out and gave his arm a playful shove.

Vedon made of show of rubbing his arm. "Do you really prefer the clouds? What about sunny days and light for the crops?

"I think where I live, I've come to think of too much sunlight as a harbinger of drought and a bad crop. The rainy season is much more promising, isn't it? And I much prefer the clouds and the rain and the shade of the trees to the bright heat of the sun.

"At night, I love to see the moon and the stars. But I love the moon like it is now. At the temple where I studied, that's called the Pomegranate Moon—when thin clouds begin to draw across the sky for the season, spinning a rainbow halo around the silver light. It doesn't only happen in the Season of Shadows, but when the rain and clouds come, it's more likely."

She kicked her legs off over the edge of the bridge again and leaned back, looking up into the sky. "I don't think your mother likes me, anyway. Do the two of you live there alone?"

"For a long time, we have. My father died when I was young, so I've helped my mother at the library as well as I could. And I don't think she dislikes you; she's just cold to unfamiliar faces."

"Maybe she's justified this time," Elsinore muttered under her breath. She looked off into the dark space of the trees in the distance, into the far-off shadows under the branches and the shifting shapes in the leaves twisting in the wind. She turned to the wandering moon, and they both were quiet for some time.

"I don't know what became of my parents," she said finally.

Vedon followed her gaze out to the moon, perhaps trying to understand what she was seeing. She turned her gaze back to him to do the same. The difference between them flickered through her mind, but what specific difference she was thinking of she could not say. Was it the difference between them as man and woman? Librarian and dancer? Or was it something more metaphysical? His place as someone wholly of the mundane world and hers as . . . what, exactly? A witch? A dreamer?

A changeling?

"What happened to you?" Vedon asked.

Elsinore started a little and looked away. "What?" she replied defensively. "What do you mean?"

"Why did you leave the town? Why did you leave us? How did you come to grow up so far from here, in Nin?"

Elsinore was silent a moment. She rarely spoke of her past fully, though her mothers knew the most. She had told the story only once before, to the one who had meant the most to her heart, but . . .

This boy—he was there, Elsinore thought. *He was there before anyone.* She still wondered if there was something he could tell her about herself, about where she was from, about where she belonged.

Sighing, she looked back at him and brushed her hand against his.

"The last time you and I saw each other would have been twenty years ago," she said. "I could not have even been three years old. It was late in the year: this same time, in the Season of Shadows, and the same moon—the Pomegranate Moon. I remember the leaves and bare branches of Summer's End and the misty skies when I could not tell night from day. When I could not tell how long the days lasted.

"That autumn—the year I was found—the women

who later raised me had stayed here in Tudur. One of them, Milanda, is a fortune teller as well as a healer, and when word spread that they were in town, I wanted my fortune told—my future read by the witch. But my parents wouldn't take me to see her. They told me it was inappropriate for a child like me to take part in such strange rituals. I was heartbroken; I remember having this sense—this feeling—that there was a secret message somewhere that I was meant to hear, and that, maybe, if I could speak to a seer, they could tell me what it was.

"There wasn't much food to go around; it had been a poor, hard year, verging on famine. I learned this later because the supplies were low in the caravan Milanda had traveled in, as well. We can't trust the seasons to always bring fair harvests, as the Old Ones could. But the hope of having my fortune read had nourished my young spirit, and whatever trauma I experienced later, I think my fond memories of my parents were diminished by their refusal to take me to see the witch. Or maybe . . . maybe I never had any fond memories of my parents? Sometimes it's so hard to remember . . ."

Elsinore closed her eyes tightly and sat in silence for an unbroken moment. It was not so much to remember or recall the details as to find the courage to speak them aloud.

"One night late in the year, they said they were taking me on a trip. They dressed me as warmly as they had the means, and we walked out some miles from the town. Sometimes they carried me, and we walked so long and so far off the ancient paths that I lost where we were, but I trusted that my mother and father knew.

"We came, at last, to a forest at the edge of the great Mountain. I remember the Mountain in the distance, silhouetted against the moon. It was the same Pomegranate

Moon as this season's, and the embers in the dying sky were colored purple. In the moon that year, the Mountain glowed with shadows and wore a lunar halo about its peak, and I was afraid. Something about the sight of it—it drew me. All these years later, I see the Mountain in the back of my dreams, looming over everything, whatever else I'm doing.

"I've asked my mothers, teachers—everyone I could— what the Mountain was called and where it was, but they refused to talk to me about it. It's not even that they refused. It was more that they couldn't, as if there were some taboo placed on it, and they were too afraid of coming so near it as to speak its name, even while in a place far away.

"My parents led me into the forest, and I remember thinking they were looking for something. They took me to a grove of immense trees, larger than the others; as a child, I imagined them to be the oldest trees in the forest. They sat me on a little root, and they spoke to me. They had been silent this whole journey, even when I asked where we were going, but they spoke to me then."

Elsinore paused. There were tears in her eyes, and they fell softly down her cheeks as she continued.

"My father . . . my father struck me, and I can't remember what he said, but I remember he called me a changeling and said I'd taken his son away and replaced him. My mother—" Elsinore choked back a sob. "I think she stayed his hand from drawing a knife, saying I was only a child. 'He's' only a child. 'My little boy,' she said. I wanted so badly to reach out to her, for her to hold me, but I couldn't move. It was so terrible; it was like I couldn't process that it was real. I didn't react at all. I didn't reach for my mother; I didn't cry. I only stared at them, my mouth and eyes dry and my mind empty of any reaction. As a grown woman, I imagine what I would do now, what I should have done, what I should have said. But I was a frightened little girl, and my mother and father were saying such horrible things to me, and I couldn't even will myself to move."

Elsinore stopped talking and brushed tears from her cheeks with her hand. Vedon gave her a handkerchief, simple and gray but clean. Drying her eyes, she smiled at him and went on.

"My mother came to me then and picked me up. She carried me into the central tree, to a hollow in the dead husk. She kissed my cheek and squeezed me as she sat me down and . . ."

Pausing, Elsinore shut her eyes tight, bit her lip, and sobbed. Her whole body shook as her face melted into tears. She turned away from Vedon, but he put a hand on her shoulder, then put his arms around her and held her as she wept.

Elsinore laughed once, involuntarily, her body's way of concluding her sobbing. She spent a moment breathing, regaining her composure as Vedon gently caressed her back.

It felt good to be held like that.

Finally, she caught her breath. "And then she left me. They left me." Smiling sadly, she looked up at the moon. "When they were gone, the full weight of it finally fell on me—that this was real, that they were gone—and I started to cry. I cried and cried, I don't know for how long. Incoherently, desperately. First, I tried to cry for them—for my mother, my father—to come back and take me home, but then I just sobbed and wailed.

"It went on for so long, and I know I must have blacked out. I don't know how long I cried, whether it was moments, hours, or days. I never moved from the tree, from the spot my mother had left me. I stayed where I was put—though it meant my death—because I was a child. Because it was where my mother put me. Because I was afraid."

The vivid pain of the memories faded as quickly as it had come, creeping indistinctly behind the trees in the deep forest of her mind. The flashes dimmed, as if they had been another person's memories, intruding into her mind like a stage show, only to draw back and away into the forest, forgotten once again.

All that remained, as ever, was that final night. Her father's voice—his cruelty, his callousness, the words that echoed like a nightmare—came to her mind unbidden. She felt her mother's final kiss, before she turned her back and left her daughter in the woods. Had that cruelty been as great as her father's? Had it been greater?

"I passed in and out of consciousness, through sleep or delirium, and at long last, I heard . . . whispers or the buzzing of insects. Like the wind or the rustling of the trees, but somehow, I knew they were voices, and they were saying my name. Only . . . I had never heard my name before, never knew it before that moment. They whispered my name—Elsinore—and I knew that was me. And their voices . . . they weren't even sounds. More like ideas in my mind, but real, substantial. They had no echo and only dropped silently after falling through the air, and I was so frightened.

"Those voices, those creatures—I think, in a way, I belonged to them. I think they came to take me someplace where I know, deep down, I belong. In the dark chambers of my heart, I think they were right, my parents. I think that . . . I think I really was a changeling. I think their boy, whoever he really was, was taken by the People of the Mounds, and I was left in his place. It's why I never felt right here—not in the world, not in my own skin. I think it was easy for my parents to see before the end.

"I could barely see through the tears, but I . . . I thought there were shapes out beyond the threshold of the trees. Shadows, vacant spaces in the moonlight, with cloaks like folded feather wings and faces like hooded birds and empty eyes darker than the shadows looking down at me. It was so long ago, and I could barely tell where I was, but I swear—at least, I know I was more afraid then than I've ever been, except once as an adult.

"But then I heard a new sound—a real sound. It was footsteps and hushed voices, and I stopped weeping. I had cried for so long, begging the gods for anyone to come help me, but when I heard someone come, I froze instinctually, desperate not be found."

Elsinore turned her gaze from the trees in the distance to Vedon. "Is that strange?"

When he only took her hand and held it tight, she felt relief. She wasn't sure she wanted her question answered.

"It was Milanda," she said, picking up the story again. "Milanda and her partner, Glamis, who would become my mothers. They took me in and raised me, and I've been with them ever since. One of the people traveling with Mil and Glamis at the time even said—

"But they thought I couldn't hear because I was a child and I spoke little, and people think quiet children can't hear you when you speak about them. But they do. Of course they do—

"They even said I was a changeling. That I was a fairy left in the woods as a trick to lure travelers to their deaths. I still say I was a changeling, but we joke about it. I'm in on it now, I tell Glamis. I'm in on it now, I tell myself.

"Somehow . . . I don't think any of them saw those

shapes. Those Others that surrounded me before Milanda found me. I don't even know if they were real. But I remember them—when I sleep, when I close my eyes. I remember I saw them in the woods near the Mountain. I remember I felt so afraid.

"But I've never known what to believe. I have . . . so few memories of my parents before those last few nights before they took me to the forest. Before they left me. Just dim feelings, senses. A rocking chair of my mother's, a drinking mug of my father's. Are these memories even real?"

"You remembered my name," Vedon finally said. He hadn't spoken once since Elsinore began her story, and his voice comforted her now. "You remembered playing with me by the tree and by the bridge."

"Did that happen afterward?" Elsinore asked, looking deep into his eyes. "Was that after I was . . . exchanged? Or were those memories left in me, given to me, stolen from the boy I was exchanged with? Did any of that really happen, to me or to him or to you or to someone else?"

Elsinore looked away from Vedon, suddenly embarrassed. When she turned back, she shied away from his eyes and gazed at his lips.

"Who am I?"

"I think you're someone miraculous," Vedon told her. "Someone beautiful and wise and strange. I would never have imagined you as someone who didn't know who she was. When I look in your eyes when you dance, all I see is confidence and a woman so sure of herself, it's infectious."

Smirking, Elsinore giggled and grabbed the hair at the back of Vedon's head.

"You learn a lot of little tricks like that when you

perform in front of an audience. Faking confidence becomes self-fulfilling after a while.”

Pulling his head in, she kissed him deeply. She drew back after a long time and opened her eyes, only to be dazzled momentarily by the light of the Pomegranate Moon. When she saw Vedon’s dumbfounded smile, she giggled again, jumped up, and holding his hand, pulled him along.

“Come with me.”

Vedon looked around shamefully. “My mother will still be awake, tending the library with me gone.”

Elsinore smiled. “Then I’ll show you where I’m staying.”

She led Vedon back to the tavern and guided him around the edges of the main room, past tables of people sleeping off drink or huddling around lanterns, wary of the growing darkness of the season. She didn’t think anyone noticed the two of them as she led him to her quarters and to her bed.

Her rooster doll of soft multicolored cloth sat on her pillows and linen-lace sheets. On a shelf against the wall, she’d set the book from the library, bottles, and the makings of potions.

A table at the foot of the bed had been covered with a scarf and consecrated as a makeshift altar, where she had placed her magical implements: a ritual dagger of iron; candles; her thin pipe for smoking cannabis; a shallow mirrored-silver dish for water; and a small piece of natural black glass, its surface pitted and pocked like that of a meteoric stone.

These sat around a pendant bearing an eight-pointed

star, which Elsinore often wore around her neck. This was the symbol of the goddess Tiranna, to whom women like Elsinore were sacred. She was the goddess of love, sex, prophecy, and resurrection.

Her star stood vigil on the altar as the two made love in the candlelight, and She blessed them.

When they'd finished, Elsinore lay in bed, exhausted. She followed Vedon's hand languidly with her eyes as he ran it softly along her leg, up the curve of her hip, across her belly, and to her small, full breasts. He kissed her lightly, conversationally. Smiling, Elsinore closed her eyes, content.

"I should have known you would move so beautifully," Vedon said gently into her ear. "You are a dancer, after all."

Elsinore rolled out of his arms and playfully shoved a pillow in his face, and they both laughed. The rooster doll fell out of the covers and onto the floor, and Vedon bent over the side of the bed to pick it up.

He toyed with the red comb on its yellow head and the rainbow of cloth that made up its tail. "This is adorable. Where did you get it?"

"It was a gift." Elsinore took the doll from him and kissed it. "From a lover I had once."

Vedon ran a finger over her cheek and pushed a lock of hair behind the point of her ear. "What happened to him?"

"She died." Looking away, Elsinore rolled away from Vedon and set the doll on a shelf by the bed.

"I'm sorry," Vedon began, but Elsinore silenced him by pulling him down onto the covers and kissing him.

"Do you usually sleep with women rather than men?" Vedon asked, sounding doubtful and, perhaps, insecure.

"I've loved many types of people. Lately, I've mostly slept with men. Don't worry, though," she assured him, "I think you're very manly."

She playfully squeezed between his legs. The boy squirmed uncomfortably, and she drew away. After a moment, the two laughed together and pulled back into each other's arms, kissing again.

"Your body is incredible. How did you . . . ?"

Vedon trailed off as Elsinore's brows knitted warningly.

"I only mean," he continued sheepishly, careful of his words, "you're very lucky."

Elsinore sighed. "It isn't luck." Sitting up, she wrapped the sheet around her breasts and under her arms. With deliberate mischief, she said, "It's magic."

"Magic?"

She laughed. "Well . . . medicine. Drugs I have to take regularly. It . . . changes me. My muscles, my fat. My cheeks. My breasts. It makes me more feminine. More . . . like myself."

"It's miraculous. How did you learn spells like that?" Vedon's hand still explored Elsinore playfully, trailing a pleasurable tingling sensation across her skin.

Giggling, she pushed his hand away. "My mother Milanda is the healer and spellcaster of our village. She taught me how to mix herbs into bubbling tinctures for healing, root-craft, and where and when to find the flowers and fungi that produce the right effects.

"I never had much affinity for healing, but I wanted to learn to make potions and drugs that could create or dispel illusions in the mind or facilitate the removal of the mental barriers that produce our everyday illusions and make the world appear to us as it does. I became rather adept at brewing the drugs that made my body closer to my true self—that displaced the virilizing hormones in my body—and other medicines that feminized me as I grew into adolescence.

"I learned other tricks from my mother, of course, like reading future events from cards and stars and dreams. I love to flip through the cards with their arcane sigils and peer deep into a subject's eyes, especially with pretty women—or men. Usually, it takes only a combination of stagecraft and a little bit of subtle sorcery to read their fates. Less flashy and exciting than my dancing, I suppose, but strangers are always so enraptured by my uncanny readings of their pasts and the tantalizing hints I whisper of their futures.

"I practiced the kind of dancing that draws in crowds of young women and men like you, who lingered to get a little closer to me after the show."

Elsinore paused, smiled, and kissed Vedon slowly.

"These tricks kept the audiences amused, I suppose, but none of the spells I learned ever felt as efficacious as the real, potent magic of the drugs that give form to the image of myself—the self I know deep in my heart."

Pulling away, Elsinore stared thoughtfully across the room, lost in thought or memory.

"And . . ." Vedon raised an eyebrow and nodded between her legs.

Elsinore sighed again, exasperated. She picked up the long, thin pipe from the altar, delicately and gracefully holding it by the stem. Taking the last of the dried, shredded cannabis from the pouch Astra had given her, she filled the bowl and lit it with a small fire spell from her finger. She inhaled sharply and exhaled slowly.

"The medicine changes how it feels," Elsinore said,

her breath trailing smoke, "but in the end, it took more than drugs or spells."

She stopped speaking and smoked in silence. When they made love, he had fingered her empty, sensitive scrotum and kissed her soft, barely erect penis. In their sharing a bed, he of course knew of her castration, but to share secrets of the Goddess's rites in detail was another matter entirely.

It seemed to her Vedon understood, for he didn't press any further. He cuddled her from behind, arms around her belly, face in the crook of her neck, nose buried in her full, blue-green hair.

"Is what you're smoking the drug?" Vedon asked after a while. "The magic that makes you like you are?"

Laughing, Elsinore turned her head away from him and exhaled a thin column of smoke. "Weed? No, silly, this is just cannabis. I was talking about potions. No, I just wanted to get high." She offered the pipe to him, but he shook his head timidly.

"What are the potions you take made of, then?"

Elsinore smiled and squinted at him. "You'd be disgusted if I told you, I promise."

"I'm very open minded."

"Well . . ." Elsinore glanced side to side in mock conspiracy. "It's compounded with a tincture of honey and herbs . . . but primarily it's based on mare's urine."

"Ah." Vedon made a face and dropped the matter after all, apparently open minded only to a certain point. "Forgive me if this is too sore a subject, but that makes me wonder. May I ask you a question?"

Elsinore looked at him curiously. Sometimes, weed loosened her inhibitions, raising her tolerance for the innocent but rudely intrusive questions people like Vedon tended to ask. Perhaps that was why she took a final drag of her pipe, cocked her head to the side, and said, "Go on."

Vedon seemed unsure how to begin.

"Well, from what you said earlier—and chastise me if I approach a subject that brings you pain in any way!" he hurried to assure her. "But it seems to me that if you were indeed . . . well, if you were indeed a fairy, some creature left as a changeling in place of a mortal boy, then, well . . . what need would you have of these potions, this medicine, these arts regarding your body? Could you not just perform your natural magic and glamour and restore your true form? Does that not mean you are as mortal as myself?"

Elsinore considered for a moment how best to respond. This was more insightful than she'd given Vedon credit for. Of course, she'd puzzled over just this question periodically, recurrently, her whole life. She had thought on it, reflecting on each facet, but she'd never really had the chance—or to admit it honestly, the emotional space— to articulate it in so many words. She attempted to now that she had the opportunity.

"That could be true," she said slowly. "I could be just as you say. But as my mothers often tell me, the People of the Mounds follow strange laws. It could be that my fae spirit—feminine and ethereal—was enchanted to take the form of the boy I was changed with. Many say this is the method of the Fair Folk when they leave a changeling behind, to better entrance mortals. I could be so malformed that only mortal drugs have the power to confirm my body's true form, to reveal that which dwells in my deepest heart.

"It could be, likewise, that the fae are grotesque, as others maintain—as I always knew the masculinity of my body at adolescence to be. They say the People use glamours and magic to alter their appearance, to change the form of a hag or an ogre or a ghoul into a fairy princess or a luminous knight or an innocent in need of help from a naive traveler. Is that not exactly what I effect with my magic and through my drugs? Must their glamour be a simple act of will and rhyme? Perhaps I use the very same tools a fae would be expected to use in making my body match, even a little closer, the form I see in my mind's eye."

Vedon was silent for a moment, lost in thought. Whether he was considering his next question or simply how to put it to Elsinore gently, she could not tell.

"If what you say is true—if you really are a fairy and were left as a child with your parents for some fey purpose—then . . . forgive me, but what became of the boy your parents knew? Their 'real' child, the boy I'd have played with so long ago, whose replacement led to you being—"

He caught himself before he could recall that traumatic memory for Elsinore once again.

"Well . . . while you've been here in the world with your new mothers—what became of him?"

Elsinore lay back, clutched her arms to her chest, and closed her eyes. This was something else she had considered, but only shallowly. For if true, that would mean only one thing—something so frightful, her mothers had always refused to speak of it. It would have been an act of great injustice, both to Elsinore herself and to the boy she was left for.

At last, she opened her eyes. "He would have been taken under the hills—under the Mountain. Into the place I would have come from—the place in the background of everything I've ever done and dreamed, the place to which, in my heart, I know I wish to return."

Elsinore paused, her breath catching in her throat.

"He would have been taken into Faerie," she concluded. "Past the woods and the hollow hills beyond, through the door in the Mountain to the underworld below."

She met Vedon's gaze, her own trembling with fear and doubt.

"He would have been taken into Hell."

✳ 4 ✳

CROSSING OVER

The following morning, Vedon left early to open the library—not without bestowing a kiss on his lover's cheek—and Elsinore returned to an uneasy sleep, dreaming of shadows and mirrors and hidden light, of forgotten memories that just barely slipped back into focus before she was pulled awake.

Astra stood over the bed with the blanket in her arms, laughing that Elsinore had slept in too late. The barkeep's partner insisted on spending the day with her new friend, and eager to begin preparations for the journey she knew she had to make, Elsinore contrived to make the most of the situation.

When Elsinore first asked to be shown the fields outside town and the road to the forest, Astra looked uneasy. However, a mischievous glint in her eye made it clear she was more interested in aiding Elsinore's adventurous undertaking than she let on. Once Elsinore had readied herself—having woken fully, washed up, and packed her scattered clothes and implements into her bag to take with her—the two set off. By then, it was after midday.

Beyond the bridge over the creek, the road diverged into two: the Northern Road, a long but gentle way that wound the length of the valley as far as Nin, and the Southern Road, a more direct route to the Great River but also more treacherous, wilder, and less traveled. Most ominously, the Southern Road sank into the rocky earth, tightly bordered by the dark trees of the fae woods, and with the approach of Summer's End, it fell within the shadow of the Mountain.

If the people of Tudur feared to venture far from their homes in this bleak season, they most especially shunned the Southern Road, for it skirted much too near the foot of the Mountain.

Within a short distance of the forest, a monument sprawled across a wide, circular field—unusually flat in the country of growing hills and resting hidden within a vale. Its edges were marked at regular intervals by large standing stones. It looked to Elsinore like a place for festivals or gatherings.

Crossing her arms, Elsinore scanned the perimeter of the field. "I imagine if I danced in the center, I could bring in a crowd that would fill the whole circle, with many climbing the stones to get a better view." She spoke not with pride but with a distant, almost resigned tone. She was tired, though not only from being woken early.

"No one dares cross into the circle anymore," Astra said. "Certainly not during the Season of Shadows. It's not clear what the circle's original purpose was, though I think you're right. It does seem like a place of gathering, especially for sacred or ritual meetings.

"At one point in its history, this place served a rather dark purpose, or so local legend holds. The apprentice librarian, Vedon, used to like talking about it sometimes, along with the other nonsense he would read in his old books." Astra smirked Elsinore a knowing smirk, and the young witch blushed and snorted.

"He's a very nice boy!" Astra clarified. "A little odd, perhaps. Anyway, it's said this was once used as the entrance to the forest and the realm of . . . well, to the other place. You see there"—she pointed toward the far side of the large field—"where the stones of the ring vanish into the tree line? One side of the ring is in our country, and the other is in theirs. In the forest.

"Back when it was more common for our folk to venture forth into the lands of the People of the Mounds, if not to the Mountain itself, those who dared set forth would begin their journeys by passing into the forest at that point, where the stone ring crosses the border. And there was a time—generations ago, I think, but I don't remember what Vedon used to say—when village elders who were tired of the uncertainty of the seasons, had long been preceded in passing by their partners, lovers, and friends, and were at last certain that their time in the world had come to a close . . ."

Astra sighed and looked out at the dark trees on the far side of the circle. "In twilight during the Season of Shadows, they would rise from their homes in town, walk to the crossroads and onto the Southern Road, cross this side of the ring, and . . . vanish into the trees. Never to be seen again."

Astra turned to Elsinore, who had watched her intently as she told the story, and studied her as if trying to gauge the young woman's reaction.

Elsinore looked out at the tree line and the shadows that rose beyond. "That's one way to do it, I suppose."

Laughing, Astra hit her lightly on the shoulder.

Elsinore laughed ruefully. "They probably died of exposure. Taken by wildcats and vultures."

"Either way, this forest is a treacherous place. And the place beyond it . . ." Astra sighed. "I know you want to go there, though I'm afraid to ask why. I also know all the warnings I could give you would do no good. Be careful, Elsinore. We don't need anyone contributing more to the legends of that place."

Smiling sympathetically, Elsinore raised her wide black hood to shade her face as the sun broke free of the clouds. But her eyes remained fixed on the trees—on the shadows between them and under their leaves, unbroken by the light from above.

Rosario stood waiting at the crest of the bridge on the edge of town as the women returned. Astra waved, but he responded not with laughter but with a frown, visible even from afar. As they met on the bridge, he took Astra's hand and sighed.

"What's wrong?" Astra asked, her eyes growing dark.

Elsinore shivered, strangely unnerved. She could hear voices in the distance, carrying over the bridge and the water of the creek. There was a commotion, someone yelling over the din of a crowd.

"There's something going on in town," the barkeep said at last. "It's those no-goods, Escus and Pars. They have the whole crowd whipped up in a frenzy at that poor boy from the library, but . . ." He looked at Elsinore and shook his head. "It's you they're after, dear."

Astra shot Elsinore a look of concern, and the three made haste into town. As they came closer to the buildings, it became clear the crowd was gathered in the square, in greater numbers than any Elsinore had attracted with her dancing.

Rosario ushered the women into an alley to keep out of sight and led them along narrow paths to the back of the tavern. When he let them in the back door, the tavern stood empty; it seemed everyone was gathered in the square, raising a clamor that practically shook the building. The barkeep led them upstairs and down a hall to a wide bay window that overlooked the town.

As Elsinore had feared, Escus and Pars were the ruffians who had accosted her. They had Vedon bound to a post at the shrine, and all eyes were on them—though Elsinore's were drawn only to the boy.

At first angry and worried, she hurried to think of a way to free him. However, after a moment of staring, she realized there was something different about Vedon. His humiliation aside, there appeared to be some change from the night before, some difference in his face and manner or perhaps his body. Precisely what it was, though, she couldn't decide.

The shouting of the two men broke her concentration, and she turned her mind to listening to what was going on.

"Do you see what she's doing now? It's exactly as we feared!" hollered the man who had attacked Elsinore with a knife—Escus, as Astra angrily identified him. "One of the People of the Mounds—a creature! You can say it, can't you? A *fairy*! She's entranced this poor boy and given him a poisonous concoction to weaken his will, cloud his mind, and *change* him!"

Escus ripped open Vedon's shirt from the collar, exposing his flat chest and pink nipples. He made a show of pinching Vedon's nipples and grabbing at what there was of his chest. There was nothing there, of course; Vedon was thin and slight and had no muscle to speak of. But the ruffian's motions were miserably familiar to Elsinore.

"Can you see, good people?" the terrible man cried, goading the crowd. "It's already begun! Soon, the good boy you knew from the book house will be gone, drawn away into the paths under the hills beyond the forest, and a *changeling* will be left in his place! A fairy, just like her! It's what she wants! It's what she's doing! And it's what she'll do to your sons once she's finished with him! Unless we stop her! Unless we find her and make sure she never fascinates anyone else in this town, one way or another!"

"My son and I will never give up that girl to the likes of you!" The shout came from the old librarian, who was pushing forward through the crowd. Gratitude welled in Elsinore's heart, along with relief that the woman wasn't as bad as the wretched men who had her son.

"You don't think so?" The other man, Pars, raised one hand to display something to the crowd. "Look at this! The source of her fairy charms! You see what she's dosed him with!"

Elsinore strained to see what the man held. It was tiny, small enough to be concealed in a fist, but even from this distance, the witch recognized it. She knew it well because she saw it, or others much like it, every day.

At once, she opened her bag and dug around, shoving aside her spare clothes and rooster doll so she could pull out a pouch, which she unfolded and laid out on a nearby table. It had a number of pockets, each of which contained a tiny glass bottle about the size of Elsinore's thumb. Examining each pocket, she counted the bottles. Then she counted them again.

One bottle was missing.

Elsinore folded up the pouch, replaced it in her bag, and glared out the window into the square. Astra looked at her, concerned.

"That eggy little bitch," Elsinore finally muttered to herself through gritted teeth. Astra and Rosario stared at her in confusion. "I can't believe it. Vedon stole one of my hormone potions last night."

Was she surprised? Perhaps she shouldn't be.

She stared back down at Vedon, still surrounded by the jeering crowd. Of course, nothing was really different about him; the potion took months of regular use for any effects to start showing. But there was a way about Vedon now, and a look in his face like a veil had been drawn back. Even enduring the humiliation the men put him through . . . there was pride and relief in his face, where before Elsinore now realized she had seen only doubt.

Perhaps it was clear in retrospect; perhaps it only seemed so. It was always that way, wasn't it?

"Elsinore?"

The witch shook her head. "But how did those goons find out?"

"They're Vedon's friends," Rosario said. "If he stole something from you, maybe he bragged about it?"

"I wouldn't say they're friends," Astra added. "More like bullies that strong-arm him into keeping them company and goad and abuse him for their own amusement. Vedon puts up with it, as much as he can. He's a strange boy, and that happens. I think it's more likely they noticed he had something and bullied him until he told them about it. Then they escalated things into what we see before us."

Elsinore glowered darkly under her hood. "I know what to do. Wait for my signal. When there's an opening, grab Vedon and his mother and take them to safety."

"Elsinore?" Astra asked.

"Wait here." Elsinore disappeared into the shadows, leaving the two alone in the dim hall.

It was clear that Vedon saw it first. The men who had taken him were too busy laughing, trying to rile up the crowd. Yet poor Vedon's gaze was fixed not on the faces around him but on a white-and-yellow flower growing from a tree by the tavern, near where Elsinore had danced.

Its bright petals practically reflected the faint sunlight, flashing in the lengthening shadows. Gradually, the flower grew, its petals lengthening and spiraling into one another, taking shapes at once familiar and eminently strange. After a moment, it was undeniable: the flower had become a face, longer petals mimicking hair, while others formed lips, cheeks, and pale, sightless eyes.

By then, it was clear the bullies saw it too. Escus froze, going silent before the crowd as he watched the face. Pars dropped the bottle, which rolled to Vedon, who dragged it between his boots. The crowd, clamoring for Elsinore to be brought to them for whatever justice they imagined she deserved, continued their commotion.

The face behind them remained silent, its blank eyes meeting the men's gazes and seeing their every intention.

In a moment, the men were engulfed in plant life deep as a thicket, and though they tried to back away, they were barely able to take a step without getting tangled and tripping. Vines curled up from the roots of each tree in the square, and soaking-wet weeds crept out of the cistern of the shrine. Before the crowd could comprehend what was happening, they were surrounded by arms of leaves and vines, moss rising monstrously all around.

The two men, first frozen with terror, were now entrapped and held in place. The crowd's mood turned at once from hate to fear, and the people began screaming and trying to run. But the vines grew longer, leafier, and wilder, and the square was now surrounded by twisting nets of plant life.

The face of flowers crept above the crowd to the level of the two men, who now writhed, fully bound on the ground. It hovered at the end of a long serpentine neck of stem and weed, lingering over the first man, then turning to the other.

It reared back, taking the crowd in with its dark, enigmatic sight. Where eyes should have been was only sunken shadow, within a face puzzled together from white petals veined in yellow.

The lips parted very slightly, and a voice hissed out of the darkness. It seemed to come from the open mouth and echoed all around the square, silencing the cacoph-onony of the new thicket.

"You two," hissed the voice, "flee the shadow of the Mountain and never return. If you ever behold the peak again, even clouded in the distance, we will see you. We will know. Thereafter, you will never again be allowed to escape our grasp."

The vines and weeds parted at once, leaving the men bare, frozen with fear on the muddy ground. They looked not at each other nor at Vedon but kept their eyes locked on the face, as if too terrified to turn away.

"Fairies! Things from the hills and under them!"

Elsinore didn't know which shouted, but both ran in haste toward the bridge. From her vantage point in the tree, she could just see them cross the water of the stream, and in a moment, they were gone in the highlands of the road out of town.

As the barkeep and his wife appeared beside Vedon, standing between him and the crowd, the youth found himself free of the rope that had bound him to the post. His mother ran up and past Astra and Rosario, who let her through to her son.

As the townsfolks' fervor rapidly cooled, the barkeep berated them, shouting at them for letting their fear get the better of their reason. Many hung their heads and slunk away, no doubt hurrying back to their homes to hide their shame from their neighbors.

The librarian spoke words of comfort to Vedon, but he didn't hear her. He only looked out over the bridge that led to the forest and thought he saw a shimmer in the air under the mist.

At last away from town, from people, and from anything else holding her back, Elsinore stood in the ring of standing stones at the edge of the forest. Securing her bag and her sword once more, she flew across the circle to the other side and vanished into the trees beyond.

$$* \ 5 \ *$$

JHE VALLEY OF THE MOUNDS

The forest was so ancient that, like the Mountain, it had no other name, and people for leagues around knew it only as the Forest. Old, wide, misshapen trees of an unknown species dominated the Forest, and their broad forked leaves grew yellow and green, reaching down from the branches like the grasping hands of some many-armed monster.

From the highlands outside town, one could see the foothills that rose near the Mountain, beyond the forest, and the tops of blue-green pines and noble, fragrant cedars of deeper green. Folks who had been through the Forest—and been fortunate enough to return with their senses—maintained that the trees growing from the Mountain's sacred, poisoned soil were the most ancient and bore forth the magic of the fae who dwelled deep beneath the mounds.

It was speculated in rare books, and among those who traveled along the rivers and valleys from season to season, that the Mountain had once had a name, in the faraway past when names were given. Back when the seasons fell evenly and the moon measured time predictably. Before the crops failed and came back just enough for people to live off them once again. Before the rivers ran with poison and then flowed clean once more. Back in the Ancient Times, when the Old Ones built cities and named mountains and broke the moon.

Then the earth was burned and blighted clear of all forests, due to the sickness, greed, and arrogance of the Old Ones. The clouds of the sky grew thin, scattered by Lord Wind, and rain fell but sparingly, withheld by that same god as punishment. What little remained of the earth's bounty once the Old Ones had eaten their fill was taken away from them by Lord Wind, and humanity was nearly eradicated.

Little by little, the clouds covered the sky again, and little by little, the grass grew and trees stood tall. But only after countless centuries of death—the Age of Devastation.

The people who lived in the Age of Regrowth gave thanks to Lady Water for sheltering life in her hidden aquifer and, likewise, to Lord Wind for at last ceasing his wrath. They did so out of deference and out of fear he would lash out again.

But most of all, the new people gave thanks to the Great Goddess, the Queen of Heaven, from whose body the universe emanates, for sustaining and daily recreating the world. The people in those days listened closely to the enigmatic voice of the Goddess, as the Old Ones had failed to do. And as they listened to the voice of the Mother, She told them that Her seat was the Mountain and that the children of the Mother of the Mountain were the fae.

For centuries, it was taboo to approach the Mountain. Around it were menacing structures that legend held the Old Ones had erected, and around those structures grew the Forest. Some said the oldest trees were born in the Ancient Times and survived Lord Wind's purges, but most believed that to be impossible. They insisted that all the trees, even the strange old trees, grew during the Age of Regrowth, after the vengeance of the gods had worked its course.

Whatever the truth, for as long as the people had known of the Forest, they knew to fear it, to fear what lived in it, and to fear what was found beyond it within the Mountain. For though the trees in the forest were young as the Goddess reckons time, the beings that had come to live among them were ancient beyond measure, creatures from an era unknown, already ancient when the Old Ones were young.

For the dwellers of the forest had come out of the Mountain.

Elsinore passed from tree to tree in the pathless woods, the floor a crunching carpet of seasons-old fallen leaves beneath her soft boots. In her dark hood, it was easy to keep to the shadows, her teal-dyed hair blending in with the grass and the leaves. In any case, the forest was dark, the canopy thick enough to block the light of the moon, and with any luck, whatever might be watching from the shadows was occupied with other concerns.

She could not see the Mountain through the trees, but she cast a simple cantrip upon her eight-pointed star pendant, intending to use it for navigation. Once under the cover of trees, she held the pendant before her by the cord, the silver glinting from an sourceless light, and under the enchantment, it swung ever so slightly to point in the direction of the Mountain. Though unnatural, this made her navigation much simpler, and following the guidance of the silver star, she felt sure she would pass through the forest safely.

Here and there in the distance, through the trunks and branches, Elsinore could see dull, steady lights. She knew better than to follow such things; they were sure to lead not to safe dwellings but to pitfalls and death. Whether they were burning gases over swamps or deliberate traps set by forest dwellers—human or otherwise—made no difference to a traveler who wished to keep safe.

Yet the lights persisted in harrying the young witch.

Soon enough, those that hung steady beyond the branches began to drift and wander, such that Elsinore feared they might be lanterns carried not by supernatural creatures but by bandits or brigands. She felt for the grip of her sword over her shoulder; though she was better trained in magic, her blade might be defense enough if she were set upon by assailants.

But the lights grew more elaborate in their motion, spinning and dancing in a manner entirely unlike any light borne by mortal hands. The lights whirled to and fro, around and overhead, casting about like falling stars, flickering beyond the branches of the trees in the darkness, and coming to rest all around the girl. She tried to persist on her way, following not the bewildering dance of lights but the focused swing of her pendant, but at last, a cluster of lights fell forward and spread out ahead, impeding the witch from moving on without approaching them.

Elsinore froze in the litter of leaves that carpeted the space between the trees. Though the lights still hung in the distance, they surrounded her nonetheless, and she feared proceeding any farther into the reach of whatever was coming. She stayed still and closed her eyes, but the lights burned deep into her vision in the darkness behind her closed lids, and she could feel them drawing nearer. She imagined the hands of whatever held the lights reaching for her, stroking her arms, folding around her cheeks, and pulling her into the trees, into the swamp, and out of the world.

Elsinore shuddered and snapped open her eyes.

Snapping her fingers, she produced the witch-light fires, which flashed into being in the air above her palms, dispelling the darkness around her. She set them adrift in the clearing and, with a slow, simple rhythm, waved her arms in an arcane dance. Two more lights circled away as she cast them, then another two, each a pale yellow green, spinning and flashing in the night. Elsinore controlled them with the rhythm of her dance, and they followed a pattern only she could determine. She sent them farther away, slowly at first, carefully directing them through the trees of the ancient woods.

Before long, the mysterious wisps responded as the witch had hoped. They began to follow her lights, to match their movements and dance with them between the branches.

Finally, as the fires she cast moved farther away, they began to fade, dying as they danced and leaving the darkness deeper than ever in their absence. Fortuitously—and better than she could have planned—the wisps of the woods, too, faded with the lights of Elsinore's spell. Each of the mysterious fae fires had danced with a partner cast by the witch, and with the departure of the latter, the former seemed to lose hold on the world and fall away into the ether from which they came.

Elsinore alone remained in the deep darkness, which obscured the path ahead, but she was too cautious to cast another light spell and risk summoning another of the wisps. Holding out her pendant, she faintly made out the direction it pointed and resumed a steady pace toward the Mountain.

Moving ever forward, Elsinore came at last to a place where she could see beyond the edge of the trees. The pale light of a growing dawn poured through the branches ahead, and she picked up her pace to just under a jog, eager to be out from among the trees and in the open air. Perhaps she was hidden by the trees from whatever might be watching her, but by the same token, she grew uneasy not being able to see what such things might be. Were there creatures in the branches looking down or things beneath the ground peering up through the roots, waiting to draw her in?

Beyond all those fears, Elsinore feared stumbling on one thing most of all. Was there any chance, however slight, that she would recognize something here in these woods? A tree, a root, a stump—something she had spent her whole life trying to forget—once more before her waking eyes? What would she do if she saw it? How would she bring herself to go on?

In her haste to leave the woods behind, Elsinore stumbled on a raised gnarled root hidden beneath the shadows of the trees. She managed to keep her footing well enough not to fall, but her hand flew out and her pendant went flying.

Though she would no longer need the guidance once she was out of the Forest, the necklace was special to her, a memento of a love she lost. Peering at the ground in search of it, she could see very little in the low moonlight, but a sharp glint of light reflected from the ground nearby, and she bent closer to look.

The necklace lay half buried in the leaves. Kneeling on a soft patch of earth, Elsinore picked up the necklace and fastened it safely around her neck.

Before she could rise, a familiar sound reached her ears, so untraceable in its source that Elsinore was overcome by a wave of dizziness and had to sit down and lean back against a tree. It sounded like a child crying in the Forest, back in the direction from which she had come. Soft at first, the crying rose in ever greater waves of sobs.

While Elsinore sat and listened, tears welled up in her own eyes as her mind drifted back. Wrenching pain and aching loneliness racked her entire body, as if she were still lost in the Forest, abandoned, hopeless. This loneliness, this pain—were these what the boy was experiencing now, his suffering swapped for hers, their mingled cries echoing from the long-ago past?

The guttural sobbing rose again and shifted slowly until it became a sharp, cutting wail, and the tears burned down Elsinore's cheeks. *I have to go back,* she thought. *I have to go back into the Forest and make sure this child will be all right.*

Standing, she turned almost automatically and started walking back into the trees. As she did, the voice changed again. A high-pitched giggle rattled out of the trees, only for a moment, then resolved into an intermittent buzzing, like that of insects, hosts of unseen flies in the darkness.

The forest, already in shadow from the density of the canopy, grew more obscure as a gripping gray mist rose out of the ground. Hidden in the mist and darker than the shade of the trees hiding the dawn, shapes drifted here and there. Cloaked and hooded, ragged as the feathers of bedraggled, unclean birds, the figures drifted closer, threatening to encircle Elsinore. Their eyes focused on her; somehow, she could feel their unnatural gazes, despite the black hollow eyes sunken in their strange hidden faces.

Elsinore closed her eyes, and a focus took shape in

her mind. She concentrated on the star of the Goddess, tracing its eight points continuously as if following a labyrinth, and in doing so, freed herself from her trance.

No longer spellbound by the child's cries, Elsinore ran desperately toward the tree line, away from the fey, uncanny sounds emanating from the shapes in the mist. She didn't stop running until she was clear of the trees—of the Forest—and fully in the light. She didn't stop until the reaching mist of the forest was far behind and the air around her bright and clear.

Reaching back, Elisinore raised her black hood, hiding her pointed ears, and tucked her messy blue-green hair in behind her slender neck. Wishing there were something to hide behind, she turned back to make sure nothing had pursued her from the forest. She was no longer surrounded, no longer hounded by fingers of mist, but nevertheless, she felt certain something was watching her from the edge of the woods.

Nothing moved. Not a hint of shadow fell from the tree line into the light. Unsatisfied that she was truly alone, Elsinore felt she was at least as safe as possible from her pursuers. Tentatively, she turned her back on the Forest—not entirely letting her guard down—and observed her surroundings.

The land was doubly illuminated by the faint light of dawn to the east and the soft glow of the Pomegranate Moon slinking through the clouds above. The moon's opalescent halo cast an unnatural shade of amethyst over the valley that spread out before her.

Dotting the valley almost randomly were artificial-looking mounds. From the center of each jutted an immense, menacing spike, and together, they gave the impression of some titanic underworld monster pushing its claws disastrously up through the earth until they towered above the valley. The spikes were not parallel, not orderly, and not graceful; they were angled at random, a scene of chaotic ruin, a horror growing as it liked with no rhyme or reason.

What kind of people were the Old Ones to have built such architecture? And why did they?

Beyond this horrible landscape, the land swelled with cedar-covered hills that grew ever taller as they marched toward the Mountain, which rose above it all. The Mountain stood wide and majestic, diminished not at all by the fearful mounds before it. Crown bright in the twilight dawn, the Mountain watched the young woman in the hills, awaiting her arrival at last after calling for so long.

Elsinore set out at a determined pace, her eyes scanning the valley but her heart never straying from the terrible destination before her.

As the sun rose, the pillars cast long, harsh shadows, which Elsinore instinctively dreaded crossing. Though she was less exposed within them than she was in the open light, she couldn't help but feel that something was watching her—something *other*—that could see her more clearly in those long, narrow shadows.

Yet avoiding the shadows was impossible, as the pillars stood many stories tall and seemed to average about ten feet in width. She didn't approach them too closely, avoiding the mounds the pillars were set in, but these structures were clearly artificial, made by something other than natural forces—if not strictly by humans. But what their purpose could have been, other than to threaten and menace intruders, Elsinore could not guess.

She traveled through the vast Valley of the Mounds as the morning wore on. Now and again, she thought she saw shapes flit past, from pillar to pillar, trailing long, narrow shadows in their wake.

But whenever she looked back, there was nothing.

Was it just clouds passing before the sun? Or was something following her, watching her from atop the grim mounds? Was it something from beneath them, watching for the intruder, waiting for a chance to pull her underneath, to teach her the true, terrible secret of this wasteland of warning and ruin?

Elsinore dismissed these thoughts as best she could but remained alert.

As she drew closer to her destination, she came to a mound ringed by a wall of white quartz that shone brighter than she'd have thought possible beneath the grim sky. Unlike the other mounds, this one bore no spike. Perched in its stead on the crest of the mound was an amazing creature—some composite entity that, whether divine or fae, was surely unnatural.

It had a body like that of a golden lion, with black stripes all along its torso and legs and massive paws with shining silver claws. Huge feathered wings spread out from its back, folded casually along its sides as it lounged, relaxed yet alert. It had the mane of a lion, black like its stripes, which encompassed its head and fell in braided bands to its chest.

Most astonishing was the face enclosed within the mane: a beautiful human visage with lovely eyes rimmed in kohl and long lashes—a curious blend of feminine, masculine, and feline.

It wore a tall columnar crown encircled by six curved horns, three on each side, which grew from the back of its head and wrapped up and around to the front, where they curved upward when they might have touched. Instead of a cat's tail, the scaly, chitinous tail of a scorpion curled around its legs, tipped with a wicked stinger like a curved knife.

As Elsinore approached, its kohl-smeared eyes followed her intently, assessing the level of danger she posed. Elsinore slowed warily. A wild cat was dangerous enough, but this monstrous chimera compounded that danger with a face that displayed wily human cunning, if not human reason.

But something, some intuition, made the witch think she had a chance to pass unharmed. She continued her approach evenly, calmly, without sound or sudden movement. The creature continued to regard her languidly, curious but untroubled. Perhaps it was little used to visitors, more curious than defensive.

Morbidly, it occurred to Elsinore that nowhere in the valley had she seen a pile of stray bones, even in the fearful shadows of the pillars. She supposed this creature might not be in the habit of stripping the flesh from intruders—or so she hoped.

Maybe it was a divine entity, untethered by the earthly demands of hunger and thirst, a spirit that posed more threat to one's soul than to one's body.

Or perhaps it was only an illusion.

The creature uttered a great purring growl, dashing all these optimistic thoughts from her mind and bringing her to a halt. In a single motion, it leaped to its leonine feet and stretched its black-feathered wings out to the sides, opening its pink humanoid lips wide in a yawn. As it did, Elsinore could plainly see in its great mouth at least three rows of sharp, knife-like teeth glinting in the veiled sunlight.

When it finished stretching, it padded down from the mound and, in an instant, stood before Elsinore. She had not even had time to move or consider what action to take. It hadn't even appeared to run. It had just stepped slowly, casually, catlike from the mound and was instantly before her, as if it had stepped over the intervening distance with a single stride.

Now that it was beside her, Elsinore could see that the feline entity was immense, larger than a horse or a bull. The girl was paralyzed with fear as the creature paced around her, lowering its head to sniff her as a cat would, deciding what to do with her. She made no motion, no action the creature could possibly interpret as a threat. If it became aggressive, she stood no chance against its terrible claws and nightmare of a maw. Instead, she waited while it made its inscrutable assessment.

At last, the creature gave a resigned-sounding puff, padded calmly back to its original resting place, and threw itself to the ground. It gave her one last lazy glance, slowly blinking at her, before it put its head down on its paws and appeared to go to sleep.

Had it judged Elsinore and found her worthy of passage?

It made no further movements as Elsinore tentatively pressed on past the quartz-ringed mound. She didn't wish to dwell on the creature; she wanted to move on while she had the chance.

Beyond the mounds, she could see another wooded region beginning at the edge of the foothills—the tall, old cedars of the Mountain, their branches reaching high and their leaves blue green and glossy. They were distant yet; Elsinore still had a mile or two—or more—before she reached the trees, let alone the Mountain beyond.

And what exactly do I expect to find once I reach it?

She had no chance to consider the answer as her thoughts were disturbed by the echoing, bone-shaking roar of the creature.

Was I wrong? Will it not let me pass?

Spinning on her heel, Elsinore stood ready to flee

or . . . fight? She didn't draw her sword; it wouldn't have been of any use. How could she hope to fight and survive against such an astonishing foe?

The creature had leaped to its feet, wings spread, mouth wide and wild, eyes pained. It paid no attention to Elsinore, instead rapidly scanning the landscape beyond her.

Elsinore turned trying to follow its gaze. *What happened? What's it looking for?*

When Elsinore spotted what was out of place, her heart skipped straight into her throat. By a pillar on the crest of a nearby mound stood Vedon. His face bore a look of overconfident determination, his posture wide and arm outstretched, as if from a throw.

Did he attack the creature? Why?

Another roar indicated the creature had located what it sought, and it dashed toward the foolish boy, its front claws bared.

"Vedon!" Elsinore shrieked.

Stopping suddenly, the creature turned toward Elsinore and roared again, not in pain but in rage. The roar, still that of an animal, was hostile and sharp with uncanny intelligence, a cry of disappointment. Rearing, the creature pawed the air and spread its great wings wider. Each wing split to reveal another, and two pairs of great luminously black feathered wings spread out majestically, circling its body and casting shadows that seemed to absorb the light around it. The beast raised its head, somehow perceptibly less human now, its visage one of fury and its rows of teeth glistening in its incredible maw.

Dropping back down to all fours, the beast tore across the ground toward Elsinore.

The moment it had taken to rage, however, had given Elsinore enough time to ready herself for its attack.

As it sped across the field, passing through the shadows of the pillars, Elsinore maintained a concentrated calm. Focusing on the notes of the spell, she drew her tympanum from her bag and quickly drummed a rhythm on it—two beats, then five, then two with long pauses—while she softly sang an ancient verse in the rhythm of the trees and the hills.

She raised the hand on which she wore the enchanted ring, and the tiny mirror surrounded by filigreed silver flashed and reflected the light of the sky. With her other hand, she swung her drum in a wide circle, counterclockwise. As she completed the circle, she suddenly clapped her ringed hand against the taut surface of the drum, and the sound thumped and echoed through the valley.

At the same time, she spoke a final word of command that she did not know—a word of such magic power, it fled her memory the instant she uttered it. Until the word disappeared from her mind, she was afraid the spell would fail; now, if she did not stop the beast, she knew it would not be from failure to cast correctly.

Before her, the circle she'd drawn with her tympanum glowed, a rainbow in the dimness, and within its bounds, the colors merged into a brilliant white light. As she watched, the rainbow circle expanded, and the creature, which couldn't check its momentum or turn away, ran into the light at full speed. Instead of passing through, it fell into a tunnel of color and was rapidly engulfed in the brightness.

The circle spun and sparkled and collapsed, until at last no trace was left of its presence but the afterimage in Elsinore's vision. She had been too afraid—no, she had been too enthralled by the majestic workings of the spell— to shut her eyes and look away.

Feeling safe for the moment, Elsinore walked to the mound where Vedon crouched beneath the angle of a pillar.

"Goddess all around us! Vedon, what are you doing here?" Elsinore shouted as she approached him. "How did you even pass through the Forest, with its spirits and witch lights?"

He didn't answer right away but crouched sheepishly as she climbed the mound. When she finally stood before him, she imagined she looked as imposing as the raging monster had moments before.

"I'm sorry," Vedon said. "I followed you. I ignored the lights, the voices—everything—and followed you. You saved me in the square, and I thought to do the same for you. I had to come with you. When that . . . that thing attacked you, I thought to come heroically to your rescue, to repay you for what you did for me."

"Heroism?" Elsinore scoffed. "To have my abilities doubted, to be followed and watched like a child, and to be undermined, waylaid, distracted, and endangered? Yes, that's what heroism is, isn't it: disregarding a woman's life so someone else can do whatever they imagine is best for her."

She sighed, exhausted, and sat on the ground beside him, her back against the pillar. Grass grew over the mound right up to the edge of the spike; in fact, the whole of the Valley of the Mounds was green with grass, faded and discolored in the cloud-filtered light.

"Are you hungry?" Elsinore didn't wait for a response before she pulled a package of rations from her bag—sweet bread, dried beans, and water, the latter of which she poured into a little cup, insisting Vedon drink.

They ate in silence, Elsinore only glancing at the boy

when she needed to pass him food. She didn't know what to say, either about their near escape or about the rest of what remained unspoken between them. Vedon focused only on his bread.

"You can come with me for a little while," Elsinore said at last, her eyes never straying from the Mountain before them. "But if you don't turn back soon, I'll have to make you go back. I can't keep watching out for you like I did just now, and what I'm doing here I need to do alone."

Vedon didn't look at Elsinore either, his expression one of shame. Head downcast, he looked out across the valley and nodded. Reaching into his pocket, he took Elsinore's hand and pressed something into it. When she looked down, she found he had returned the bottle he had stolen from her bag.

It was empty.

"Are we going to discuss this?" Elsinore asked, unsure what his answer would be. It was unusual for her to be uncertain in situations like this.

"I don't think I can right now," Vedon replied. "I'm sorry. I shouldn't have stolen it from you." Elsinore sighed, understanding.

"Did you drink it? You could have just asked me. I would have given it to you." Vedon avoided eye contact, and Elsinore shook her head. "No, I suppose you couldn't have asked, could you?"

Vedon didn't respond, instead changing the subject.

"How did you do that?" he asked, his voice more amazed than ashamed, lifting his head to look up at the clouded sky. "What you did to the creature? Was that magic?"

Elsinore turned and stared at Vedon as if he were

mad. "I'm a sorceress, Vedon." She raised one eyebrow incredulously. "I know you saw what I did to those buffoons and the crowd in the square."

The boy looked away. "I thought you only performed . . . stage magic? What you did then was an illusion, wasn't it?"

Elsinore laughed quietly but brightly enough to raise both their spirits in this menacing place.

"Usually, prestidigitation is all I need for a performance." She took his hand in hers. "But even then . . . I really am a mage. I know a few spells with real power to alter fate or change the material world in little ways."

"Where on earth did you learn a spell like that one you just cast? You made that creature disappear."

"Magnel's Prismatic Door?" she asked, as simply as if it were a name he should recognize. "My mother—Mil—taught me many of my spells. But there are a few others, like this one, that I learned . . . elsewhere."

Vedon laughed, mouth agape. "Is your mother aware you know spells like that?"

"She doesn't recommend casting them, but yes."

Elsinore stood, brushed herself off, and helped Vedon to his feet. Taking his hand in hers, she led him onward, down the mound and toward the wood of cedar trees growing up the foothills of the Mountain. They walked on for a time in peaceful silence, before Vedon broke the quiet with a question.

"Why is it called such a strange name? The spell, I mean."

"Spells are usually named for and by the mage who discovered them."

"And can you cast it again?" Vedon asked. "If there are more of those things?"

"Not for a day or so." Elsinore turned to look at him for a moment, then turned back to the Mountain and walked on. "It takes a certain degree of concentration and preparation, and now that I've cast it, I'd need to rest and recover and ready it again. I've already cast that and Earth Maiden's Renewal—the plant-growth spell—but I have others prepared. If another creature appears, I'll have to see what I can do."

"What if that one returns?" Vedon asked. "That thing was incredible; you can't have destroyed it, can you?"

"Oh no, of course not. That was a dimensional door," Elsinore said, as if that were obvious. "But its destination is unknown. No one has really gone through it to find out because of the very high risk of being torn apart."

Vedon stopped, eyes wide. "Torn . . . apart?"

Elsinore grinned. "By the friction of crossing between planes and through bent space."

"So that thing . . . it could have been dismembered, then? It could have been killed?"

"Oh, almost certainly not! That creature was far too magically strong to have really been harmed by any spells I could cast. That's why I didn't want to have to fight it in the first place." She smiled at Vedon sardonically. "So thanks for enraging it and sending it after us!"

Vedon averted his eyes.

"So . . . what was that thing?" he asked after a moment of walking in silence.

Elsinore sighed. "I'm not sure. It could have been a sphinx or a manticore or a lamassu. They're similar; they're all guardians of the sacred places of the gods, and they're all unspeakably dangerous for mortal travelers to encounter. It was a guardian, anyway. It was something I shouldn't have had to fight."

She looked away from Vedon in annoyance, but the boy persisted in questioning her, though out of worry or a deliberate desire to be a nuisance, Elsinore could not tell.

"But it could come back, then? If it wasn't destroyed, it could come back and come for me again? For us?"

"There's still very little chance of that," Elsinore said with certainty and, she feared, a hint of contempt. "Nothing that goes through the gateway has ever come back. At least, nothing I've ever seen."

Elsinore grew suddenly sad, and though Vedon said something else, all she caught was the uplifted tone of a question. She didn't respond, only staring out into the distance, over the dark cedars hidden in shadow. The day had not yet grown late, but the light of the sun was occluded already by the height of the Mountain ahead.

She walked on ahead as Vedon trailed behind and kept quiet. They walked for over an hour, until finally they approached the cedar forest, very close to the Mountain.

"Did you bring any weed?" Elsinore suddenly asked without turning around.

"No, I don't smoke."

"Shit," Elsinore muttered. She let him catch up with her, and they walked on together side by side, neither a word nor a glance passing between them until they came at last to the edge of the wood and stopped.

"I want to come with you," the boy said.

Elsinore's back was to him, and she considered the trees before her, before closing her eyes and remembering the valley they had passed through. She remembered the town they had started in—the town she had come from so long ago.

At last, she looked at her companion. "You're not happy in Tudur, Vedon." She laid a hand on his cheek.

"I don't know what it is you want. To be like me? To remake your body, your life, your place in the world? You can do that anywhere, with anyone, in your own time. There are witches, potion makers, in every village who can help you. Is it that you wish to travel, to see the world? I think you're far too inexperienced for that kind of danger. Is it to be with me? To stay by my side always, to show me what it is I mean to you?"

Tears welled in her eyes. "Do you know what I mean to you? Am I just a pretty girl you like to kiss and make love to—*to*, I think, not *with*. Or am I something from your past, something you knew, something familiar but different enough now that it pleases you to think how much you've grown since you were a boy?"

"Are you describing me? Or are you describing yourself?" Vedon asked after a moment.

Elsinore didn't respond. She only stared into his face, her mouth unmoving, her eyes hard and steady but for the welling tears.

"I'm sorry," Vedon said. "That was cruel of me to say. I'm sorry . . ."

"No, I'm sorry. I . . ."

Elsinore breathed a little laugh, held Vedon's face gently in both of her hands, and pulled him in close. He softly stroked the small of her back, and they kissed while the wind of the Season of Shadows rustled the branches of the cedars at the foot of the Mountain.

Pulling back from her lover, Elsinore reached into her bag and pulled out the book she still carried: *Love Poems and Songs of Intimacy*. She placed her ringed hand upon the cover and said a word that, afterward, neither of them could remember. The book briefly flashed blue light, then faded back to red cloth.

She handed the book to Vedon, who looked at it curiously. Then he looked back up at Elsinore, unable to even ask what she meant by the gesture.

"Keep it safe, and the spell should protect you till you're back home," she said. "Please return safely, Vedon. May you pass through the Forest unharmed. Go find what will make you happy and take hold of it, whether or not you ever see me again."

When Vedon looked as if he were going to speak, Elsinore placed a finger on his lips and smiled. Then she turned and walked into the woods, leaving him behind.

✳ 6 ✳

THE PLOUTONION

The cedars of the Mountain grew tall and ancient, rising with the foothills before clinging to the slope of the Mountain itself and disappearing up it into the clouds like a forest of heaven. But the way through these cedars was brighter than in the trees of the Forest, the path well-lit by the late-day sky, despite the heavy clouds hiding the sun.

Before long, Elsinore heard the crashing and beating of rushing water. Following it, she came to a break in the trees, where a waterfall cascaded down from a large hole in a rock overhang high overhead that jutted out over the edge of the wood. Despite the power of the falls, the water appeared darker toward the bottom, as if the rock behind it fell away, hiding a path behind the curtain of water.

Unease crept through Elsinore as she stared at the falls and the hinted darkness beyond, tingling at the base of her skull and zipping down her spine. She shuddered. This was the place, she realized, where she would need to alter her sight. There was a fissure, a magical one, somewhere in the air around her.

Or was it in the Mountain?

Whether the fissure was as aspect of the waterfall itself or something beyond it, she could not tell. Either way, she feared crossing through unprepared, and she knew she was not yet prepared.

Not at all.

Elsinore regretted once again that she no longer had any cannabis. Fae spaces like the Mountain were shifting, wild realms; being able to alter one's consciousness, to channel and focus through the mind the divine that surrounded all things, could enable sorcerers to perceive more of that realm than mundane consciousness permitted. Smoking cannabis probably would have been a simple way to achieve that.

Just as well, she thought. *The weed most likely would have been too weak.*

The witch desired to identify the folds of the curtain that lay across the matter of the world and pick the right place to draw it aside and step through. This would be possible with meditation, but she wasn't centered enough to achieve such a state on her own. Other methods taught by the mages she had studied under might be easier; while they still required focus, Elsinore's mental state would be less of a concern. They might even be easier than stepping through the waterfall, as that would require her to gather her will.

Elsinore looked back into the cedar forest she had come through. The trees stood in ancient silence, deeply aware in their roots of the secrets of this place, but of course, they refused to speak of it to any who trespassed at the foot of the Mountain.

If they won't tell me, perhaps I can feel what they know instead?

Laying her hand on the nearest trunk, she closed her

eyes and felt the tree's life flowing around her. The tree grew from the earth and was part of it, reaching up to the stars like everything else: the trees, the spires in the valley, and the Mountain itself. As she opened her eyes, a bright fiery-red arc flashed into sight upon the ground deeper in the forest, illuminated by light from the fading sky that cut clearly through the clouds and branches.

Elsinore walked carefully toward it. Perhaps it was unwise to be drawn away into the woods, but the energy in the tree, its life, reassured her.

As she came closer, she realized that the bright spot was a fairy ring—a circle of mushrooms in the grass—centered around a tremendous old cedar. The mushrooms were large, white stems with fiery red caps speckled with white spots, like stars emerging in a red dome of the night sky. The witch recognized the mushrooms from her herbalist studies; they were poisonous when ingested at certain quantities, but the right amount could produce the alteration of spiritual sight she needed.

A fairy ring was a sacred place, bound to and drawing from the life of the earth. For a mortal to disturb any part of one would be incredibly dangerous and invite deadly retaliation from the spirits who tended them. But Elsinore was a sorceress, a priestess trained and initiated in the mysteries of the Goddess, and she knew how to respectfully request what she needed from the earth.

At least, she thought she had some idea how to try.

Elsinore knelt before the ring, careful not to cross or disturb the mushrooms. She took from her bag one of her packs of rations, and from that, a small sweet cake of bread and sugar. Laying it aside, she drew from her belt the ritual dagger she had kept on her altar. It flashed silver in the fading daylight, and she reflected the light from the blade onto a spot on her arm.

Gently, she pierced the spot she had indicated with the sharp tip of the blade and let the first drop of blood fall onto the cake. With the knife, she then cut the stem of one of the smaller mushrooms as close to the earth as possible, immediately setting the cake in its place.

Elsinore cleaned the blade on the earth and sheathed it. Taking the mushroom, she stood and lingered over the ring. "Thank you," she whispered to the base of the tree.

Though there was no response in the wind, the air, or the earth, Elsinore felt a gentle sense of calm.

When she returned to the falls, she looked around again. She was on higher ground than before, in a place obscured by the woods around her. She saw no one, no creature, no other people. She had kept an ear out since entering the cedar forest, and she was confident that Vedon hadn't followed her this time.

The sun was now setting behind the Mountain, and the wind had cleared the sky of clouds. The brightest stars and planets began to emerge as twilight fell. Sitting on a rock by the edge of the pool beneath the falls, Elsinore began to undress.

First her boots, then her black hood and jacket, and finally her dress and undergarments. All her clothes she packed into her bag with her other supplies; the bag was not watertight, but it would do well enough for passing the falls.

But the witch did not move on yet.

Still seated on the rock, Elsinore held the mushroom in the palm of one hand and cupped her ringed hand over it. After some concentration, she opened her hands to reveal the mushroom, now dry and withered and more potent than ever. She broke off a piece of the cap and wrapped the rest up in a cloth, which she tied and placed in her bag.

At last, Elsinore put the piece of dried mushroom under her tongue. Closing her eyes and focusing on the sound of rushing water, she let the mushroom soak in her saliva for a few moments before chewing and swallowing.

A chill settled within her, and when she opened her eyes, the falls ran purple, as if they carried the light of the moon instead of water. Shouldering her bag and sword, she walked into the pool, its water sloshing about her knees, and passed through the waterfall, running her hands through her teal hair as she did.

On the other side, the light was dim. It filtered through the falls behind her, but there was another source ahead, flickering in the mist that wafted from the falls. Climbing out of the pool and onto the damp stone floor of the cave, she wandered toward the flickering light, though for how long she could not tell in her current state.

At last, she wandered into a grotto with another, much smaller waterfall. The water poured over the ledge of a hole in ceiling, through which Elsinore could still see some stars and planets.

Passing through to the other side of the grotto, Elsinore came to a stop, at last, in front of a smooth, solid stone wall. It was smoother and more even than it should have been, standing perfectly perpendicular angle the floor.

Is it artificial? Elsinore examined it but could find no door or other method of passage forward.

In the sky visible through the nearby hole in the ceiling, blue stars thrummed softly in the violet night. Sitting cross-legged before the wall, Elsinore closed her eyes and focused on the material world around her. She could feel every part of her body individually. She was aware of every pore and felt every breath. She felt the air permeating her lungs, the blood coursing through her veins, her eyes shifting behind her eyelids. She ran her fingers along every part her body: through her wet hair, over her cheeks and lips, down her chin and neck and shoulders and breasts, over her belly, her penis, her hips, her thighs, her knees, her heels.

As she opened her eyes, she could feel every individual atom of the world around her. She could feel every particle flowing through and around and in her, see their paths through the immediate past and future as they dipped into the depression she caused in the fabric of the universe, the gravity well of her body.

The drug she had taken was in full effect, bestowing a unique single-mindedness, a meditative state with which she could focus on what was in front of her and see beyond it.

She stared at the wall, at a single point in the center. The purple and blue light of the sky shaded the walls of the grotto lavender, but it was a lavender that grew stronger the longer she stared.

Her eyes never strayed from the single point she had chosen. But after a few moments, the purple, blue, and teal that colored the smooth rock face in the periphery of her vision began to swirl and form triangles, then circles of triangles—mandalas interlocking and rotating and pulsing on a wall she knew was gray and unmoving.

The mandalas kept spinning together, working toward something, a shape Elsinore could see coming yet couldn't delineate or express until the exact network of colored lines locked together just so.

As the mandalas lined up, the sheer face of the wall shifted with them, giving way to a passage beyond. Elsinore stood and passed through, and the door sealed shut behind her.

Elsinore wasn't certain if what she saw on the far side

of the portal was a hallucination brought on by the drug or a real place she had entered. Though it was dark, at last hidden from the rainbow light of the Pomegranate Moon, this place was lit by the same amethyst light as the night.

In this weird light, Elsinore stood before a kind of temple, a stone structure with pillars that were too close together to pass through but far enough apart to see between them. A stone doorframe stood in the center, carved with concentric rings that centered on the portal. On either side of the door stood a statue of the kind of creature she had encountered among the mounds: a recumbent lion's body, wings straight off its back, horns encircling a crown set on a humanoid head, mane coifed in ringlets and braids framing wide, blank, staring eyes of stone.

Assuming the temple really existed, Elsinore stepped through the doorway and down a short flight of stone steps. Beyond it stood another structure—older, more utilitarian, more real.

She never wondered whether this one was a vision.

It was a simple gray cubic building. It was made not of stone but of a compacted composite material of stone and cement, which looked solid and unbreakable. An unadorned rectangular doorway stood in the center of the near wall.

Elsinore stood still in amazement, trying to make sense of the things around her and maintain her balance as waves of the drug washed over her, though the height of its effects had passed.

How long had it been since she passed through the waterfall? It felt like minutes, but she could have been meditating before the wall for hours. In here, with no view of the stars and moon, it was impossible to say.

Stepping forward, Elsinore entered the structure. It was empty, the plain surfaces veiled in thick layers of dust of unknown age. But set in the back wall was a monolith larger than Elsinore, made of the same composite material as the building itself.

Carved into the slab was text, though in what script and language, the witch could not tell. She couldn't read a word, couldn't even tell if the text used an alphabet, a syllable system, or hieroglyphic characters.

Elsinore was highly literate; in addition to understanding the script of several forms of languages local to the valleys, Elsinore had learned from her mother and other teachers several ritual languages—some foreign, some dead. These were for magical use only, and she knew the arcane scripts and runes to scribe them.

Yet still, most of the writing before her was a mystery.

After a moment of study, she realized the monolith included multiple scripts—many languages—though not one could she read any more than the others. Only as her eyes neared the floor did she at last find a block of text she could recognize.

```
    YOU ARE NOW           THE PLOUTONION.
              NOT A PLACE OF HONOR.
        ABANDON HOPE ALL WHO ENTER HERE.
        NOTHING                 DYING
          WE CONSIDERED             TO BE
                        CULT
                PART OF   SYS     OF WARNINGS.
        THIS FACILITY                  LONG-TERM
          STOR     AN  DIS       OF HIGHLY
        RADIOA        MATER             KILL.
                      PARTIC L    LOC
          INCRE       TOWA    THE CORE
              THE HEART      THE MOUNTAIN.
                    STILL PRESENT IN YOUR TIME.
              DANGER IS UNLEA
                        DIS       THIS PLACE.
        NO MAN    RN            NO WOMAN    N A GIRL
            MAY RETURN                    PLACE.
                  FLEE WHILE    U
```

It was archaic, amazingly so; she knew it as one of the runic scripts she had learned in her magical studies. It took her a moment to parse it, a struggle that was not helped by the cracks in the bottom of the monolith that broke through the only portion she could even remotely recognize. Lines were broken and words were missing, and what she could see perplexed her without the full context.

The cracks converged on one side of the ominous tablet, creating a fissure so wide that Elsinore could have fit into it if she chose. A few moments after she finished reading the text, an eerie green light appeared within the fissure, accompanied by noxious fumes that made her slightly dizzy, similar to how she'd felt under the full effects of the mushroom.

Stepping aside, she leaned against the tablet away from the crack and tried to catch both her balance and her breath. As she did, the light spilling from the crack grew brighter still.

After a few minutes, scratching sounded from inside of the wall. Before Elsinore could react, a cat crawled out of the fissure, much to her amazement.

It was a mostly ordinary cat, seemingly domestic, with solid-colored fur that might have been black. It was hard to distinguish its natural color, though, because the dim green light appeared to emanate from the little creature's body.

Looking at the young woman, the cat meowed once, insistently. Then swift as they had arrived, the cat disappeared back into the fissure.

Elsinore looked around at the dust and the stone and the tablet and the crack. "How strange. Do you wish for me to follow, little cat?"

She looked back through the door at the temple

structure and the backs of the statues at the entrance. She read the message again, its ominous words echoing from some ancient past reverberating in her head as her mind reeled and recovered from the drug.

Considering all these things and the place she was in, the place she had come from, and the reason she had come, Elsinore clutched her bag and her sword and lay on the floor as flat as she could. Crawling on her belly, she descended into the crack after the weird, unearthly light and on into the Mountain.

✳ 7 ✳

JHE KUR

Elsinore crawled through the fissure for so long, she completely lost all sense of time. Had it been hours since she followed the cat? Minutes? A day? She began to fear the tight, claustrophobic tunnel would never end and, instead, grow smaller and smaller until she would be trapped, crushed, lost, or all three.

The one saving grace was the illumination provided by the eldritch green light. She had a light spell, but she lacked the concentration to cast it in so restricted a space.

She pressed on, hoping an end would come to the tight, squeezing, rocky tunnel before she was driven to panic, lost within the sepulchral veins of the Mountain.

She had lost sight of the body of the cat she had followed in here, but they must have been close, as the illumination always spilled from around a bend or curve of the tunnel.

Finally, eventually—though not soon enough for Elsinore's comfort—the ceiling began to rise, allowing her to breathe a little easier. As the tunnel filled with the damp, earthy scent of petrichor, Elsinore was able to push up onto her hands and knees.

Not long after, the space opened up further, and Elsinore found herself standing in a cavernous chamber, lit all around by flickering lamps bearing crystals or stones that burned with the same green light as the cat. The creature was nowhere to be seen.

How long had she followed the light of this room in the cat's stead?

The chamber was so deep, its ceiling so high, that even in the bright green light of the lamps, the walls stretched up into an impenetrable darkness—a starless, underground night. The far end of the chamber was likewise shrouded in distant obscurity. What she could see was a mound of some kind some distance ahead of her, and for lack of any other goal, Elsinore made her way toward it.

The slap of her bare feet on wet stone echoed endlessly into the distant shadows. It seemed impossible that she could have gone deep enough yet for the ceiling of a mountain cavern to reach so high above her, yet where else could she be? She already felt so far away from the surface, and the echoes made it feel farther still.

She knew such impressions to be lies, tricks played on the senses by the distance and the darkness. But still, the loneliness in her heart grew deeper.

As she approached the mound, the ghastly truth became clear: she was approaching a large midden of disarticulated bones.

Once she was close enough that the echo of her footsteps fell upon the mound itself, a few bones shook loose and rolled down the pile. When the whole mass began to rattle and shake, Elsinore stopped and stared.

The great curved ribs of some huge unknown creature began to stack on top of each other, creating a great pillar of bones that towered over her. As the bones piling atop the pillar narrowed to human width, arm bones and hands with horribly long fingers attached themselves to the upper ribs. The spinal column at the back terminated in the lolling white skull of a giant owl, with a terrible, sharp black beak and vast empty eye sockets, the depths of which burned with pinpoints of bright green light the color of the lanterns.

The creature waved its fingers through the air and called out in an inhuman voice that echoed across the vast cavern.

"Well met, traveler from Eridu! You are come to Kur, the Mountain! Sidhe-Kur, Burial Mound Mountain! Orkur, Mountain of the Oath!

"But be warned! No woman born a girl nor man born a boy may enter the Kur and ever again return to Eridu, the world above! The inhabitants of this realm are Orcs, People of the Oath; Aos Sidhe, People of the Burial Mounds; Kurgarra, People of the Little Mountain! So say I, appointed guardian of the gate!"

As the gatekeeper spoke, Elsinore felt she should wither before it, but something—the frightful experiences she had already had, perhaps, or the loosening of her inhibitions by the lingering effects of the mushroom—kindled enough courage for her to reply to the terrible thing. Raising her head, she spoke with a clarity of purpose that rose from a forgotten part of herself, drawn from she knew not where.

"Then I should be allowed to enter and to return home, by the law you have spoken."

"Wait!" the creature said. **"Speak more! Speak to me again! Speak!"**

"What do you want me to say?" she asked, voice low and doubtful.

"Anything! Speak longer!" The gatekeeper leaned as far forward as it could upon the column of bone that made up its lower body.

Elsinore closed her eyes, shutting out the sight of this underworld creature and the cave of darkness and grim phosphorescent light. Focusing, she spoke slowly, without opening her eyes. Her voice was deep and soft, and she was aware of every sound and syllable she made.

"I have come here for answers—for the key to the door of my past. I have come because . . . I think I was brought out of here as a child and left in exchange for a mortal boy, who is now unjustly imprisoned. I think I was left in the world above—in . . . in Eridu—so I might impersonate him, which I did poorly, before becoming true to myself. I wish only to know why, if not to free the boy so imprisoned. I think I am from here, the Kur, for it rises in my dreams before the moon. And further-more, though I was thought a boy by the mortal parents with whom I was left, I am now a woman—of my will, in my heart, and in my life—and so I am free of your ban on entrance and return."

Elsinore opened her eyes and met the gatekeeper's green-light gaze, which sparkled with amazement in the deep, dark sockets of its skull. "Let me enter here."

"The depth of your voice! Your breasts, and the shape between your thighs! Your scent, the sweat of a woman!

"You are an Orc! Kurgarra! Bean Sidhe, Woman of the Burial Mounds, and one of the Tuath De, the Tribe of the Goddess!

"You are a *Gala*! The special people of the Goddess! A younger daughter of the Moon! A Galla, a ghoul from out of the Kur and under the Sidhe! Welcome, my little sibling. May I say . . . my sister?" The gatekeeper leaned forward expectantly.

"A galla? How did—yes, I am . . . a sister." Elsinore stepped back from the creature's reach, as internally she stepped back in her memory.

How does this gatekeeper know of the gallae?

"She/Her! Sidhe/Kur!" The creature spread its arms exultantly. **"Your name! Tell me your name, little sister!"**

Elsinore's voice caught in her throat. To tell an entity like this one's name was a great risk. Knowing a name gave power over the named.

Yet she had borne many names besides her own. There was Elsie, the pet name her mothers had given her, but that was a gift and not really hers to give away. There was her surname, Ningala, but that was her name as a child of her home village of Nin.

And there was the name Vedon once knew and that her birth parents knew and had used for her so long ago. But was that even her name? It certainly wasn't anymore, if it ever had been. It was the name, at least, of the boy she had been exchanged with, the boy she had come into the Mountain to rescue. She would need it to find him.

But what name could she safely give the gatekeeper?

As she hesitated, the owl-headed creature spoke again.

"Careful! Cautious! As a fae witch should be with her name! But I ask in good faith! I take your name and beautify it! I exalt it! And I give it back, as

a veil that shall cover your Deep Name. This I swear by the light of the New and Full and Crescent Moons, and by the rift in heavenly Gallas, the Great River of Stars!"

Satisfied by the oath, the young witch consented. "I am Elsinore," she said at last, speaking her true name, the only one she had to give.

"Elsinore!

"Ensinurma!

"You must be! You must be allowed to enter!

"EN.SIN.NU.UR.MA!

"High Priestess of the Pomegranate Moon!

"With such a name, you must be allowed to enter the Kur! Your Deep Name: EN.SIN.NU.UR.MA!

"You were wise to be cautious, but I warn you against being foolhardy. With your name, you may enter the Kur, but do not give it to another, in Kur or in Eridu. 'Elsinore' is a veil that hides your Deep Name. Keep your Deep Name well and do not use it recklessly, or the power to destroy you will follow. It can be a powerful key to open the way, but otherwise, I must caution you: if others are able to hear you, keep your Deep Name ever behind your lips and in your heart.

"Enter, Ensinurma, Galla of the Goddess Heqakigal! Enter! The doors open for you! Flit through them like a fly! The barriers will not be barriers to your name! You are welcome here and welcome to return to Eridu, as are all gallae and pilli! For no woman born a girl nor man born a boy may enter the Kur and return to the world above!"

The gatekeeper's owl skull dropped from its shoulders and rattled to Elsinore's feet, where it lay lifeless, its eye sockets empty. Meanwhile, the ribs and spine clattered and clashed and fell, reforming into the arch of a gate, a portal of bone revealing a tunnel previously hidden by the pile of bones and the body of the gate-keeper.

Seeing no other way to proceed, Elsinore stepped timidly over the skull and descended into the tunnel. It was steep, with dusty brown stone steps cut directly into the earth. She moved slowly, carefully setting her bare feet on each narrow step and steadying herself on the rock walls. The staircase spiraled down, deep into the earth—how deep she did not know.

When she came, at last, to the bottom, there was a little doorway cut into the rock face. Beyond was a hallway, lined on either side with open doors leading to rooms that, while not very large, were each as big as a generous bedroom at an inn. The rooms were lit by candle lamps burning with natural fire, a nicer atmo-sphere than the one created by the green spectral crystals of the gatekeeper's chamber. All the rooms, however, appeared to be empty of occupants.

Walking down the hall a little way, Elsinore chose at random a chamber of stone and clay warmly fur-nished with hospitable trappings. The floor was covered in a wide round rug braided out of rags dyed many col-ors, humble but soft beneath the traveler's feet.

In one corner, a bed dressed with white linen sat by a table draped in a red tasseled blanket. On the other side of the room was a small pool and basin, and a door in the far corner led to an inner chamber for relieving oneself, all featuring drains and running water like the cities of the river valley.

Elsinore was suddenly aware of her body. She had never dressed after stripping to cross the waterfall, and her bare skin was dirty all over from crawling on her belly along the crevice in the mountainside.

Before doing anything else, she looked back out into the hallway. There was a thin wooden door at the entrance to the room she'd chosen, and another stood on the far end of the hallway, leading farther into the realm under the Mountain—the Kur. There was no means of barricading the entrance to her room save for the bed and small table, but Elsinore had prepared a spell, having expected to have to rest in such a place. She didn't know how much danger she faced, but it was best to take precautions.

Closing the door to her room, she spun around, drawing a circle around her body with her ringed hand. Once it was complete, she brought her ringed finger to her lips and whispered the word that cast the spell. The walls of the room flashed blue, and Elsinore knew the ward was set: no entity that meant her harm could cross the threshold until she left the room, dispelling the ward.

Thus protected, she left her bag on the floor, sword leaning against the bedpost, and sat in the inner chamber to relieve herself. She then took a pitcher and the basin to a smooth tiled corner of the room with a drain in the floor and washed the filth from her body—her breasts, her arms, her hair. Soaps and perfumes sat on shelves in the wall, and with them, she soon felt clean and refreshed. Once she had washed, she filled the pool and eased into the warm water, poured it over her face and hair, and rested.

In the bath, Elsinore fell into first sleep—her first since leaving Tudur—a peaceful sleep during which her body and mind alike drifted in the water. When she woke, softly and gradually, she could not tell how long she had slept or if any dreams had haunted her.

Rising from the pool, she dried herself off with a towel waiting nearby and walked to the bed, where she found white linen robes. Dressing in the robes, she sat beside the pillows.

Elsinore usually spent first waking in meditation and recuperation. Reaching into her bag, she took out a vial containing her dose of medicine for the night. She uncapped it and took the potion, holding it under her tongue to let it absorb into her mouth as she had the hallucinogen at the waterfall. Crossing her legs, she sat on the bed in silent meditation as her body absorbed the hormones.

Afterward, she took her spell book from her bag and studied the arcane writing within. In this way, she restored the mental energy she had spent casting spells the day before.

Most of the entries were not so much formulas as they were poems, songs, stories, or even visual depictions made out of words—not describing the spells with language but rendering the shape of the spell using text in a manner known only to a rare few talented mages. Elsinore reflected on each spell's meaning, purpose, and place, and the sound of them drifted through her mind.

She meditated, first on the spells she studied, then on the shape of her body and the world she lived in. Thus prepared, she could cast those spells stored in the ring once again.

She decided, however, not to prepare the Prismatic Door. She had a nagging suspicion that the destination of the portal was somewhere within this land—in the Kur—and she would rather not risk finding out for certain.

Having completed her meditation and study, Elsinore threw herself into a pile of pillows and sighed. She reached into her bag for her rooster doll and hugged it to her breast. She then gazed into its eyes, as she did most nights in the dark when she was alone.

As she stared at her reflection in the polished black buttons, she started to drift into second sleep, her mind skimming back over her life and the journey that had brought her to the Mountain. She thought of her parents abandoning her in the woods. She remembered her new parents finding her, saving her, recognizing her identity, and adopting her as their daughter. She contemplated being raised by a healer and traveling to those in need throughout the valley. And she considered the seasons after her adolescence, when she traveled from her home to Sanisa, the jeweled city of the Great River Gallas, where she studied at the temple of the goddess Tiranna and was initiated into Her mysteries.

✳ 8 ✳

JHE CHANGELING

The wagons were old and solid, reliable and mundane. Their age belied their stability, worn but durable, seemingly as old as the ancient road they followed. They were led by two women in the carriage at the fore. The smaller woman adjusted her colorful scarves and the dark hair that framed the cunning face of a witch, even as she managed the reins of the horses. The larger of the pair, tall and muscled enough that she might have been a giantess, gazed apprehensively beyond the long, waving brown grass at the edge of the road, to the forest in the highlands nearby.

"I still don't see why we have to pass so close to the Mountain," the giantess said. "In ordinary times, it's unsettling and makes the horses uneasy. During the Season of Shadows, it's dangerous."

"It's not yet the Season of Shadows, I'm quite sure. Do you see, Glamis?" The witch pointed dramatically into the distance. "In the stars? The Sign of the Reaper falls close to the horizon in the west, but it will not touch the earth at sunset till Summer's End."

It always amused Glamis that her partner tried to make herself look grand and mysterious before making such pronouncements, like a storied temple astronomer in some great city rather than the simple traveling hedge mage she was.

Glamis was wary and superstitious, but she trusted the witch's knowledge of the secret lore of the earth and the stars. Milanda might lead the caravan, but it had not been her decision alone to pass by the forest at the foot of the Mountain as the twilight season approached—though she had welcomed the shortcut. Glamis had stood alone among the company in voicing her objection, and she had deferred to her partner's wisdom.

"Still, it's close enough to it," Glamis replied. "It must be nearly Summer's End. And I think it's foolish to put our lives at risk . . ."

"Going near the Mountain would make you uneasy even at the peak of the Season of Light."

Milanda punctuated the statement with a twitch of the reins. Glamis was always amazed by the hidden strength in her slender arms, matched as it was by the depth of her wisdom.

"And besides, our lives are at no such risk. Or rather, they would be if we took too much time by going all the way around the whole Mountain region—forest, foothills, and all. We're low on supplies and can't spare the extra night it would cost us. You weren't there when I had to barter at the market for what we could get. The famine fell upon this poor region worse than other parts of the valley.

"Anyway," she concluded, "the people of the Faerie mounds are very fastidious about following the ancient laws. They wouldn't act out of season, and we all know it."

Glamis conceded the point. The People of the

Mounds followed strange laws, but they kept to them strictly.

Still, to know all the laws was more than could be expected of even the most cautious mortal, and who was to say if they were broken? The turn of the seasons was guided by the phases of the moon—irregular phases in these late days of the world, when the slowly falling moon was huge and strange in the sky, her changing face unfathomable to all but a few—and of course, to the People of the Mounds themselves. The edges of the seasons were hazy, obscured as if by the mists of the forest and the high clouds that hung around the moon, casting strange halos of light; any boundaries between them might be easily crossed by the unwary.

The witch and her partner made their home far from the Mountain, in a town called Nin, but they traveled the valley from season to season, visiting town after town for Milanda to practice her work as a healer, midwife, and fortune teller. Glamis was skilled as a laborer and could be of use wherever their wagon carried them. Nevertheless she always felt most comfortable at her own forge, following her calling as a blacksmith.

They traveled with a few others who made their way east toward the river, away from the forest and the Mountain. Their companions on the road varied with each trip, of course, but Milanda and Glamis were known in many of the towns and quickly endeared themselves to anyone they met. They had little trouble finding companions and fellow travelers to share the long journeys, especially given the protection such an obviously capable fighter as Glamis could provide.

They were eager to return home and had most recently set out from Tudur, a town many months' journey from Nin. They had been meant to move on to the next town in their itinerary by the end of the full moon and the show of its horns as a crescent. But the moon waned more quickly now, and their time on the road was short.

Driving on the Southern Road, they passed along the edge of the Forest, beyond which lay the broad wasteland dotted with ancient mounds that was said to be haunted by the People, who took unkindly to the tread of mortals.

And beyond the mounds stood the great Mountain.

The true danger, the true fear, the true magic, emanated from the Mountain. The Forest was but the conduit through which the magic flowed into the mortal world. Either way, Glamis felt they were too close to the wasteland, even with the forest. On the Northern Road—the safe road—the Mountain would still be visible in the distance. But here by the forest, she thought she could see, in the faded light and unnatural cast of the moon, the uneven spikes and spires said to jut at random from the mounds like the teeth of a deformed dragon.

What would become of them if they came closer? Too many tales spoke of intruders stricken dead, shot by the invisible bolts of the People of the Mounds. Or worse—rare warnings spoke of those who came away from the wasteland in fine health, only to wither and fade to barren shadows of their former selves over months or years, a changeling left in place of the hale youth who intruded among the mounds and was taken by the People.

And no tale Glamis or Milanda knew told of any who approached the Mountain itself and returned.

These dark thoughts grumbled in the back of Glamis's mind as she kept watch, and she would not have been surprised to know they were also in Milanda's, though the latter humored them less. Even the learned mage could not deny that strange things happened in the region of the mounds, and she would never have insulted the People so harshly and so dangerously by disbelieving in them.

As if conjured by Glamis's dark imaginings, a distant cry pierced the night, gripping her heart with a chill. It was the cry of a child—anguished, afraid—but surely such a sound was likely a trick of the People.

"Milanda, don't listen!" Glamis said, prepared by her fear to react immediately. "It's a trick, like a will-o'-the-wisp or a jack-o'-lantern, and you know as much! The craft of the People to lure us in and drag us below the earth!"

Milanda had heard the cry herself, and a fear crept into her heart—fear of what would happen not if they stopped but if they kept riding on.

After a moment, Milanda squeezed her eyes shut tight, sighed, and brought the lead wagon to a halt. Those behind followed suit. Glamis gave her a hard look that mixed warning with resignation, and then she, too, sighed before leaping to the ground and drawing a short sword she kept behind her seat.

"Come on, then! Kef, Brakko!" Glamis called to the travelers in the nearest wagon. "Please, I need you both with me. There you are, brothers!"

A quick explanation, and the two were eager to follow the strongwoman to interrogate the source of the cries. As eager, it seemed, as Glamis now was to lead the way.

"Let's get going—the voice is coming from there, those trees by the edge of the wood. Let's be quick!"

Feeling a soft hand on her arm, Glamis turned to find Milanda looking up at her from her side. "Why the sudden change of heart?"

"I could see in your face that only one thing was going to get us moving again," Glamis said. "That, and the thought of a real child out there, alone on the hill where even I'm afraid to go . . . well, I have to make sure, don't I?"

The giantess took her partner's hand, looked her softly in the eye, and kissed her quickly, before she and her crew strode off toward the hill. "Though I still say it's a trick," she called back over her shoulder.

She'd gone barely fifty paces when she found Milanda had caught up, striding beside her, her hood shading her eyes from the moon.

"Shouldn't you be staying back to keep an eye on the wagons?"

"I left Capan in charge," Milanda replied with a grin, referring to one of the horses that drew her carriage. "If this is a child, after all, I know for a fact I'm better with children than you."

Glamis didn't turn to look at her partner, though she smiled.

"I'd imagine I'm better at dealing with fae, as well," Milanda muttered, and Glamis chuckled. The quiet laughter made the darkness of the forest ahead seem less grim.

The four of them walked on silently, listening for the voice to call out again. By the time they came to the tree line, the louder cries had died down, but they were close enough that Milanda could hear a soft, steady sob.

Kef and Brakko cleared the brush as they entered the wooded spaces at the edge of the forest. No one said a word, and as they moved deeper through the trees, farther from the road, the sobbing grew louder and louder.

The voice was near, they all knew, and when Glamis stepped on a brittle fallen twig, causing it to snap, the sobbing halted suddenly with a stifled gasp. Milanda turned to the others silently and held out a hand, telling them to wait.

Moving forward without a sound, Milanda pushed branches aside with her arm to reveal a wide, ancient grove. In its midst stood a great hollow trunk—the husk of a dead tree that must have been taller than the hills in life—and perhaps just as old.

Moonlight spilled through the space in the branches overhead, dancing off the dew on the moss and the glitter on Milanda's scarves. The scarves swung softly as she proceeded into the grove, sliding over the knots and roots of the massive old tree. Though the field was brightly lit, deep shadows hung in the hollow, and Milanda crept toward them, her footfalls padded by the moss. She steadied herself on the uneven root before vanishing into the tree.

The men looked at Glamis. *Should we go with her?* they seemed to ask. But the giantess pointedly avoided their gazes, tightening her grip on her sword as she stared at the spot where Milanda had disappeared. She had no idea what good blade and muscle might be against what-ever unearthly creature lurked inside the tree, and she knew no reassurance she could give her companions or herself. Milanda was learned enough in the ways of the People to know better than Glamis—learned enough, at least, to feel confident descending into a shadowy pit in an ancient rotten tree in the Forest beneath the Moun-tain, to a fate the nature of which Glamis could not guess.

For a long moment, there was nothing. In the still air, sounds echoed, multiplied, shimmered, and struck; an er-rant breath would have been heard back at the caravan as clearly as the cries that drew them to this place. Yet in this moment, there was nothing—no sound, no breath, no cry, not a whisper.

In the silence, Glamis saw them. Like deeper shadows in the darkness, patches empty of moonlight, figures stood near the tree, watching. Some looked into the hollow where Milanda had disappeared, but others looked back at Glamis and her crew.

They were robed in black, and their eyes were hidden in darkness, hidden from the moon, in what must have been the shadows of masks. Their heads were inhuman, with untidy black feathers and long, narrow beaks like crows or ravens. Whether these were their natural faces or sinister hoods was unclear.

Glamis stood frozen, not in fear but with caution. None of the figures moved, not toward Glamis nor into the hollow after Milanda. They all merely stood vigil, watching silently.

Not taking her eyes from the figures, Glamis turned her head, attempting to silently signal Kef and Brakko, but neither spoke, moved, or signaled a reply.

Then, so suddenly that Glamis jumped with fright, leaves rustled, branches parted, and Milanda stepped out of the gap in the ruined tree and into the bright moonlight, scarves trailing from her loose hair and her cloak wrapped around a child in her arms. A girl? Glamis was unsure, though they were surely no infant and, by size, seemed two or three autumns old.

"Hurry ahead to the wagons and bring me back some water, Kef, please," Milanda said.

Glamis looked past her, to the figures in the trees. However, in the moment she had focused on her partner and the child, the figures had vanished, as silently as they had appeared. No branches moved in the moonlight, and not a trace indicated there had ever been anyone there.

"Let's get out of here. This is no place for anyone, much less a child."

Brakko led the way out, and Glamis kept to the rear, her eyes sweeping all around but mostly trained behind them on the grove of the tree husk, where the feather-garbed, bird-faced people had disappeared. Only when they had gone far enough that the moonlight was visible through the trees ahead did Glamis feel safe enough to speak freely.

"Is she . . . ?" Glamis was unsure how she meant the question to end: Safe? Hurt? Human? A girl at all?

"I don't know yet," Milanda replied after a moment, answering all the questions without needing to hear any of them. "But they're—she's—alive and needs water."

Glamis motioned to Milanda that she would take the child in her own arms, being much larger and stronger than the smaller woman, but Milanda only walked on, perhaps not with ease but showing no sign of struggle.

There's strength in those slender arms that the world can't always see, Glamis thought. *And I guess a midwife like Milanda surely is better with children—and fae—after all.*

Keeping pace with Milanda, the crew walked steadily out of the woods and into the weird light of the moon. Only then could Glamis make out the child's face, illuminated by the halo in the sky—wan, emaciated, and smudged with dirt from the rotten tree—but the mystery surrounding the child was no clearer.

On the way back to the wagons they met Kef, who brought water, a little cake, and some medical supplies. A cunning woman skilled in the application of medicines and herbal tinctures, Milanda looked over the child, who bore no grievous injury but was fatigued, severely mal-nourished, and slow to trust and speak to any of them.

The child had not made a sound since emerging from the leaves with Milanda. Once their tears finally dried and they had ravenously eaten some of the cake, they at least seemed calmer. Once they returned to the caravan, the witch ventured to ask a question.

"I'm so sorry you were out there alone. My name is Milanda. My partner and I heard you crying quite a lot from the woods. Do you have any parents? Caretakers? Friends?"

Avoiding Milanda's eyes, the child gazed deeply into their cup of water. They tightened their lips as if holding something back, before starting to squeak out a word.

"My—"

The child choked and started sobbing softly, quietly. Milanda brushed the child's hair from their eyes, planning to wipe away the tears, and found the left side of their temple bruised. Tutting sympathetically, she told Glamis to heat some water and soak a rag.

"Your . . . ?" she asked the child gently.

"They . . . they . . . they left me. My mama and . . . in the woods . . ."

Fully crying again, the child spoke no more. Milanda embraced the child right away, letting them mourn as her body absorbed the tears and wails before they could echo out into the night all alone. She held them tightly in her arms, her face over their shoulder so the little one could not see her eyes harden, her rage boiling faster than the water Glamis fetched.

Had this child been abandoned, exposed in the woods? It was rare for a child to be exposed, though not unheard of in times of leanness and famine. Still, for someone to do this to their own child was more than the healer could comprehend or forgive.

The child gradually stopped shaking and crying, comforted by Milanda's embrace. She smiled at them, and they laughed. The warmth of a protective affection settled in Milanda's heart, though it could not quell the anger she felt toward any who would let this child come to harm.

Glamis finally sent the others back to their wagons and told Milanda to gather the child up into the back, insisting she would take the reins herself. "We can't afford to linger any longer, after all. An extra night would cost us too much in the way of provisions, and doubling back to the town is out of the question. We bartered dearly enough for these supplies, as it is."

Milanda eyed her partner, puzzled, but Glamis didn't meet her gaze, instead looking back at the forest with something terribly like fear.

Rather than press or tease her as she had before, Milanda agreed. They were moving on, after all, and they had a new responsibility to tend to. Glamis's changes of opinion came as freely as the wind tonight, with the urgency of a storm, but whatever she knew—whatever she had seen in the trees—it could wait until another time, until sunlight shone down on them, far from the Forest and the Mountain.

It could wait.

Milanda found some pillows and blankets for the child to rest on in the body of the carriage as the horses picked up speed beneath Glamis's whip, and the caravan continued their journey. The child fell soundly asleep almost immediately despite the rumbling of the wheels on the ancient road, worn from however long they had spent shaking with terror and tears.

When the child woke the next day, after a night of mumbling darkly from nightmares Milanda could only guess at, they were prone less to weeping but still reticent to share details. Even the child's name proved impossible to tease out, leaving the women to address their new companion as "little one."

Milanda and Glamis tried not to voice the doubts that remained in the backs of their minds, which Glamis had put there with her worry when she heard the child's cries from the woods. The doubts had weakened and sunk away, but they lingered just the same: didn't there seem to be something a little uncanny about the foundling? In moments alone, Milanda wondered, in a dark corner of her mind, if the child was a changeling after all.

But when she heard the little one laugh at a face Glamis made, kick their legs over the side of the carriage, or run to play with the giantess in the field where the caravan had stopped, these dark thoughts fell far away. Yet still, they remained; buried and out of sight, perhaps, but not gone.

The travelers came at last to a little town by a stream and set up camp. The child's face brightened when Milanda offered to replace the filthy, torn rags they had been found in. She went into town while Kef and Brakko joined a few others from the company to repair one of the wagons, and Glamis and the child played. When Milanda returned with some clean robes she'd acquired from a shop, she took the child to the stream to bathe and dress.

As she cleaned them, she thought at first that Glamis had been mistaken that first night about the child's sex—this was a boy, apparently. Milanda tried addressing them as such to build a better rapport, but this only made the child shy away, even dispelling the trust they had built up over the past few days.

Once clothed, the little one's tears returned, and they

ran from Milanda, back to Glamis and the carriage. The witch stopped herself from running after them; instead, she sat on a stone at the edge of the trickling little stream, running her fingers through the water.

After some contemplation, she smiled.

When the child came running to Glamis in tears, Glamis dropped to one knee and embraced them, awkwardly trying to comfort the little one despite being unused to showing such affection.

"What's wrong, girl? Was the water too cold? Milanda can be a little cold herself at times."

Brightening up at once, the child laughed and fell into Glamis, burying her face in the woman's side. Though confused, Glamis laughed with her as Milanda returned to the carriage.

"I'm very sorry, but I think I made a mistake," Milanda said to the child as she sat beside Glamis. "I think we can be friends . . . if I try again the right way this time. But first, I hope you will finally tell me your name, little princess." She wore an expression of quiet calm and welcome.

The child laughed again brightly. "Elsinore! I'm Elsinore!"

"And where did you get a name like that?" Milanda asked playfully.

Elsinore suddenly became very solemn, in the way of a child wanting to seem serious and grown up. "They gave it to me in the woods. It's a girl's name, and I love it, and it's for me."

Milanda knew enough of the ways of the People to be wary of asking more, no matter how she wished to. Though worried, her face softened, and she smiled at Glamis.

"That's a pretty name," Glamis said playfully, "but it's a mouthful for a grown-up like me. How about I call you Elsie?"

Elsinore laughed again, blushing, and nodded.

"Elsie," Milanda said, her wariness subsiding. The child looked up at her shyly. "I think you're a very special little girl, and I'm glad you're with us." The girl threw her arms around the witch's neck, and from then on, she seemed much more comfortable around them both.

She accompanied them back to Nin, where the townsfolk came to know her only as the healer's new ward. She quickly grew to consider Milanda and Glamis her mothers, and the two women loved her as the daughter they couldn't have had otherwise. The new family took care of each other as the seasons passed, the stars fell by, and the months turned into years.

Nin was a little town, one of the lesser that lay in the bends of the Great River. The houses were flat-roofed, built of clay and brick, shaded by palms, simple gardens, tents, and flying awnings. The cool climate of the river kept the pace of the town easy and slow, and Elsinore loved playing in the communal fields of clover and wild-flowers within the residence block with the other children.

A few months after she was found, Elsinore accompanied Milanda to the stables at the edge of town. Though barges and skiffs made travel along the river swift and regular, carriages and wagons were the norm for travel deeper into the valley. The horses and oxen were shared among the people of the town and well taken care of, and those who made frequent journeys, such as Milanda and Glamis, kept good relations with the ranchers.

The town healer brought her daughter on this trip to accustom her to the animals, and the girl soon shyly asked to pet one. The ranch hand laughed and led her to a fence, then brought one of the horses over to meet her.

The animal was so huge compared to the little girl. It was actually quite small, perhaps a pony rather than a horse, but to little Elsie, it was a giant. She screamed and cried in fear and ran to Milanda, who laughed gently as she comforted her child.

Milanda had taken so easily to the role of mother. In no time at all, she knew just how to take care of a worried little girl who had survived such great pain, no matter the truth of her background. She took Elsie to the fruit stand nearby, gave her a little basket of juicy, ripe berries, and the girl was soon content.

When she finished her berries, Elsie approached Milanda timidly and asked to try petting the horse again. Her mother waved her hands in a flourish, producing an apple from nowhere. Elsie laughed with delight, and this time, she stroked the horse's ear as it ate from her hand.

Elsie quickly grew fond of the horses and accompanied Milanda whenever she made arrangements to travel. The moon changed her uneven face many times.

One year, in Elsie's eleventh autumn, Milanda took her adopted daughter to the stables, but the girl knew not what for. She and Glamis had no plans to tour; perhaps Milanda was here to plan another trip or on some other business. All she knew was she loved visiting the ranch to ride, see the horses run free, and feed them apples and stroke their beautiful manes.

When they arrived, Elsinore met a friend she talked with often; the girls had known each other for years now, and they played with the horses, gossiped, and laughed while Milanda engaged in whatever business she had.

When Elsinore went to look for her mother, she found her conversing with a young person the girl did not recognize. Their style of dress was quite queer. In a town where everyone's dress had become predictable to Elsinore after years, even Milanda's colorful costumes, this stranger's outlandish attire drew the girl's attention immediately.

The right side of their head was shaved clean, and the hair on their crown and left side, which fell to their shoulder, was dyed bright purple. Their ears and nostrils were pierced in several places and decorated with sparkling metal rings, and their eyelids and lips were painted black. They wore a short black tunic with a yellow scarf the color of sunflower petals, and a blue-green traveler's cloak with a black hood drawn down around their shoulders. Their arms were adorned with black bracers studded with blunt steel spikes.

Milanda and this woman laughed over something only they could hear. Or was this person a woman? It dawned on Elsinore quite suddenly that she couldn't tell, and that ambiguity stirred up feelings of strange familiarity in the girl.

"Elsie!" Milanda said when she saw her daughter half-hidden behind a stall, lost in thought as she gazed at the stranger. "I'm glad you're back. There's someone I'd like you to meet. This is my friend Ardena. I knew them when we were younger, but they've been traveling, and we've been on the road so much lately ourselves. It's been a long time."

"I'm very happy to meet you, Elsinore." Ardena had a very sweet voice, with an inflection Elsinore could recognize but not place. It wasn't an accent; it was a tone of voice, a manner of speaking that sounded familiar somehow. Their face was kind, despite their dark eye shadow. They smiled gently. "Your mother was just telling me she's teaching you magic? Can you show me any spells?"

Elsinore didn't respond out of shyness, but she shut her eyes tight, drew a flower petal from a pouch she carried on her belt, and then made a few simple gestures in the air in front of her. She whispered a word over the petal, and it lit up, casting a bright rainbow light visible even in the midday sun.

Ardena's face lit up as brightly as the petal, and they laughed. "Elsinore, that's beautiful! As bright as the full Pomegranate Moon they're predicting for tonight."

"I want to learn a lot of prismatic spells." Sheepishly, the girl added, "I just like rainbows . . ."

"Well, of course," Ardena said. "They're very pretty and very special, just like you." Elsinore blushed.

"Elsinore," Milanda said, "Ari was just telling me about the temple in Sanisa where they studied. They're one of the priests of the Goddess. They spend time at the temple, and at other times, they wander the valley, visiting towns and meeting with old friends like me."

Elsinore's eyes widened with wonder. "You studied in a big city like Sanisa?"

"Well, magic, yes," Ardena said. "The acolytes there learn deep spells from the long-ago days of the Old Ones, and from before even that cursed time—"

"Ari!" Milanda muttered under her breath. "I don't think you need to go into that just now."

Ardena grinned. "Of course. But more important than the magic, we also learn the proper worship and theology of the Goddess. It's the temple of Tiranna, Mother of the Mountain and Source of the River."

"The goddess of love." Elsinore wrinkled her nose in

disappointment. Romance was something unpleasant and unnecessary, something adults wasted their time with and bored everyone else by talking about.

Ardena laughed. "She's much greater than that. Maybe someday when you're older you'll understand. Not everyone hears the voice of the Goddess, after all. But it is also a magic school, and maybe when you're old enough, it's the sort of place you'd like to study?"

"Can I, Mil?" Elsinore asked, taking her mother's arm. "When I'm old enough? Can I learn magic in a city like that?"

She didn't mention the real reason she wanted this. There was something familiar, something luminous about Ardena, like the warm window of a well-known inn after traveling at night through the woods, or a bright star cutting through the clouds to light the way through the darkness. Elsinore wanted more than anything to be like Ardena—more than learning magic or following any goddess. It was as if seeing this queer person had somehow stirred up memories of herself from in the future, as if she suddenly remembered that this was what she had always been meant to be like, what she had to be like to be herself.

Studying her daughter thoughtfully, Milanda smiled. "I think that would be lovely—when you're older. We have to let Ardena get going now, and head back home to Glamis. But I'm very glad you had the chance to meet cousin Ari."

They parted ways, but after saying goodbye to Ardena, Elsinore felt suddenly, inexplicably lonely. She realized that in all the years since she'd been rescued from the woods, she had known no one else like them. She had mothers and a community who loved her, but this was the first time she had met someone like herself.

* 9 *

THE TEMPLE OF THE GODDESS

Milanda had known about the temple, of course. Most folks in the Great River Valley knew the followers of the Great Goddess Tiranna, and witches like Milanda knew more than that, being familiar with the seats of worship of the most widely venerated gods. Tiranna was one of the most beloved: Mother of the Stars, Queen of Heaven, Queen of the Divine Mountain, Lady of Resurrection. Most popularly, She was the goddess of sex, of the mundanities of women and men, and of those in between or otherwise.

The latter were especially beloved by Her. Her priesthood consisted of those who traversed or blurred the conventional boundaries of sex. These priests and priestesses traveled around the Great River Valley as mendicants, wanderers, singers, fortune tellers, and dancers, and they frequently crossed paths with traveling healers like Milanda on the road and in towns.

Elsinore never forgot how she felt when she met her mother's friend Ardena in her childhood, and she studied the spells Milanda taught her diligently in preparation for the day she could attend the temple of Tiranna in Sanisa.

Seasons passed. Elsinore grew into a young woman like many others: pretty in her way and awkward as any her age. She was sullen at times, like many who were no longer children but far yet from adulthood.

Yet there was more to this melancholy, in Elsinore's estimation. A feeling lingered in the back of her mind that there was somewhere she was from, somewhere she was meant to go back to, some place she had only seen glimpses of in her dreams. Then there were the brief meetings with folk like Ardena who, it seemed to Elsinore, were travelers from this foreign country. Though she had friends around Nin, at times she felt the weight of an aching loneliness that threatened to grow unbearable.

The young witch made the most of her solitude by haunting libraries, in Nin and in other towns of the valley that Milanda visited as a healer. But study as she might, seeking answers in spells, old books, and ritual mysteries everywhere she looked, the pieces Elsinore so desperately sought continued to evade her. In all the years since she'd been rescued from the woods, Elsinore had never been able to find the answers she needed about herself.

Milanda and Glamis did what they could to help their daughter, as mothers try to do. Elsinore's adolescence started at a late age, but she eventually began to show signs of a boy's puberty. Her skin grew greasy, a little body hair began to grow, and to Elsinore's sorrow, her voice began to drop—not very deep, not yet, but she knew what it meant and wept despairingly to her mother. Consulting her book of recipes and spells, Milanda found a potion that could halt the unwelcome march of alien masculinity in Elsinore's body, letting her grow into the woman she knew herself to be.

Within the next few months, Milanda taught her daughter potion-craft so she could brew the medicine herself. The mysteries of these techniques had been discovered by devotees of the Goddess long centuries ago; none could even be certain if it had been before or after the time of the Old Ones. The urine of pregnant mares formed the basis of a potion of great magical power, a potion that would grant or restore the features of womanhood to the body of any who used it.

Being of the age that a girl with a womb would have begun to menstruate, Elsinore began taking the medicine regularly.

Soon, what body hair had begun to grow melted away, her skin and hair grew smooth and soft, and most of all, her breasts ached and budded and grew like any other girl's in her adolescence. Her voice remained a little strange for a girl, but Elsinore felt mostly at peace with her body, for the first time that she could remember.

Still, though, a longing remained in a deep part of herself—a gap calling out to be filled, though she never could see clearly how.

As the seasons flew by, Elsinore spent her time like any other girl in the village—playing, studying, making mischief with her friends, and laughing at the agony of the world—as she tried her best to push aside the unintelligible call she heard, carried on the back of the wind. Many years had passed since the night in the wood, and as the dry, sunny Season of Light danced with the rainy, fertile Season of Shadows, Elsinore grew into a young woman.

One morning, she noticed Milanda making preparations for travel. The older woman told her daughter to gather her bag, for they were going on a journey.

"But we just returned from time on the road,"

Elsinore protested. "I thought you were going to spend the rest of the year here in Nin?"

"I am, dear. Glamis is staying in town, and I plan to return soon. After I see to your safe arrival."

"Where?" Elsinore asked, even as she began to pack clothes and supplies. She trusted Milanda, of course, so she knew she had a plan, but her curiosity got the better of her.

A half smile crept into the corner of Milana's mouth. "Isn't it time you went to study at Sanisa?"

Elsinore's eyes widened, and she laughed, unable to respond otherwise. Pouncing on Milanda, she embraced her, and after packing, the two set out for the city on the river.

Sanisa was a larger, more populous metropolis than Nin and the smaller towns Elsinore had visited with her mothers. Stone buildings multiple stories tall, with columns supporting overhanging eaves and roofs, towered over smoothly paved streets, steps leading to wide terraces, and bright but narrow alleys. Colorful pennants flew from balconies of residential insulae, bearing personal devices, symbols, letters, and messages in every language known to Elsinore, as well as many she did not recognize. Lanterns floated in the air, supported by posts and pillars, lines and chains; unlit in daylight, the lanterns promised the ambient radiance of the stars brought down to earth come nightfall.

Graceful bridges and walkways spanned the gaps between towers and rooftops, and people of all kinds and origins climbed stairwells and gently curving ramps on each level. From atop the tallest bridges, one could see the glittering magnificence of the river Gallas, a name that, by way of some wordplay in one of the old languages of the valley, meant simply "river."

The word once meant "voice" or "song," like the speech of a person or the call of a bird. It had drifted over the centuries to also mean "lip," as in the mouth of the speaker or singer, and from there to metaphorical edges or rims, like the shore of the sea or the marshland along the edge of the river. From there, the word must have been applied first to the marshes and then to the Great River itself. So the river flowed like the words of a song, carrying the praise of the children of the Goddess to the Great Mother.

If the river was the lifeblood of the valley, Sanisa was its heart, the city from which ships with flying sails sped all along its length and abroad upon the sea, for trade and surveying and travel. Visitors came from every corner of the valley to marvel at Sanisa, to study at the library in the temple, to stroll in the shadows of its gardens, and many could not help but stay indefinitely, to become part of its cosmopolitan wonder.

But the beautiful architecture of Sanisa was dominated by the temple of Tiranna—a large complex with a paved pavilion, from which rose a tiered pyramid, a ziggurat with wide irrigated gardens on each level. The lush vegetation was like a forest being lifted up to heaven.

To Elsinore, the city felt like a paradise. But what she found most amazing, most wondrous, was not the architecture but the people.

The city thrived with activity, with folks performing on the streets, trading food and items, singing, wandering, and enjoying themselves in every way. People from all lands came together as one community. And all around her—not everyone, but many more than she'd ever seen at once—Elsinore saw people like herself. Street performers here and there, folks strolling with their friends down the avenues—Elsinore could tell that they had been born to one role but their hearts had decisively led them to another.

Women like herself, who in another time and place would have been thought to be—would have been conscripted into—the role of men, but here were free. Likewise men, who in other circumstances may have been forced into the domain of women, here proudly walked the city as equals with their brothers. Others Elsinore saw whose sex she could not guess—folks who blended the appearance of men and women, or who eschewed signifiers entirely, who were singularly unique.

The temple was hung with banners and curtains of purple and blue green. Many bore a bright-yellow design; Elsinore thought at first that it was a flower, its pointed petals revealing a circular inner floret. Upon further consideration, she decided it was likely meant to be a star, with eight rays shining in the night.

When they entered the courtyard, Elsinore and Milanda saw others wearing robes and sashes of these same colors. Some had their hair dressed and dyed to match. Elsinore later learned that these were the colors of the Goddess: purple for the sky that surrounded the rainbow halo of the Pomegranate Moon; turquoise for the Great Ocean that surrounded the world to the south, as well as for the blue cedars that reached for the heavens in hilly regions surrounding the valley; and yellow for the flowers that bloomed at the dawn of the Season of Light, as well as for the stars that burned in the heavens and flowed in the currents of the galaxy. Each—sky and sea and earth in between—dotted with brilliant stars and gentle flowers, formed the body of the universal Great Mother.

"These are the gallae and the pilli. Temple personnel," Milanda said. "The sisters, brothers, and siblings of the order, the Stars of Galattis."

Elsinore was reminded at once of Ardena, who had dressed like those of the order when she saw them years ago.

As if summoned by Elsimore's memory, a familiar voice called out, "Mil! Elsie! It's so good to see you again!"

Ardena approached from across the pavilion. Elsinore swore they looked not a day older than when she'd last seen them, and they were dressed much the same. Their hair was now full, braided, and black, and they wore a purple dress with a teal shawl.

"Welcome, both of you. Mil, I got your message, of course. I'm so glad Elsinore wants to study here. Will you be staying, Mil?"

"I wish I could stay for longer than just the night, Ari, but I'll be leaving to return to Nin in the morning. Elsinore, though, can stay as long as she needs and wishes to. With the permission of the temple, of course."

"Certainly she may." Ardena focused on Elsinore. "There is no hierarchy here. No hierophants, pastors, kings, or masters. Those of us here who are blessed by the Goddess, the Stars of Galattis, are all equal in Her eyes and all open to Her revelation."

Elsinore turned to look at Milanda. "I always thought the temple was dedicated to Tiranna."

"Galattis is an emanation of Tiranna." Ardena motioned for their guests to follow and began walking the courtyard to the grand stairway up to the first level of the temple. They picked a flower from a tree along the path—a flower with white pointed petals like a star.

"The emanations are forms Tiranna takes to manifest in disparate parts of the universe. Imagine a sage—a learned woman of great wisdom, such as your mother."

Milanda scoffed, and Ardena laughed gently.

"This sage composes a poem, and that poem exists

in her head. She may transcribe it with ink on paper or chisel it in stone, but it originates from her mind. She later composes another work, perhaps an essay on flowers or herbs. Then another—a set of directions for constructing a house perhaps, which her partner may use to bring the building into reality.

"Each of these works is part of the sage, a view into her mind. They are part of her, but not exactly her. Each is limited to part of her thoughts but may be used to extrapolate other thoughts she may have kept hidden in the work.

"Tiranna's emanations each form a part of material reality—a galaxy whose emanations are the stars, a star whose own emanations are planets, planets whose further emanations are the flowers and animals and people who live there. But each thing ultimately proceeds from the Mother."

As they finished speaking, Ardena handed the flower to Elsinore, who looked at its petals, considering its form.

"It's so beautiful," Elsinore said. "Like someplace I've seen in my dreams. The place where they're all set." She had a faraway, wondering look as she gazed from the flower to the majesty of the temple gardens.

While Milanda and Ardena talked over dinner that night, Elsinore explored the living quarters of the temple. Many came to stay, study, and worship, for a few months or years at a time, before moving on with their journeys or pilgrimages or to return home. When her mother left to return to Nin, Elsinore's studies began. Disciplined practice of old spells in the library and crafting potions from ancient formulas occupied her waking hours for months.

Most importantly, Elsinore's mind finally cleared of the fog of alienation and loneliness that had fallen over it in the last few years, which had darkened her hopes and her view of herself. She began to feel not as she had as a child but as if she were growing into the woman that child should have become.

At the temple, Elsinore learned the word for women like her: gallae, women of the river, of the flowing, changing water and the marshland that blurred the boundaries between the water and the land. Women who sang with the voice of the Goddess. Now that she was surrounded by girls with bodies like hers, she felt a sense of belonging to know there was a name for the kind of girl she was.

She also met many boys conversely cursed at birth with bodies like those she wished she had. They were known as pilli, men of the tall reeds that grew in the marshes; men of the thrusting spears, who fought for the bodies other men were granted by birth.

At last, the acolytes saw that they weren't alone, that others shared their particular afflictions, that they were more normal than they had ever felt out in a world where everyone else seemed to have bodies that matched their hearts. Being together helped them all finally feel understood. Being understood helped them feel less afraid.

Elsinore had lived as herself, with her own name, and as a girl for as far back as her memory reached, for as long as she'd been with Milanda and Glamis. Many of her brothers, sisters, and siblings of the heart here at the temple were the same way; they had been heard by their loved ones when they spoke of themselves and had, in one way or another, been living their own lives truthfully before coming to Sanisa.

But a few had been less free to express their true selves. Though rare, these unfortunate youths had been opposed, denied, even ostracized by misunderstanding communities. Mostly, they had journeyed from far outside the Great River Valley to come to the temple of Tiranna. Her religion spread far through the known world, and the temple was known to be a place of refuge for those who needed safety. Elsinore couldn't help but feel a sense of solidarity with them. Though she had been able to live most of her life without hiding, she, too, had once been abandoned, and being here brought them all some measure of peace through camaraderie.

One morning, when chores were given out, the girl who volunteered to tend the chickens caught Elsinore's eye. The roosters and hens were kept by the temple in a garden on one terrace, mostly for eggs, and this same girl was sent to look after them week after week. She always seemed cheerful when she offered herself to the task, but Elsinore had begun to recognize a resignation hiding in the back of her voice. She never joined the other acolytes at meals and always kept apart to eat and read alone. Yet whenever her temple siblings greeted her, she always responded with a smile that shone like a star, masking a sadness Elsinore wished she didn't recognize in herself.

That morning, Elsinore volunteered to help her look after the chickens for the day. The girl's name was Folia.

"Most days you help the potion makers at the stables, don't you?" Folia asked as they scattered feed in the coop. "Isn't it beneath you to spend a day tending to these silly birds?"

"I don't know about that. I think the girls are rather clever, in fact." Laughing, Elsinore picked up one of the chickens and cradled the bird in her arms. "And there's something about them I find relatable. Don't you?" She held the chicken in her arms out to her new friend, who stood back a little and grimaced.

"I almost think I dislike them for that reason," Folia said. "They remind me too much of myself."

Suddenly, the bird kicked and squawked, thrashing about in Elsinore's hands, and jumping forward, flapped at Folia's face. They laughed as the bird pranced away.

Still smiling, Folia pointed at Elsinore's chest. "You should be careful when holding the chickens."

Elsinore looked down at her breast to find a long drop of bird shit streaking the front of her dress. She laughed again, and Folia couldn't help but join her. The laughter seemed more sincere than the sad smiles she'd offered before.

"Go on," Folia said, still laughing. "You're free to go, if you want to change to fresh clothes."

"Will you come with me? I'd like to talk." Folia turned, looking around the coop, but Elsinore insisted. "They'll be fine alone for a few minutes."

There was a lavatorium on the same level, not far from the coop, and Folia sat nearby, soaking her feet in the pool, while Elsinore bathed in the inner chamber and changed into a clean dress. The sunlight slipping through the narrow windows above danced off the water, casting patterns of shifting light into the shadows on the tiled walls. Folia watched the light and splashed, and Elsinore, drying herself from washing a little more than was necessary, sat beside her on the tiles around the little pool.

"Why do you offer to tend them so much, if they make you so sad?" Elsinore asked.

Folia looked away. "I didn't mean that." A ray of sunlight caught her eyes, and they shone as silver as the moon.

"I know you didn't. But I noticed it anyway."

Elsinore leaned forward over the pool, trying to get a better look at Folia's face. At her beautiful eyes. Folia grinned widely at Elsinore, with a look in her eyes that mixed accusation and resignation. Her smile was so beautiful, acne-scarred cheeks and all.

"I have experience with them," she admitted. "I used to tend chickens for my uncle." She paused with an air of finality, but Elsinore's gaze willed her to go on. It was clear she wanted to and only needed permission.

Folia relented. "I was raised by him after my mother died of an affliction. Uncle said it ran in the women of the family, that they were weak of heart, not as strong as men like him and . . . and me. He was a hard worker—we had to be to survive—and he put a plow in my hands at a young age. Whatever other plans or wishes I had didn't matter—I was to work in the fields, with him and his sons, to toil as it was fit for men to toil. When I failed to get much done—too weak, he finally said—he would give in and let me tend to the animals, especially the chickens. I enjoyed their company. It was a reprieve, at least, from tilling the soil with the men."

Her voice grew sadder. "Still, he cropped my hair short and gave me rough clothes that were stiff and thick, and we had to wake and be ready each morning to work before dawn. He made us greet the sun as it rose every day. He belonged to a religion that worshipped above all others their sun god, Rudash, and he hated what he blasphemed as the false faith of the . . . what he called the 'whore goddess,' even more than he hated the worship of Lord Wind and Lady Water and all the other small gods. I kept my faith in the Great Goddess a secret from my uncle for years, a memory of my mother, who I missed so dearly."

Folia's hands went automatically to her pendant, the eight-pointed evening star of the Goddess that she and the other acolytes had been given at the temple.

"Until finally, the night came, not long ago, that he decided I was to marry a girl from the village and start a family. It was my duty, he said. He said it was the duty of every man to marry and lead a family to serve Rudash, who portions life out for men and for women. He had been tending the fire when he called me in, and the light the hot flames cast on his face was lurid and terrifying, like the face of the sun, his horrible god. He was fanatical; he said at more than twenty summers, I had waited too long, that I should have become a father and begun service to God the Sun years before.

"Something in me—years of abuse from my uncle, years of the voice of the Goddess whispering to me in my dreams—I had finally had enough. I told him I didn't ever want to marry a girl, that I was a girl myself, and that I would never bow before the sun cross of Rudash and forsake the star of Tiranna.

"That's when he called me a fairy and said the boy I'd once been had been taken away by 'that devil goddess from below the hills,' as he put it. He said I was a changeling sent to damn his family and that I would waste away and die like my witch of a mother had done. He took up a hot poker he'd been heating in the fire and came at me, and it was only by the grace of the Goddess that he missed. I was so afraid; I didn't have time to take anything but the clothes I wore. I ran and came here, and that's me."

Thereafter, the two of them spent much of their time at the temple together. Folia took meals with Elsinore and her friends, and they worked and laughed together during class, making potions and studying spells. And of course, Elsinore continued to help Folia tend the chickens. In short order, Elsinore shared with Folia the story of being abandoned in the forest and found by her mothers—the first time she had shared her full history with anyone. Folia listened silently and held Elsinore as she cried. Their flirtation carried on day by day, during which time they became lovers, awkward and experimental and shy as any in their youth. Elsinore's fears and doubts melted away when she was with Folia, and her time at the temple was full of peace and belonging.

✳ 10 ✳

THE DREAM

The months flew by, and the Season of Light arrived with its southern winds and clear skies, bringing with it the time for the final initiation into the mysteries of the Goddess. By tradition, this initiation began at a ritual held at the season's equinox, known as the Day of Blood. Elsinore knew she had more studying to do to fully comprehend the meaning of the ritual, but she had begun to neglect her books for other pursuits. She spent whole days with Folia, the two gallae doing little but enjoying each other's presence.

Whenever they were alone, the new lovers explored each other's body, fully and enthusiastically. But Folia never let Elsinore play with her penis; it caused her too much distress to even remember it was there. Instead, she preferred to be entered through her bottom, for which her lover used her own penis. Elsinore never had any reason to associate this with anything but femininity, having been raised by women who loved each other. At other times, Elsinore pleasured Folia with her mouth and tongue, which caused her lover to laugh with joy.

Whenever Elsinore dove down and buried her face in her lover's meticulously cleaned bottom, she thought of diving into a cave, a fissure in the body of the earth devoid of air but leaking suffocating fumes. She wouldn't breathe for almost a full minute as she used her tongue to pleasure Folia, then she would surface, gasp for air while her eyes adjusted to the light of the surface world, before descending once again, until her mission was finished.

Folia had never experienced anything like it, only a brief flirtation with a girl from a neighboring farm who her uncle had pushed her together with and who she hadn't particularly liked. That brief arranged affair had ended with an awkward and embarrassing kiss.

Elsinore, though. showed her that she should be proud of her own pleasure, of her own body, even as Elsinore admitted she herself was only learning to feel so.

Late one night, when they had finished, the two girls lay in bed together, embracing. Folia was taller than Elsinore, and it was more comfortable for her to lay with Elsinore's back curved into her front, their legs intertwined and Folia's arms folded around Elsinore's chest, cupping her breasts. She had started taking medicine to halt virilization and feminize her body much later than Elsinore, not until she came to the temple, and it showed in her body in ways it hurt to think about. But the potion was deep, ancient magic and had worked greater miracles on others in the past. Elsinore thought her lover was feminine and beautiful, even if Folia had never before seen it herself. But it seemed now as if, sometimes, she finally could see it, if only through Elsinore's eyes.

"I can't believe you're going to keep it," Folia said. "I can't wait for mine to be reformed into a vulva during the initiation."

"Oh, I'm going to have my balls removed, at least,"

Elsinore replied thoughtfully, kissing the back of Folia's hand. "I can't ever allow the chance they could cause my body to become more . . . masculine. The medicine helps, of course, but I always worry—what if I lose it and can't brew more? What if I miss enough doses? It was like my heart had fallen under a fog as I grew up, and I could barely see the world around me, let alone myself. I've been so much freer, so much better since I started taking the estrogen potions.

"But I don't mind my penis at all. Some women have one, and it doesn't make me wrong. It's even feminine, in its own way; only a larger clitoris, after all. Sometimes, I even enjoy it." She playfully reached back and tickled her lover's thigh with her fingertips. Folia giggled and jumped as Elsinore rolled over to face her, and they kissed.

"Do you mind making love to me?" Elsinore whispered into Folia's ear. "Despite that? Even though I'm the kind of girl you are?"

"I love you because you're like me," her lover replied. "It used to hurt so badly, being alone."

Folia grew serious and drew away a little. Elsinore sometimes feared that her friend would become melancholy, that her good humor and bright smile would be overshadowed by the past she'd endured.

"But sometimes I wonder if there's more to you than that, isn't there?" Folia combed her finger through her lover's hair, looked softly into her eyes. "There's more to you than girl or boy, woman or man. I think there is to many of us. More to some of the gallae and the pilli, but more to some of the other people who aren't like us too— the 'dry-land people,' I call them, people whose bodies already match their hearts from birth. But couldn't the dry land fade into water by degrees, after all? So subtly, you can't even tell? I wish there were a word for it. I think I've seen it, sometimes, when I look into your eyes. It's what I love about you." She kissed Elsinore, lingered, and pulled back.

"It's what I love about myself," she whispered.

Folia and Elsinore were inseparable, always together even when surrounded by their other friends. They had grown close to another girl, a galla like themselves, named Nissa and a boy, a pillus, named Uras.

One evening after dinner, the four friends adjourned to a wide pavilion on a lower level of the temple to practice dancing. Elsinore and many of her sisters learned the art—not the erratic childish dances she had played at with her friends as a girl in Nin but erotic, seductive dancing that somehow echoed the curve of the wind over the fields and the shapes the planets drew in the night sky.

Uras joined in only for fun—he'd had rather enough of dance lessons from his youth, before he realized he heard the call of the Goddess. Nissa practically dragged him along, and they both laughed at the boy's missteps.

Of course, Elsinore partnered with Folia, the girls' movements silvered in the moonlight with flashes of their love. Elsinore was more adept; Folia was a novice, but her body flowed with an unpracticed grace that matched her lover well.

Nissa cried out in pain and laughter; Uras had kicked her in the shin as he untangled his legs. The two stopped dancing, but Elsinore and Folia hardly noticed, lost in the movements of their bodies. At last, as their dance wound to a close, Elsinore caught Folia's eye, and the two girls smirked and broke out laughing about nothing at all.

Uras rolled his eyes and scoffed. "If you lovebirds are finished, would you mind helping me get Nissa to the healers? There's an infirmary on this level."

"I'll be fine, Uras," Nissa insisted. "I just need to lie down. I think we can leave the girls to themselves; clearly, their thoughts take them elsewhere." She smiled knowingly, and Uras sighed.

"That isn't true," Elsinore protested. "We just . . ."

The young woman trailed off looking at Folia. When Uras snapped his fingers, Elsinore laughed brightly again.

"Well, maybe it is true. But we don't mean it to bother you two, really. I've started to pick up on how much you don't care for displays of romance; I'm sorry to subject you to that." Blushing, Uras looked away, then smirked and laughed.

"Besides," Folia added, "we know we have a lot of studying to do; we've been giving as much thought as everyone else at the temple to the preparation for the equinox. Haven't we, Elsie?"

"Hmm? Haven't we what?" Elsinore asked, startling herself out of dreamily gazing into Folia's eyes as she spoke.

Uras sighed. "It's not that I'm not glad for you both. I love it when my friends are happy. I just can't sympathize."

"Some people don't feel that way about love," Nissa said. "It's perfectly fine. Come on. There's some comfortable lounges in the library where I can rest my leg. I want to study; there's something I still don't understand about the rites of the Goddess. Something I know is important."

"I don't think we're meant to. Not until the initiation to the mysteries," Folia said. "But you two go on for the night. I know how to make Elsie focus."

Elsinore giggled, and Uras mock gagged. The four friends laughed and split up for the evening.

When the two women were alone, they retreated to the nearby lavatorium to wash up and then went to stroll the gardens. The trees had blossomed during the rainy Season of Shadows, their fruits now ready to be picked as a chore by the gallae and pilli who volunteered. The seasons could not be relied upon to bring forth predictable crops in the late age of the falling moon; the Stars of Galattis were among those who tended the earth, nurturing its body to ensure fair, full harvests using spells of fertility and growth taught at the temple. Many of the gallae in particular strongly identified as embodiments of the flowers of the Goddess, a sentiment mawkish enough to make Uras roll his eyes.

The girls walked under a pergola with hanging ivy and settled under a quiet bower, a place of privacy. The mossy roots of a tree formed a natural bed, and Folia pushed Elsinore gently against them, kissing her. Elsinore's back pressed against the gray bark, her brown hair mingling with the white star flowers of the long, dangling branches. Their bodies pressed together, eyes closed, hearts racing, each beating in time with the other's. Their shared breath mingled with the wind in the blue-green leaves all around them.

Elsinore fluttered her eyes open briefly as she turned from Folia's lips for a quick breath of air, but in that blink, a shadow passed over the bower and across the two of them. Gasping, Elsinore jerked back as Folia turned to look, her short feathery hair whipping around her ears.

When they realized it had only been a branch heavy with leaves and flowers bending in the wind, they giggled and rolled into each other's arms as they fell back to the soft earth below, overcome with laughter. They lay together for a long time, the sky above growing darker, the stars winking to life and peeking through the leaves and flowers above.

"When did you first hear the Goddess call to you?" Folia asked, her head resting on her lover's breast, her eyes still on the sky above.

Elsinore looked down at her, puzzled. "Call to me? What do you mean? To come to the temple? I met Ardena when I was a little girl and recognized myself in them. I thought there would be a place for people like me here. And I was right, I suppose."

"I don't mean that. Not exactly." Folia turned onto her side to look at Elsinore and laid her hand on her lover's soft, smooth cheek. Elsinore kissed her palm and listened.

"It's why I have such faith in the Goddess. She wasn't unknown in my part of the Great River Valley, but my devotion came from Her message to me. For as long as I could remember, at least since I was orphaned, She spoke to me in a recurring dream. It wasn't every night, but it was often enough that I knew it was a true dream, intended for me deliberately.

"In the dream, I would wander a maze in an old temple, someplace I knew to be from the days of the Old Ones. Someplace I knew also to be from long ages before their fall, in the dawning of their era. Someplace that had been walked by my sisters and mothers who came before me. But now it was old, empty, and abandoned, hallways carpeted with dust, the water in the cisterns overgrown with algae, the bowls in the corners that emptied into sewers clogged with ancient shit and echoing with the buzzing of flies.

"I wandered through the twisting, bending hallways, unsure why I was there or of the way out, till finally I saw a slant of light lying across a path, and I went toward it. As I approached, the hall opened into an inner chamber with a washing fountain, like we have in the temple. On the wall was a smooth sheet of black obsidian, as clearly reflective as a mirror. I went to the fountain to wash my hands and face, for fear of the smell of old shit from the labyrinth, and then I looked up into the mirror.

"And I was . . . beautiful. Back then, in waking life, I was a mundane-looking boy, unremarkable and gawky, with cropped hair and acne and eyes full of regret. But in the mirror in the dream, I was a grown woman, my hair long and flowing like uncut grass, my cheeks smooth and unblemished, my eyelids decorated with kohl and my lips smiling with life when I saw my face and my breasts. I reached out to touch my hand in the mirror, and it passed through, rippling the obsidian like the surface of water in a bowl. I immediately wished I hadn't reached out, so afraid the image was gone forever, that I hadn't had enough time to study the reflection that showed me how I should always have looked. I would see this face so often, in this very same dream, but it was never for long enough.

"When the ripple subsided and the surface grew still again, the face looking back at me had changed. Another woman was there, no longer me. Her flesh was the blue of a moonlit sky, deep and luminous like lapis lazuli. Her hair was black, and her eyes shone like stars. She smiled at me joyously and held her hand out, palm open, invitingly. But the light from the exit of the labyrinth would always distract me, and I would turn and look away and awake.

"The woman in the mirror was Galattis, the form Tiranna takes on earth. I know it. Her body like the night sky, Her eyes like the evening star. I felt Her speaking in my heart, when my waking mind was inactive, unable to distract me from hearing Her voice.

"Nissa told me something similar once. That the Goddess spoke to her in a dream and showed her that she was really a woman. Hers wasn't exactly the same but similar enough. A few others around the temple have told me the same thing. I think it's common for us to hear Her. Not always—not everyone. But often enough that I think we can tell.

"So did you hear Her? Something about you, Elsinore . . . I feel you must have. In fact, I'd wager you've felt it more strongly than any of us."

Elsinore turned away doubtfully, looking back up at the sky and the inner branches of the tree, lit only by the stars and the moon. She'd experienced no such dreams, heard no such voice. She simply had always known she was a girl. Was there more to it than that?

Elsinore realized she felt a twinge of jealousy.

As a witch, Milanda brought Elsinore up to respect, if not worship, all the gods. Like all other things, the gods were part of the natural world, of the flow of magic that pervades the universe. She tended to pay more frequent homage to Tiranna as goddess of the earth and the stars. Until coming here to the temple, Elsinore had not particularly thought more highly of Her than of any other gods, but Folia's faith was inspiring.

"I'm sorry to disappoint you," Elsinore said softly, not meeting Folia's eye. "But I just . . . have always known? It's just me, I'm afraid. No one told me. I doubt I was worth telling anything. I just knew."

Folia looked at her, puzzled. "Why would that be disappointing, love? You are yourself, with or without the Goddess. I'm just glad you're here with me now. For as long as I have here."

The way Folia said those last words brought a question to Elsinore's lips, but Folia silenced her with a finger across her lips. The two women curled up in the soft earth beneath the tree, Folia's face in the crook of Elsinore's neck, Elsinore's nose buried in Folia's hair and her lips pressed to her head. They fell asleep in the starlight, until the first light of dawn awakened them together.

Over the next few days, as the acolytes prepared for the ritual of the Day of Blood, Elsinore found Folia keeping to herself more often. She missed lectures where they studied spells, rehearsals for the ritual, and even meals with her friends. When Elsinore asked, her lover only told her she was feeling a little poorly but doing what she needed to prepare.

Finally, one morning, Folia was not at the chicken coop when Elsinore arrived to feed the hens. She had been late for appointments a few times that week and missed other obligations, but she had never failed to arrive to help Elsinore with the chickens.

As the morning wore on to midday, Elsinore's concern grew to real fear, a distant apprehension that lurked hooded in the back of her mind. At last, she ran to Folia's room, knocked on the door, and when there was no answer, let herself in—the door was not locked.

On the floor, unconscious beside a broken clay bowl and scattered pomegranate seeds, lay Folia.

The healers came at once when Elsinore called for help and took Folia, unconscious, to a bed in the temple's infirmary. They examined her: her breath was shallow and halting, her cheeks sunken, her pulse weak. Elsinore sat vigil all night, talking to the healers.

Folia's heart, they said, was failing, grown weak from a degenerative failure in her body. She was afflicted, Elsinore realized, with the same birth defect in her heart that had taken her mother so long ago. Elsinore begged the healers to tell her if the surgeons were going to operate on Folia; if there was anything they could do for her. But they told her she had come to them too late. Folia had been kept from the city, from the temple, and from the healers by her uncle's selfishness for so long that her condition had progressed past the point she could be saved.

Finally, early before daybreak, Folia's breath quickened, and she opened her eyes and smiled faintly.

Elsinore squeezed Folia's hand. "Why didn't you tell anyone? Why didn't you tell me?"

"Tell you what? That I was broken? That I was soon to die, like my mother? Would you have wanted me to burden you with that? But maybe this is the greater burden. Maybe by not telling you, I increased its weight on you now. Maybe I was wrong, and I'm sorry."

"Please don't be sorry. You have nothing to be sorry for."

"I'm not really, love. I'm sorry for . . . ha, there I go again." Folia laughed weakly. "I only mean I didn't intend to worry you. That's all I really regret."

"Worry me?" Elsinore said. "There's more important things than that, love."

"I know," Folia said. "I don't mean that. I mean . . . I'm grateful. Despite everything, I'm so grateful. Grateful for you. Grateful for the moon and the stars and the wind. Grateful for my body, even so broken and sick. The Goddess made my body; She made me like this, and I'm so grateful She made me the woman I am."

"I wish . . . I wish I could hear it," Elsinore whispered after a moment.

Folia looked at her strangely. "Hear what?"

"Her voice," Elsinore said. "I wish I could hear it as clearly as you do. The voice of the Goddess. There's just a . . . a space, a silent hollow in my dreams. There are times when it doesn't leave me; even when I'm awake, if I close my eyes for too long . . ."

Elsinore looked away, and Folia found the strength to sit up. She took Elsinore's hand and let her lover put her arms around her in turn. They pressed their foreheads together.

"There's something about you, my love," Folia whispered, and Elsinore felt her smile. "Some fae thing, like me . . ."

The two women lay together in each other's arms until the healer returned and Elsinore reluctantly withdrew.

Later that day, once the healers had finished caring for Folia and Elsinore had finished tending to the hens and roosters, Elsinore came to visit Folia again. She was sitting up, smiling and talking softly with Uras and Nissa, who sat in chairs at the foot of her bed. They all stopped talking when Elsinore knocked and entered. Uras smiled gently and took Nissa's hand, leading her as they silently stood to leave. He placed a hand on Elsinore's shoulder as he passed.

Elsinore sat on the bed beside Folia and said nothing. She didn't know what she could say that would be adequate. Folia looked at her with love in her deep eyes, unable to decide either.

Finally, Folia reached down beside the bed and produced a doll, a creature like a dragon made of yellow cloth with rainbow-feathered wings like a rooster or a . . .

"A chicken?" Elsinore smiled and gave a little laugh.

Folia held it out to her lover. "I sewed it myself; I was working on it before my fall. I made it for you. Once it became clear to me that . . . well. I want you to have something to remember me by."

Elsinore gasped, trying with all her heart to hold back tears. "Folia, no . . ."

"It's you, Elsie. My beautiful little hen. Thank you for helping me. Thank you for everything . . ."

She trailed off, her eyes falling to the floor.

"I'll—"

Both women stopped speaking, shared a glance, then giggled.

"I'll miss you," Folia said. "Very much. I hope you find whatever you're looking for."

Elsinore didn't really know what she had been going to say. *Miss you? Remember you?*

Always love you?

Elsinore didn't finish her thought. She hugged the doll to her chest, then turned gently to Folia, careful not to disturb her in her delicate condition. She cradled her lover until the sick young woman fell asleep, head resting peacefully on the pillow.

Elsinore held back her tears and kept herself from sobbing for fear of waking her love. Standing, she headed for the door but stopped on the threshold. She turned and looked at Folia for a long time, not wanting to leave but struggling to keep her grief silent.

She didn't know if Folia would wake before she returned.

She hoped she didn't.

Folia understood so much about herself—she saw

herself so clearly—but Elsinore couldn't bear the thought of leaving her alone. Elsinore hoped the last thing Folia knew would be Elsinore's arms around her.

But Elsinore could no longer hold back her tears. She slipped out of the room, leaving Folia to sleep without saying another word.

Alone in the garden outside, as the tears finally broke free and spilled down her cheeks, Elsinore decided that holding them back had been the hardest thing she had ever done.

✳ ‖ ✳

THE DAY OF BLOOD

Folia's life ended on the eve of the Day of Blood. The whole time Elsinore had been at the temple, she and the other acolytes had been preparing themselves for this ritual, not just by learning the recipes for the potions that confirmed their heart's true image in their bodies, and studying the spells that drew upon the quintessential presence of the Goddess, but also by listening to stories told by initiates about the birth and history of the Mother Herself. They knew pieces and jumbled accounts, Her roles in myths of other gods and brief stories that served as natural lessons, but only on the Day of Blood was the final story of the mysteries revealed, allowing them to become initiates. The story was never to be told to outsiders, and once initiated, Elsinore would never share it, not even with Milanda and Glamis. It wasn't a secret, something exclusive; it was a key, a puzzle piece. Those who had not seen the other pieces and neither knew nor needed to know the location of the lock would have no use for it.

With Folia's death, the scene of the ritual was to be changed. By tradition, on the evening of the equinox, the

143

Stars of Galattis gathered within the inner chamber of the high sanctum on the upper level of the temple and remained until the sun rose among the Seven Sisters in the constellation of the Bull of Heaven. But now, Ardena and the other senior initiates prepared for a procession out of the temple, along the banks of the river, to a secluded place on the outskirts of Sanisa called the Place of the Mound.

Ardena went to each of the acolytes in the early evening and called them to the terraces in the light of the setting sun. They wore their ritual robes; Elsinore's was the turquoise of the sea, over which she wore a shawl the purple of the weird night sky. She pulled the shawl up over her hair as a hood so it slouched over her eyes and across her shoulders. Only her nose and mouth remained visible, and she felt mysterious and arcane. She wished Folia were there to tell her she looked no such thing, only silly and adorable. A wave of grief washed over her, but Uras and Nissa came to her side as they were called from their quarters, and Elsinore swallowed her sorrow and walked with them.

The gallae and pilli drew together from every level of the temple ziggurat, gathering in a solemn procession down the central stair from the upper levels to the lower. Behind them, the temple rose to a pinnacle, where the sanctum stood high above the city—an open-air shrine large enough to accommodate all the acolytes and priests, though there were at least a score more than a hundred.

Instead of going to the sanctum, the followers of the Goddess paraded slowly and grimly through the evening streets, following Ardena and the others who bore Folia's body on a litter decorated with flowers and pine wreaths.

From the temple, they processed for miles beyond the boundaries of the city that was the Jewel of the Great

River Valley. The earth was the body of the Goddess, and the Great River was Her lifeblood. The fertile land of the valley glistened in the setting sun and the rising moon, and the beauty of the earth made Elsinore's breath catch. She knew of nothing more sublime, nothing more important. Though the world was old, weary, and dreadfully fragile in this late age, it was still the body of the Mother, and Elsinore couldn't help but feel awe.

As night fell, the lights of the city danced on the water and mingled with the reflection of the stars, leaving the river awash with sparkling lights—a mirror of its counterpart in the night sky, Gallas the Great River of Stars, the galaxy. Sometimes, as the stars flickered into view, the celestial and terrestrial Gallas seemed almost to flow into and out of each other, in truth the same river, one continuous circle from heaven to earth and back and beyond.

The procession crossed through a marsh just outside the city. Reeds danced gently in the cool evening breeze off the river, and lilies drifted across the water. Where the river shore met the grassy fields and low shrubs of the lowlands, the distinction between water and land was obscured, the transition gradual in places and dramatic in others. The marsh was at once river and soil, both and neither, but above all, its own place with its own beauties and dangers.

Casting light spells that hovered above their uplifted palms, Ardena and the other senior initiates led the procession along the safe path through the marsh. Following the witch lights prevented the acolytes from falling astray in the gloaming darkness and becoming lost in the pitfalls along the way.

A flash of color away from the crowd caught Elsinore's eye, and she turned her head to see something dropping from above. In the light of spells and stars, a bird alighted atop a cluster of tall, thick reeds reaching out of the marsh water. The feathers of the body and wings were black, and Elsinore would not have seen it at all if not for the head and neck; that plumage was bright yellow, like a flower.

The bird floated in the darkness, and as she walked on with the others, Elsinore glanced at the other acolytes, but it seemed to her that no one else saw what she did. Nissa did, however, turn to her sister with her eyebrow cocked in concern. Elsinore smiled at her and turned her attention back to the procession. She stole a final glance into the marsh, but the strange bird was lost in the night—perhaps flown away while Elsinore's attention was turned.

Finally passing beyond the reed marsh, the procession climbed to a highland above the river, ending in a wide grassy field. The acolytes spread out in a great crowded semicircle before a high mound of raised earth. The mound was perhaps three hundred feet across and ringed in a wall of glossy white quartz that reflected the violet wavering light of the glittering night sky. At regular intervals around the wall stood great megalithic stones, far enough out that the whole procession fit inside the outer ring. The river cut a chasm below them to the east, and a good many leagues of the Great River Valley were visible, stretching out to the edge of the sky in the west.

Looking down the Southern Road toward the horizon, Elsinore saw—she imagined—something in the great distance. It must have only been a mirage in the fading light, but it was something she at once knew and never knew. It was something she saw in her mind daily, something she tried to ignore but never truly could.

By the time all had gathered in the Place of the Mound, the moon and starlight fell slanted through the standing stones around them. The litter bearing Folia's body was set before a door leading into the mound, framed with huge stones set into the mound itself and flanked on either side by the ring of quartz.

Ardena stood before Folia's body, facing the crowd. Though there were no leaders in the temple, as one of the senior initiates, Ardena was highly esteemed for their wisdom, experience, and kindness.

At the fore of the crowd surrounding them, the other senior initiates, who carried packs, bags, and supplies, spread sheets upon the ground and unpacked the supplies they carried. Once unpacked, they dispersed among the acolytes.

They gave each galla a small tympanum—a shallow wooden frame with a taught drumhead—and a metal bowl like a cymbal that rang on fingernails like a bell. Each pillus received a spear—its long wooden shaft topped with a flared blade—and a mace that ended in a heavy metal object scaled like a pinecone.

Ardena themself came to Elsinore, giving her a tympanum and bowl with a sad smile. Accepting them, Elsinore looked at the drum and caught her reflection in the bowl. She tried to recall what she had learned about the meanings of these tools. Instead, she found herself thinking of Folia's smile and how often it had distracted her from her studies.

Other initiates followed, placing pieces of bread in the hollow of each galla's tympanum and pouring a dark-red liquid—a tart, rich pomegranate wine—into each galla's bowl. When all had been distributed, everyone ate and drank, the gallae sharing with their brothers.

"I have eaten from the drum," Ardena said once tympana and bowls alike were empty. "I have drunk from the cymbal. I have read the letters in the stars, and I have stolen into the inner chamber. I am your sibling."

The acolytes repeated the prayer to their neighbors quietly. The murmur of a hundred voices rustled through the field and echoed off the mound.

"I have eaten from the drum. I have drunk from the cymbal," Elsinore said to Uras and Nissa. "I have read the letters in the stars, and I have stolen into the inner chamber. I am your sister."

Uras repeated the prayer, ending with, "I am your brother."

"I am your sister," Nissa said, finishing her own repetition.

The three friends avoided one another's eyes, looking instead to the empty space among them where they felt an unfillable void.

After long moments of silence, a low, rising keen slowly filled the air, a simple tune more of pure mourning than artful melody, but beautiful in its sorrow. It was another moment still before Elsinore realized the keen was Ardena's.

The other initiates and acolytes joined in after a moment, first those beside Ardena, then the whole procession, voices rising and falling with the simple harmony of the keening. A clash of metal rang out in the background, surrounding and underlining the wailing, the sound of blade on blade carrying the voices of the mourners farther into the night. The pilli danced erratically with their spears, each letting his blade meet his brother's, now and again striking the shaft with that of his mace or beating the head of his mace against the earth.

Elsinore's body shook, her voice channeling a deep grief she had felt in the back of her heart since she was a little girl, brought to the surface now by the loss of her love. The keening voices and the harsh clatter of the spears overfilled her, and she wept until she doubled over in pain, clutching her head. The keening song in her voice vibrated deep into her bones, joining the swelling mournful chorus around her.

When at last the song had run its course and the wave of grief that had washed over the crowd passed away, the young acolytes finally fell silent. Elsinore saw through eyes bleary with heat and tears that a handful of initiates surrounded Folia's litter, holding long cords tied to the edges of the bed. Two of them ran around the sides of the mound, their cords trailing behind them, while a third climbed the mound with theirs. Elsinore couldn't tell what they meant to do.

Ardena stood on the far side of the litter from the crowd, between Folia's body and the portal to the mound. Facing the rough-hewn stones, Ardena raised their tympanum and drummed a quick tune while humming softly. Arm fully outstretched, they swung the drum in a circle in front of them, then clapped the drum again, once.

When Ardena then spoke, Elsinore could not hear what they said; rather, she realized she could, but the word instantly slipped out of her grasp, drifting away as if carried by the wind, before she could recall it.

Elsinore shivered, though the air was still and warm.

In front of the litter, at the entrance to the mound, a wondrous prism now spun, ringing a circle of light like a hole opened in the very air to reveal the sun itself. It hurt to look at it, and many acolytes covered their faces and looked away.

Elsinore, however, could not bring herself to. The white of the center faded the longer she stared, until it seemed only soft silver. The thought came to her that this silver, ringed in a halo of rainbow light, was not unlike the cloudy Pomegranate Moon.

Ardena stepped aside, and the initiates holding the

cords began to pull, dragging the litter bearing Folia's body toward the light. As her body touched the ring, it did not stop moving. Instead, it crossed into the light as if the circle were a door, a portal to a long and unknowable path. The circle continued to radiate light, and the initiates continued to pull, until Ardena made a gesture with their hands, reversing the circle, and it spun shut. The light flickered out, leaving the mourners only in the light of the stars and the true moon.

Ardena drummed a little to draw attention back to themself. They thanked the gallae and pilli for their studies, for their devotion, and voiced sorrow that an event anticipated with such joy should be shadowed by the loss of their sister. Then they began to tell the story of the Goddess and the founding of the temple. Gallae and pilli drummed a rhythmic beat on their tympana and spears as Ardena sang.

Elsinore sat in the grass between Uras and Nissa, legs crossed, worn from grief, mourning, and the long journey to the Place of the Mound. She fingered the star pendant on her breast, like the one Folia had worn, and tried not to grow distracted thinking how badly she wished to hold Folia—arms around her waist, face in her neck—as she listened to Ardena's story.

The origin of the temple's order, the mysteries told, had been long ago, in the time of the gods.

A cry from the Earth rose up in the air.
A cry from the Earth and the children of the Earth.
The Earth was brought down,
Her body chained by fence and enclosure,
Mined and pitted and stripped of Her jewels.

Her children were brought down,
Their bodies chained by systems of oppression,
Abject and appointed to fill roles for the kings.
The kings killed people, the forests, the air.
The kings poured poison into air and sea.
A cry from the Earth rose up in the air.
Lord Wind heard Her.
Across the surface of the Earth, Lord Wind heard Her.
In the hallways of the air, Lord Wind heard Her.
Across the surface of the Earth, Lord Wind ran.
The clouds dispersed while Lord Wind ran.
The trees would not grow while Lord Wind ran.
The Season of Death spread across the Earth while Lord
    Wind ran.
Lord Wind carried his son across the Earth.
Lord Wind carried Plague, his son, across the surface of
    the land.
The children of the Earth hid their faces.
The children hid their faces and shut their mouths.
The kings and lords opened their doors to Plague and fell
    low.
Kings and lords tried to flee to their towers,
Kings and lords tried to hoard what was left.
Lord Sun found them out.
Lord Wind dragged them from their towers.
Lord Sun starved the kings,
Lord Wind took the breath of the kings as he ran,
And Lord Wind's son Plague choked and strangled them.
Lord Wind and Lord Sun found the kings and lords.
Kings whose greed caused the suffering of the children of
    the Earth.
They put an end to the kings forever, and their heirs did
    not survive.
At last, Lord Wind and Lord Sun withdrew.

Emily Wynne

To the Mountain, Lord Wind and Lord Sun withdrew.
To the house of the gods on the peak beyond the last
    cloud,
Lord Wind and Lord Sun withdrew.
Lord Wind and Lord Sun, Lady Water, and the myriad
    small gods withdrew.
From the Mountain, Lord Wind saw—
From the Mountain, Lady Water saw—
The children of the Earth walked the wasteland below.
Lord Wind and Lady Water turned their ears to the
    children of the Earth below.
The children of the Earth below cried out for breath.
The children cried out for water.
The children cried out for food.
Lady Water raised her hands to the Earth below, and
    water rose up.
The aquifer deep below the surface rose up.
The children of the Earth had water.
Lord Wind raised his feet and ran.
Lord Wind raised his feet and ran across the surface.
The children of the Earth had breath.
Lady Water held seeds.
Lady Water held seeds of fruit, flowers, trees.
Lady Water scattered them, and Lord Wind carried
    them off.
The children of the Earth had food.
The trees grew, clouds covered the sky again.
Trees grew, cedars along the foot of the Mountain.
Trees grew, red and green and orange and blue,
Trees of the autumn and the summer.
Trees of the Season of Shadows and the Season of Light.
Tiranna laughed and sang.
Fruit trees grew; from Her body and as part of Her body
    a fruit tree grew.

In the field of stars that grow like flowers around the
    house of the gods,
A fruit tree grew, a low tree with thin leaves,
Twisting branches hung with round seed fruit.
Fruit with seeds and tart juice grew.
The pomegranate grew, and the gods rejoiced.
The fruit fell from the tree as the seasons turned.
In the Season of Shadows, the fruit fell.
And its juice ran like blood and seeped into the black
    earth,
Of the field of stars that grow like flowers.
The juice ran like blood and flowed like a river.
The seeds were like the flesh of the body.
From the seeds like flesh and the black earth of the shore
    of the river,
From the juice like a river of blood emerged a body.
From the seeds and the river and the earth grew a body.
Galattis arose in the pomegranate grove, deity of the river,
    child of the seeds,
On the sacred mountain near the house of the gods,
    They arose.
They lived and grew on the height of the sacred Moun-
    tain,
In the field of stars that grow like flowers, They lived,
Outside the house of the gods in the pomegranate grove.
In the pomegranate grove and star-flower field of the For-
    est of Heaven.
The deity Galattis approached the house of the gods.
The nymph, the youth, the fae deity,
Emanation of Tiranna, Who is inside All and outside All,
    and All-in-One.
They approached the house of the gods on the peak of
    the Mountain.
Lord Sun shone down from the rooftop—

Rudash, Lord Sun, heart of the daylight sky, shone glow-
    ing from the roof of the house.
He shouted from his pinnacle and commanded Them to
    stop.
He shouted with a voice of command for Galattis to halt.
"You may not enter here; you are forbidden.
Only the gods whose bodies are perfect may enter the
    house of the gods.
Only those whose bodies match their hearts,
Who were born with bodies in the shape of their hearts
    within,
May enter this place of the gods.
The ways of the Mountain of the gods are perfect.
You are forbidden."
Galattis protested; with a voice beautiful and unheard and
    strange, They protested.
Galattis, with a voice of true Fate, the unchangeable
    course of the river, spoke,
Galattis, High Priest of Speaking, spoke out to Lord Sun
    in the house of the gods.
"I am the pomegranate fruit.
I am the pomegranate seed-stars in the mournful sky.
There is more in heaven than Lord Sun.
There is more in Earth than the fruit of the sun."
For three days and nights, Galattis stood before the house
    of the gods and wept.
The strange lamentation, the unheard voice of Galattis,
    First to Weep.
For three days and nights, They wept and lamented.
For three days and nights, Their lamentation echoed in
    the halls of the gods.
At the end of that time, a wanderer passed by.
A wanderer passed by with a cup of water.
A wanderer gave water to soothe the throat of Galattis.

"Who are you who passes by the house of the gods?"
Galattis asked.
"Who is this who soothes my voice and gives me comfort
in my mourning?"
The wanderer's face was hooded.
From the shadow of the hood, a voice spoke,
"Mourn not, sibling, for the key to the end of your suffer-
ing is near.
That which can end your suffering is below, at the foot of
the Mountain.
At the foot of the Mountain is a gateway.
There is a gateway that leads deep into the heart of the
great Earth.
The door is open going in, for all who dwell on Earth will
enter someday.
In the land below, you will find something to make your
body match your heart.
With what you find, you can make your body match your
heart.
You can enter the house of the gods to dwell forever."
Galattis quickly climbed down the Mountain.
In the space of a day, Galattis climbed down the Moun-
tain quickly.
In the grove of cedars at the foot, They found the door.
The door into the heart of the great Earth was not hidden.
It is the door into the land of the dead.
The door is not hidden.
The children of the Earth fear to speak of it.
But the door to the great world below is easy to find.
The great below under the Mountain was black as ob-
sidian.
The reflection of the obsidian is the reflection of the
mind.
Those who go there see only what is in their own eyes.

Galattis plunged into the darkness of the great below.
The deity walked in the darkness.
In the great below under the Mountain, Galattis walked.
At last, they stole into the inner chamber.
From the inner chamber, a light shone out, a sparkling
        silver light.
A luminous mirror shone in the darkness.
Its face was silver.
Its reverse was black.
Three days and nights, Galattis gazed into the mirror.
After three days and nights, Galattis saw Themself.
Galattis took the mirror in Their hands, and it reflected
        the light from Themself.
With the light as Their guide, they found Their way back,
Back from the darkness below.
With the mirror's light as a guide, all shades are reborn
        from the great below.
Galattis returned to the cedars at the foot of the Moun-
        tain.
Three days and nights They spent ascending the Moun-
        tain.
Galattis went again to the house of the gods in the Forest
        of Heaven.
Through the pomegranate grove, They strode,
Through the field of stars that grow like flowers, to the
        house of the gods.
When Galattis stood again before the house of the gods,
They called out in a loud voice for all to come.
Galattis called out in a beautiful, strange voice.
Galattis cried a lamentation for all the gods to hear.
All the gods came—Lady Water, Lord Wind,
Lord Sun, and the myriad small gods, all.
All came out of their house to see the commotion.

Galattis raised a lamentation, and all the gods came out to
    see and hear.
"Hear me, gods of the Mountain!"
Galattis spoke, Galattis said,
"Hear me, Lady Water, Lord Wind!
Hear me Lord Sun, who bars the gate to those unbound
    by his prescribed order.
He told me that none would be allowed in the house of
    the gods,
Whose body does not share the form of Their heart.
None whose body was not perfect to Lord Sun are al-
    lowed.
I see in his cruel face the glaring heat of his eye,
I see that his body shares the form of his heart very well.
Know that it is not for your sake but for my own,
Know it is for my own sake that I do this.
The ways of the Mountain of the gods are perfect;
The body of Galattis is already perfect,
For my body already matches my heart."

Now, other senior priests came forward to speak alongside Ardena, reciting different versions of the next verse.
Each was unique and perhaps contradictory, but each was
true.

    Ornina, a galla, said:

Taking the mirror in one hand and Their testicles in the
    other,
With the sharp edge, Galattis severed the organs from
    Their body.

Emily Wynne

She severed Her testicles, and Her breasts budded and
    grew,
And the Goddess stood before the house of the gods,
And Her body matched Her heart.

Then Migalo, a pillus, said:

Taking the mirror in one hand, They unbound Their
    breasts with the other,
With the sharp edge, Galattis severed the organs, one
    after the other.
He severed His breasts, and His chest was flat,
And the God stood before the house of the gods,
And His body matched his heart.

Ardena continued:

Galattis severed the organs from Their body,
Raising Their hand, They cast the organs through the
    gate.
To the feet of the gods, They cast them.
Raising Their hand, Galattis cast the mirror into the sky.
The gods drew their eyes from the gore at their feet to
    gaze upward.
The gods looked up at the mirror casting reflections of
    light in the sky.
The mirror spun around in the sky, from side to side it
    spun.

The silver face reflected light into the eyes of the gods,
The mirror turned, its thin sickle edge flashing sharply in
    the sky,
Its black reverse like obsidian, hiding the secret reflection.
The mirror spun, and back again.
The mirror became the moon in the sky.
Brighter than Lord Sun, it flashed in the dark sky.
For ages it spun, keeping time. For ages, time mattered.
The blood on the moon was flung across the sky.
Galattis's blood spread across the black sky and turned it
    red and purple.
When the blood hung all about heaven, it was the Pome-
    granate Moon,
The Day of Blood ran red from heaven into the Earth.
When at last it dispersed, the moon shone silver.
Lord Sun flashed his light, and the moon was unseen,
But the moon returned in the evening to reflect the light
    back.
Lady Water smiled, pleased with her sibling.
Lady Water let her seas and lakes and aquifer be drawn
    up by the gravity of the moon.
Lord Wind blew away from the Earth. With currents of
    air, he reached for the moon.
With currents of air, he reached up for the moon, drew it
    down.
He drew down the moon, and it falls closer to Earth.
Crescent to crescent, new to full. Its shapes became
    strange.
When it falls, will it scour the Earth?
When the moon falls, will Galattis catch it?
When the moon falls, will it reflect what is deep in your
    heart?
In the red light of the Pomegranate Moon, Galattis
    turned Their back.

On the Day of Blood, They turned Their back on the
house of the gods.
Galattis dove off the Mountain, from the Forest of
Heaven,
From the field of stars that grow like flowers, They dove
down.
Like a meteor, a black star stone from heaven,
The deity dove down.
They struck the Earth; They struck the surface where
They fell.
From the field of stars that grow like flowers, Galattis
dove down and struck the Earth.
Into the Earth beneath the Mountain, Galattis sank;
Though beneath the Mountain, Their reach encompasses
the Earth.
Far-Reaching Queen of the Great Earth They are named,
And all meet Them beneath the Mountain when we pass
through the door.
Where They fell, the earth melted and splashed away like
water.
The clay and stone of the earth melted and splattered all
around where Galattis fell.
The droplets cooled and reformed as black glass in the
crater where Galattis fell.
Tektites, base earth transformed by the touch of the di-
vine fallen star.
Base earth transformed into holy black glass by the touch
of the moon.
Transformed into holy black glass by the evening star that
dives under the Earth.
The gallae and pilli, base earth transformed by the hand
of Galattis.
The gallae and pilli were made by the deity.
They wander the Earth.

The children of Galattis wander the Earth with a message
    of autonomy over our bodies.
A message of freedom from the edicts of the gods.
Those who follow Galattis are led out of the darkness of
    death,
Those who follow Galattis are led to new life and rebirth
    in the light of the moon,
In the light of the stars that grow like a field of flowers at
    the peak of the Mountain.
In the silhouette of the Mountain of the gods that stands
    high above our heads,
And behind our eyes in dreams.

When Ardena was finished, the drums faded away, and
the initiates remained in the glow of the moon and the
stars all around them.

"What did you think, Elsie?" Uras asked.

Elsinore didn't respond.

"Elsie?" Uras turned to look at his friend.

Tears fell down her cheeks, and her breath came
shallow and fast. "Where is the mountain?" Elsinore
cried out, stifling a sob.

The crowd turned from Ardena and looked at her.

"Elsinore, what is it? What's wrong?" Uras put his
hand on his friend's shoulder in concern, but Elsinore
pushed him off and stood up.

"This mountain. What is it?" Elsinore repeated.

Ardena looked upon her with worry. "It is the idea
of the Mountain, Sister Elsinore. Just as Galattis is the
idea of a galla and a pillus. It has no one place in the
world; all mountains are echoes of the ideal Mountain. It
is all around us in nature, as it is in your heart."

Elsinore's chest heaved, and hyperventilating, she fell to the ground in a faint.

"Elsie!" Ardena rushed forward, clearing the others to make space for the girl to breathe.

Elsinore saw rainbow auras surrounding Ardena and everything around them. The temple healers came to her as she was laid back on the soft grass, but she knew no more as her vision blacked out.

In the mass of colorful stars circling behind her eyes, one vision stood out. Shadowed against the light, the black mass of the Mountain stood over her. The Mountain from the story. The Mountain from her childhood. The Mountain that called to her from the back of each of her dreams.

When Elsinore awoke the next morning, she lay in her bed, in her room. Uras and Nissa sat by the bed, smiling. She'd had a migraine and fainted, they told her. They had stayed with her all night out of worry.

"What happened to Folia?" Elsinore asked faintly. Uras and Nissa looked at each other in fear, then back at Elsinore. She suddenly realized they thought that, in her condition, she had forgotten what happened in the past week. As if she could forget anything about Folia, especially this.

"I only mean . . . what became of her body? Where did she go once through the gate? Where did the spell take her?"

Uras visibly sighed with relief.

"No one really knows," Nissa said. "Ardena told us it's a door—a portal that leads between places or worlds. They said the terrible wind between the worlds is too much for the living to bear; that no living person who passes through could survive and return. The mage who created the spell wrote that it was a pathway to the Goddess, and it became tradition to use it to bear away the bodies of the Stars of Galattis. Folia will rest now with Her, if it's the Goddess's will."

"I wish I knew the Goddess's will," Elsinore said, more to herself than to her friends. "I wish She would tell me."

With the revelation of the final mystery of Tiranna, the temple acolytes underwent their initiation into the priesthood of the Goddess. For many, this meant their decision to undergo surgery. They processed into the temple, where they were operated on by surgeons of great training and skill. Uras had his breasts removed, and since starting to grow a beard from his masculinizing potions, the boy had become as proud and confident as his brothers, or so it seemed to Elsinore.

She planned to go through the surgery she had discussed with Folia; while Folia had wished to reshape her genitals entirely, Elsinore needed only to have her testicles removed. But the operation was delayed as she recovered from her episode, and Uras and Nissa wouldn't leave her side until they knew their friend was well. After a week, the healers agreed it was safe for Elsinore to move forward with the procedure.

The process was long and recovery slow for those who had more complicated surgeries, but both were rapid for Elsinore. It was done, of course, more carefully and cleanly than in Galattis's myth; though she had to rest for days before attempting to walk very much, once that time was past, she was relatively free.

Indeed, even before recovery, when Elsinore's surgery was over, she felt immediately and instinctually free.

For a long time, in the back of her mind, the fear lingered that the life she had, the way she was, could be taken away from her. It was an irrational fear, perhaps; as far back as her memory reached, she had always been seen as her true self by her mothers, never been opposed and tormented as poor Folia had been by her uncle. But finally, Elsinore felt assured that no power could reverse the progress she had made in becoming herself.

But the feeling of freedom and release was short-lived. Though she felt an overwhelming sense of euphoria at her castration, as she recovered more fully, she realized there was still a dark feeling in the back of her mind. She slept uneasily and woke unable to recall the dreams but for a shape.

There was something looming over her—and had been for a very long time. She had thought it was her initiation, her castration, the unfulfilled longing to learn more about people like her, to meet and befriend her siblings. Now that she had found these things and was past her surgery, past her initiation, past her first love—this something was still there.

Now that the story of the Goddess had put a name to it, Elsinore finally thought she knew what it was. In her mind, behind everything, was the overshadowing height of the Mountain. Now she was certain the one in the story and that of her childhood were one and the same, in some way she struggled to articulate, even to herself.

Elsinore remained at the temple a little longer; she tried to learn a few more spells and participated in a few more rituals meant to honor and celebrate her passage into adulthood as a woman. She tried to focus, but as distracted as she had been by Folia's company, she found it was so much harder in her absence.

The only spell she really studied by that point was the Prismatic Door; its rainbow ring had burned itself into the young woman's memory. The truth of it eluded her, but somehow, she knew it was important.

Somehow, it seemed more important than anything else.

Finally, as the moon's irregular patterns shifted, Elsinore's melancholy turned to homesickness, and she decided to move on. She saw her friends rarely, even Uras and Nissa, who she avoided with a sudden, inexplicable shame. One morning, the young woman quietly packed her supplies, searched the living quarters timidly, and finally found Ardena. The two embraced as if they were cousin and niece.

With her spirit full of a bittersweet mix of sorrow, regret, joy, and melancholy, Elsinore set off to return to her mothers in Nin.

✳ 12 ✳

RETURNING HOME

In the months since returning from the temple, Elsinore had grown quiet and moody. She had set her implements on an altar by her bed: her dagger, her necklace, and a tektite stone given as a memento of the story of Galattis. They all felt empty and useless to her, and she was unable to make herself concentrate on the simplest cantrip. She had not even the desire to try. It was only when Milanda remarked that empty bottles lay strewn about the girl's bedroom that Elsinore even realized she had missed almost a week of her hormone potions. The girl's mind was foggy, and she was barely responsive to her mothers except for the most basic things.

One morning, Milanda found that Elsinore had risen early and was not in the dwelling—unless, she realized, her daughter had never gone to sleep at all. That afternoon, the young woman returned home, not quite cheerful but personable, and she was more willing to join her mothers' conversation over their meal in the evening.

She didn't mention where she had gone, and Milanda didn't ask, nor did Glamis seem to have realized, as she had slept rather late. Quietly keeping an eye on her daughter without prying, Milanda marked that Elsinore followed the same secret routine each morning for a few weeks, and her worry rose steadily with her curiosity.

One day sometime after midsummer, Milanda followed her morning rounds among the neighbors, strolling and enjoying the fresh river air and trying to banish her fears. She soon found Glamis sitting on a stone at the edge of a field just outside town, a wide circle of a few acres with edges regularly marked by standing stones. The field was used for performances and festivals but was now quiet and nearly empty. Glamis beckoned Milanda over and motioned to look to the field. She was watching their daughter, and what Milanda saw filled her with hope.

Elsinore was dancing. Her mothers hadn't seen her dance so seriously since she was a little girl, and their spirits lifted as she twisted and spun with such ease. Though she improvised, it was clear she remembered her training, for her movements were graceful and elegant.

Milanda had no intention of disturbing her and interrupting her performance.

As Elsinore danced, she spun green flames from a fire cantrip, which drifted in the air and accompanied her motions. She guided them with her hands, back and forth, drawing ephemeral pictures in the morning mist. She was so focused on her dance that it was quite some time before she noticed her mothers sitting nearby on a fallen stone, watching and smiling.

All at once, Elsinore stopped, and the witch lights faded away. The young woman was unable to meet her mothers' gazes.

After a moment, she walked over from the center of the field, still not looking directly at them. Head hung with something like embarrassment, the girl sat between her mothers on the stone, pulling her knees close to her chest.

Milanda drew on the metal mouthpiece of her cannabis pipe, its long thin bamboo-like stem gripped firmly between her thumb and forefinger and its tiny metal bowl nestled in the crook of her finger. Exhaling, she released a cloud of smoke into the foggy air.

"I'm glad to see you like that. It's been so long since you've danced; I was afraid you wouldn't even remember how."

"I danced at the temple. It's just been hard since . . . well, I've fallen away from it. But lately, I've been out here practicing every morning."

Elsinore snatched the pipe out of her mother's hand, quick enough to barely elicit a reaction. Holding it more delicately than her mother had, closer to the mouthpiece, with the length of the stem balanced along her index finger, she took a drag and let a plume of smoke rise in the morning light.

She didn't return it.

"I've just had the urge lately. It helps me to—I don't know how to describe it. It helps me to remember. I've been coming here when no one else was around so I could dance and think and grieve."

"Seeing you like that reminds me of when you were a little girl, dancing with your friends," Glamis said. "You have grown and changed so much, but seeing you like that—it reminds me that you're not so different after all."

Blushing, Elsinore turned her head. "I'm a grown woman. I'm not a child. Anyway, is that all you were afraid of?"

Glamis smiled softly. "We know you went through so much at the temple," she said gently. "Mil and I just wish you would open up about what it meant to you."

Elsinore blew a thin stream of smoke into the mist above her head, already feeling the intoxicating effects of the weed. It made her a little dizzy, particularly after waking so early and dancing without eating. She kept her balance mentally by focusing her thoughts on a point beyond the far distance—a place she knew she was meant to go.

"Why have you never told me more about the place where you found me?" she asked suddenly.

Glamis shifted uncomfortably and looked away, suddenly reluctant to talk. Milanda sat still, no less uncomfortable, and waited a moment before speaking. Despite the pause, when she spoke, it was a little too quickly.

"Tudur? In the shadow of the Mountain? It was a frightful country, and we've told you all we know."

"You know what I mean, Mil." Elsinore's eyes never flicked away from the horizon. "The place I was. Where you found me in the forest, in the dark."

Milanda paused, betraying no emotion other than concern. "Yes. Because you were in a place of pain, and I thought to dwell on it would do you no good. Because I thought it would bring you nothing but regret and make you worry. You're prone to it."

"Worry? I'm not worried; that's silly. Why should I be worried? Introspective. Nostalgic, maybe. Moody and melancholy, of course! I can't imagine why." She rolled her eyes. "I've only realized I know nothing about the place I was born, where I was abandoned. Why should I be worried?"

Milanda didn't reply—at least, not with words. She only looked at her daughter with silent assent, giving her space to find the words for her feelings. When Elsinore finally turned and looked at her, Elsinore saw eyes heavy with kindness. It was the same look of kindness she'd seen in her eyes twenty years before.

"It wasn't even my home. Not really. I don't even know what I'm melancholy for or worried about."

"You're young, and you've already lost so much," Milanda said. "No young woman knows why she's melancholy at your age. No young person in general, I should think. But the grief you've endured and the loss of poor Folia . . ."

A look of subtle mourning tightened the girl's face, and her eyes searched Milanda's for a way to say what she wanted.

Instead of speaking, Elsinore embraced both her mothers. She fought back the urge to tell them what she saw whenever she closed her eyes since Folia's death, echoes of the mourning from her childhood so long ago: dreams of mirrors, of houses full of forgotten images, of labyrinths full of shit and waste, and the Mountain that stood before the full moon in her dreams.

That night, Elsinore retreated to her room early to be alone. She slept fitfully, and when she rose late at night for first waking, she realized she would not be able to go back to bed. She knew what she meant to do, but first she had to prepare for her journey.

She packed her bag lightly yet with enough to last her for days at a time. Rations, the tools from her altar, and other necessities were all she needed. She wore a short jacket with a wide black hood and her eight-pointed star necklace, but most importantly, she donned a ring that was enchanted to store several spells for which she need only speak a word or make a gesture to cast. She packed her book of spells, though those would take longer to prepare, and really, the book was mostly only her journal.

There was room for her silver bowl and her tympanum. The drum might have been small enough to fit in her bag, but the wooden frame and taut skin could still produce a deep, primal sound that resonated in the listener's mind for ages when struck. Of course, it was also another tool for casting several of her spells and was necessary for certain rituals, but she had begun to use it in her dances for other reasons—foremost among them that it made her happy to play it.

She tucked the thin, narrow pipe she'd gotten from Milanda into her belt, along with a pouch of cannabis. But the more necessary drug was her medicine, which she carried in a cushioned packet of little vials.

In her recent depression, she hadn't had the will to keep taking it, which made little difference—for a short while. She could not miss it for too long, though; in many ways, it made up for the deficiencies of her birth, as she lacked the hormones other women's bodies made naturally. Most immediately, of course, it helped make her body more visibly feminine, more like the true image of herself she held in her heart. It also helped her center herself emotionally, bringing the chemicals in her brain to a level her body expected and keeping herself grounded and focused.

But beyond that, in another bodily sense, not deep in her heart or mind but deep in her bones, Elsinore's drugs maintained her very vitality. Now that she had been castrated, if she went long enough without the drugs, her body would become frail and fragile, her bones vulnerable to fractures, her spine to bending like a crone's. Her body would wither before her time, the lithe, young dancer becoming a haggard old witch. She had brought enough vials for another few weeks still, though she did not know how long she expected the journey to take her.

If necessary, and with a little time, she could brew more, but the caution reassured her.

By the time her preparations were complete, it was early in the morning, still dark. It was long before any others would wake and begin preparing for the day, so Nin was still quiet. Quickly composing a note, Elsinore left it on her bed in the wings of her rooster doll for Milanda and Glamis. It was brief, telling them she loved them, she had gone to the Mountain, and she would return as soon as she could.

Yet she wondered as she pulled back from arranging the rooster and note just what she really meant to accomplish. Did she really think she could find—who, exactly? Him? Was he even real? And what if she did? Was it in her power to free a captive of such a place? What would it cost her to do so?

Closing her eyes, she laid her hand on her chest. No, she had to go. Now that she had the clarity, now that the Mountain called forth from her dreams, no longer looming in the past but before her, terribly real, she had to go back to make things right at last.

Elsinore turned back to consider the note and found herself looking into the button eyes of her rooster doll. Sighing, she felt a momentary twinge of regret. Regret not that she was going to the Mountain but for something else—something she couldn't place. Picking up the doll, she regarded it for a moment, hugged it, and fit it into the corner of her bag bundled with the purple dress she would use when dancing and her colorful scarves of turquoise and yellow. She then laid the note against the foot of a statue of the Goddess on her altar.

Once she had quelled her doubts for the time being and felt she had prepared the best she could to weather the journey alone, Elsinore shouldered her bag and pulled her hood up over her head. The hood obscured her hair, freshly dyed the blue green of the pines, of the deep ocean, of the banner of Tiranna at the temple. The hood and the gray dress she wore beneath her black jacket would help her avoid drawing attention on the road, but the color of her hair would signal that she was a priestess of the Goddess when she danced.

Casting her spell of invisibility, she slipped out of her room and shut the door quietly. Then she made her way out of her home, out of the town, and toward the Northern Road, by which she planned to return to the country in the shadow of the Mountain.

The invisibility spell was simple but powerful; she had learned it for both performance and safety. It didn't just let her flit through the world unseen; it also made her feel insubstantial and unreal. The world around her became shrouded as sunshine and moonlight alike gave way to an abyssal darkness, the only light an ambient glow that shone dully from the heavy, iridescent mist that surrounded her on all sides. The environment around her—stones, buildings, and people alike—became still and sepulchral. It was not that people froze in their tracks in Elsinore's eyes; rather, their movements appeared to drift and trail, their voices an echo as from a great distance.

A heavy veil was drawn over the sorceress when she cast this spell, as if she had been hidden beneath layers of soft gossamer. Or as if the world around her had been, and she alone walked free.

Normally, she tried to walk under this spell as briefly as possible; but now, to make her way clear of the town, she needed to concentrate on the spell and move through the shadow world for a little longer than she felt comfortable. It was a relief, at least, that she did not need to dash through a crowd or tight conditions. The fields tonight were untraveled, and Elsinore hoped the way would remain clear until she made it far from the sight of windows and, hopefully, to the road.

As she hurried unseen, surrounded by the veil of mist, Elsinore found her eyes drawn to the horizon, and she halted in shock from what she saw. Though the air around her was shrouded in ethereal fog, though the moon and stars were lost in the distant darkness—straight ahead, distinct as it might be on a bright, clear night, the Mountain loomed above as if it were truly near. It stood bridging earth to heaven, as it ever had in the sky of her dreams.

If anything, it was sharper and more luminous than ever, the mists not obscuring it but hanging about it as a halo. The Mountain glowed, not in the light of the moon but with its own terrible white luminescence.

In her amazement, Elsinore's focus slipped, and she lost her concentration, dropping her spell of invisibility. The Mountain no longer stood before her, but it was still visible, now only as an afterimage illuminated by the early-morning moon in her mind's eye. The ghostly mirage radiating through the mist remained in her eyesight, and she stood still, trying to concentrate on her surroundings before moving on. She breathed deeply—once, twice—closed her eyes, and focused on the darkness that had returned when the light of the Mountain faded.

Back to her senses, Elsinore began to move on. She had only gone as far as the first gate over the road, a waymark out of Nin, when she became aware that someone was following her. Her heart sank when she realized who it was. Glamis was jogging toward her over a hillock, not far away, sword over her shoulder and a hard expression in her eyes. The hooded Milanda followed close behind.

"What do you think you're doing, young woman?" Milanda demanded, stepping in front of her daughter and blocking her way through the low gate. Glamis stood back, left behind when Milanda dashed ahead. In her hands, Milanda held the note that Elsinore had written before she left.

"How could you?" she asked incredulously.

It took a moment for Elsinore to realize her mother wasn't speaking to her. She had turned to face down the Northern Road, her eyes drawn upward across the distant horizon, toward the Mountain.

Glamis stepped beside her partner. "She doesn't owe us an explanation, Mil. She doesn't owe one to anybody. She's a grown woman. Aren't you, Elsinore?"

The young woman looked away, down the road, not meeting her mother's gaze.

"I didn't want to worry you," she mumbled.

"Worry us?" Milanda said. "Why should we be worried? You've been hiding your own worry for months, and when you couldn't, you've avoided us. All you've done is try not to worry us. And all I've done is worry."

Elsinore turned her face in shame. "You seemed encouraging yesterday morning."

"Because I want you to be happy!" Milanda said. "Because I don't want you to lose faith in yourself. You were always so sure of yourself, from the moment you came to us." She stepped forward and put her hands on her daughter's shoulders. Tears welled in her eyes. "You belong with us. How can you forget . . . ?"

Elsinore took Milanda's hands in her own. "I can't possibly forget. But I have to go there, to the Mountain. I know the answers are there. The answers to the questions I don't even know how to ask. I have to go while I have the chance."

She turned to Glamis and smiled, and Glamis turned to Milanda. The tall, strong woman held the buckle of her scabbard strap with both hands, looking like a timid schoolgirl. Then she reached over her shoulder and drew the sword, a short one she had trained Elsinore with in the girl's youth. The older woman flipped it and held it carefully by the blade, grip toward her daughter. The girl looked into her mother's eyes, then took the sword in her own hand.

The blade was short, longer than a dagger but able to be wielded one-handed, even by Elsinore, who had little in the way of sheer physical strength. The guard on the hilt was a silver crescent moon, and the blade flashed like a white beam of moonlight, reflecting the light of the true moon fading in the morning sky. The grip was the deep blue of the night, and on the pommel was a crystal that flashed and sparkled in the light like the evening star. Elsinore had named it Moonstar when she was a child, and it had always been her favorite of the tools her mother crafted.

Glamis swung the scabbard off her back and slipped it across Elsinore's, fitting it to her smaller body with the buckle. Holding the girl's shoulder, she nodded.

Elsinore sheathed the blade, feeling its weight on her back, and hoped she remembered what training Glamis had given her. More than that, she hoped she would not have to use it.

"I know I'll be all right." Elsinore bowed to her mothers. "I know I belong here, with you. But I think . . . I think the Mountain thinks I belong there too. I don't know how I know that. Not exactly. But I do."

She took one of their hands each in hers, and they stood in a ring, mothers and daughter, in the cool morning dew that covered the grass of the field. The summer, the Season of Light, was usually hot and still, but an unseasonable mist rose in the air, refracting the light of the moon and casting a rainbow that seemed to circle the women below.

Milanda lifted her gaze to the sky. "A Pomegranate Moon. The first of the season, I think."

"Maybe it's a sign that all will be well," Elsinore said, though her voice sank, mired in doubt. "I've measured my life in those moons."

"You oughtn't predict the future," Milanda said. "Make it into what you want instead, and do what you can with the fate that is spun for you."

Tears welled in Elsinore's eyes to match Milanda's, and all three women smiled sadly and embraced.

"I love you both so much," Elsinore said, tears streaming down her cheeks. "I'll return as soon as I can."

"I love you, my little girl," Milanda said. Rather than speak, Glamis rushed forward after they had released the embrace and hugged her daughter again.

Once Glamis let her go, Elsinore walked backward, her eyes on her mothers, as she started on the road toward Tudur, toward the Forest, and toward the Mountain that would be robed in the luminous veil of the moon. Finally, she stopped, turned, and hurried off toward her destination.

She didn't say goodbye. Never in her life had she learned how to.

$$ * \; 13 \; * $$

THE MARKET

Elsinore woke slowly. She'd slept peacefully after a long, strange day and night. She didn't even rightly know how long it had been, nor did she know the time; was the sun just rising, or would it be high in its arc by now? Had she gone deep enough that it no longer mattered? She was beneath the Mountain, in the Kur, and the passage of time marked by the phases of the moon and the course of the sun and the other stars had ceased to hold any great importance.

She lost track of these thoughts when she realized there was something else, something alive, sitting on the linens with her, and she jumped up in alarm. Whatever it was slowly lifted its head and ears and blinked, before curling back up into a ball, undisturbed.

It was a cat.

The same cat Elsinore had followed through the tunnel into this underworld. So that hadn't been a hallucination, unless she dreamed still. But the visionary drug she'd taken at the waterfall would have worn off long ago, before she fell asleep.

The cat had dark fur—if not black, then a brown or gray dark enough that the difference was imperceptible. The little creature's body no longer glowed strangely as it had in the passageway. Had that been a feature of the deep hall of the gatekeeper, perhaps? Or only an illusion, a hallucination caused by the mushroom?

Elsinore looked at her magic ring—the mirrored silver at the end of the filigree glowed faintly blue, which signified that the ward she had set before drifting off still held. Either this cat was a vastly more powerful magical entity than she could conceive or they meant her no harm. Or—and this she didn't truly entertain but had to consider as a remote possibility—they were just an ordinary cat, unaffected by magic.

Deciding it made little difference which, Elsinore calmed down and sat on the edge of the bed to scratch the cat's ears with her fingers. The cat opened their eyes, then squinted them slowly, looking at Elsinore. She had made a friend, then. After a few moments of scratches and leaning themself against Elsinore's warm leg, the cat stood up, slow and dignified, jumped down from the bed, and slowly walked to the door that led to the hall and farther into the Mountain.

"Yes, please give me a few moments to get ready," Elsinore said. "I've only just woken up, and quite suddenly, thanks to you." The cat meowed impatiently and settled neatly on their paws.

On a table beside the bed, Elsinore noticed something she had missed the night before. There was a tray set with food—luscious grapes and apples, sliced pomegranates wet with juice and seeds, and golden cakes with well-baked edges. A carafe and chalice stood beside the plate, the former full of fragrant wine.

Elsinore was starving after her descent and long sleep,

and she found herself reaching automatically for the wine. A warning leaped to mind, however, and she snatched her hand back as if from a hot stove. Turning away cautiously, she ate only a little bread from her rations and drank from her water before she started to strip off the linen bed clothes she'd worn during the night.

She stopped when she noticed the cat facing into the room, looking at her.

"May I have some privacy?"

The cat gave no indication of comprehending. They didn't seem capable of reason, but just the same, Elsinore was more comfortable taking no chances.

She looked around for a hook or pole, something she could hang the bedsheet on to make a curtain. Seeing nothing of the sort, she cast a small levitation spell and set the sheet aloft in the air so she could change clothes without the cat's weird eyes upon her.

Somehow, it never occurred to her to turn the cat around or cover them. That would have been much too rude.

Elsinore dressed in her short purple dancing dress, black hood, and yellow and turquoise sashes. She'd worn such colors and dyed her hair since leaving Sanisa; she did it to remind herself of her time at the temple and to remind herself of the Goddess.

It also acted as a way of identifying her to others who might know, who might tell from her dress where she came from. She liked to think that by doing so, she might give others who saw her the same glimmer of recognition and hope Ardena had once given Elsinore, so long ago. Not that she knew what sort of person she was likely to encounter in this place, but nevertheless, she had a suspicion the colors and livery of Tiranna and Galattis would be recognized in some way.

With that in mind, Elsinore took up her dagger and went to a mirror beside the pool in the corner. Letting down the top of her dress, she wet and lathered her hair with soap, then slowly and carefully shaved the left side of her head above the ear, leaving the crown and right side long. This was the style Ardena wore, a common one among Tiranna's priests and priestesses, which Ardena had once told Elsinore signified a unity or transition between sexes and their usual manners of dress. Or else a separation from them all.

She gazed at herself in the mirror for long moments, at the shape of her face, the smoothness of her skin and cheeks. The woman looking back at her was beautiful, she knew. But she never quite understood how.

Once Elsinore had dried her hair and redressed, she realized the cat had come silently around the curtain and now lay by the corner of the pool, sleeping. Gathering the shorn blue-green locks, she was wrapping them in a scrap of linen when the cat awoke and began to sniff at her hands. She hadn't noticed that the creature had come so close; they pawed at the locks she held, pulling the hairs to the ground and looking at the strands as if studying the length and color. Elsinore inclined her head quizzically and decided to leave the locks where they lay.

The witch giggled at the little creature. "An offering, then, to the Goddess—or to you, little kitten." The cat played for a few moments, and Elsinore laughed, trailing the hair along before them as they swiped and pawed.

At last, the cat grew bored in the way cats did, and Elsinore was ready to move on. As she approached the door, the cat hurried over, pressing their way through as soon as she pulled it open.

This creature certainly behaves like an ordinary cat. The thought brought her comfort; a sense of normalcy.

Leaving the room, she walked down the hall, and that normalcy was lost amid the strange sight on the other side of the door leading farther into the Mountain.

Once out of the hall, Elsinore found herself at the edge of a town square, populated, active, and alive. There were houses all around the perimeter, made of stone and clay. In the center of the square stood a larger domed building with a columned facade that had the look of a temple or shrine. The ground was level dirt, with a few sparse growths of some purple and red weeds alongside a path that circled the square and spiraled out around the town, past the houses and into the unseen distance. The sky above was black and starless, like a particularly cloudy night, and the horizon crouched very low and near in the darkness, as the road and the level rocky landscape simply ended in nowhere.

Despite these shadows, an even blue light suffused the area as if from an unseen full moon, and the town and square were fully visible. Looking back at the door she had come through, Elsinore saw that the hallway to the little rooms with baths and cushions was the interior of one of the stone houses, and only a little one at that. There was certainly no room above or behind to accommodate the stairs she had descended from the chamber of the gatekeeper; it seemed the whole part of the Mountain she had come from was contained in only that little hovel, or else it all led into that place by some impossible means she did not know.

The square was boisterous and left her little time to consider the reality of the situation. There were tents, stalls, and tables all around. Wooden poles held colorful awnings, tattered and tasseled, and strange flags with pictures of animals and wares flew in a soft breeze that whirled around but seemed to originate from nowhere.

The people were like no one Elsinore had ever seen. They had bodies like ordinary humans, many of them especially tall, fit, and healthy. A few wore tunics, but most displayed muscular arms and pectorals or uncovered breasts. Many wore gold and silver necklaces and shoulder ornaments and had skirts, kilts, or robes tied elegantly around their waists.

Most incredibly, though, all these people had heads like exotic birds. Like hawks, ravens, or fowl, they had long necks, protruding beaks, and tall feathered crests or fleshy combs. Their heads were covered in feathers of black, red, and dark gray. Their eyes were solid-black orbs, with expressions Elsinore could not even try to decipher. From a distance, their unearthly faces seemed to change expressions subtly like human faces, and they opened their mouths as if to speak quiet, shallow words that the girl could not hear. When they did, she thought she could see many long, sharp teeth and wild tongues that could not be fake.

Reluctant to approach, Elsinore remained by the door, but she was in no way hidden—merely apart from the crowd. People walked along the path to and from the under-mountain darkness of the near horizon, setting things up or taking things away from the square.

In her amazement, she had nearly forgotten about the cat until they meowed insistently. Looking down, she found them standing by her feet, gazing up at her with bright green eyes. They meowed again and walked away, down the path to the marketplace, the tents, and the people, of whatever kind they were.

The people paid the cat no attention, walking by as if they were not there or walking around them, carrying pots full of scrolls or baskets of fruit and other items to their stalls. Steeling her will, Elsinore walked away from the house and toward the tents and the strange people going about their business.

As she came closer to the people crowding the market she realized the truth: they did indeed wear masks after all. Obviously artificial, they appeared to mimic stylized bird heads, like ceremonial headdresses. Something about these people's shoulders and necks, though, made Elsinore think that under the hoods, they had faces more like her own. The darkness of their eyes was just the shadow of the slits they looked through, and their strange mouths and tongues and changes of expression had only been her imagination.

Or is that just wishful thinking? Was it really the distance that made me mistake what I saw? Or was it a lingering effect of the mushroom I took yesterday?

The drug should have passed through her system entirely by now, so the idea that she might be experiencing aftereffects almost discomforted her more than if she'd been surrounded by real monstrous creatures.

Elsinore was surprised that the people paid her as little mind as they did the cat. She felt embarrassed, and the heat of a blush rose quickly in her face, while beads of sweat trickled down the shaved side of her scalp. She was not fearful, or at least, she didn't think she was, even in the presence of these people; rather, she was nervous and awkward, suddenly overcome by the feeling that she had come upon someplace she didn't belong. She felt woefully out of place, as if it were shameful to show the face of a human here.

The cat meowed, once again by her side. They looked up at her, then turned and walked away, looking back again to see if she was following. Elsinore thought they were keeping her company, and she appreciated the gesture, if that's what it was. Giggling, she followed, and every few yards or so, the cat would stop to look back at her, then hurry on while the girl caught up to her smaller companion.

At least there's someone here who wants me around.

In the market, the stalls were set with wares, and the poles and awnings shook with the activity of their keepers, already trading with people coming and going along the road. Elsinore timidly approached one of the tables near the edge of the crowd, but the hooded figure beneath the awning ignored her, gesturing to one of their companions, seemingly carrying on a whole conversation with their hands.

The two people never spoke a word, and as Elsinore looked around, she realized no one else made a sound either. They gestured and traded items, but no one spoke in any way that Elsinore could hear. Though they seemed to understand each other's gestures, it did not seem to be a hand or sign language, like those used by people she knew who were mute. They seemed only to be pointing out what goods they wished to trade and expressing their pleasure or displeasure.

The persistent silence of these people made Elsinore uneasy, but she was unsure how to proceed. She didn't wish to wander off into the unseen darkness in the distance. The domed structure in the center of the market dominated the town, drawing her attention; it seemed as good a place as any to investigate.

Following the path, she circled the building, but she could see no door in the facade, not even one locked and barred, and there were no windows anywhere that she could find. She approached a person by one of the nearby stalls, bolder than before.

"Excuse me," she said to the masked stranger. "Can you tell me anything about that building there? It doesn't seem to have a door. Can you tell me if I might be able to take a look?"

The figure turned their head and looked at her—or appeared to, as the eyes were hidden deep beneath the hollow black sockets. The person, predictably, did not respond verbally but stood from the table, looked around, and motioned for Elsinore to follow them. They walked along the spiral path, and after a moment of hesitation, the girl followed, keeping a respectable distance, until the person came to a tent on another side of the market.

Elsinore's worry immediately fell away when she saw the marvelous fruits and sweets laid out on display at the table. Bright red apples, ripe citrus of all colors, strawberries that she at first took for flowers, fruit with heavy, hard rinds and fantastical shapes, and others she couldn't even pretend to recognize.

Her mouth watered at the thought of drinking the juice from one of the orange citrus sunfruits; her rations had been the only food she had eaten since meeting Vedon in the Valley of the Mounds and dispelling the guardian creature. The thought of this delicious fruit tempted her, and it must have been visible on her face, because the stall keeper picked up one of the very oranges Elsinore had been coveting and held it out to her, hands open in offering.

Elsinore stepped back, startled. She held up a hand in a gesture of thanks and refusal. At least, such was her intention. As badly as she wanted the fruit, the sorceress recalled old stories that spoke of the fates that befell those who took food from the land beneath the hills—that those who ate and drank what was offered were bound by some ancient oath never to return to the land above. She resolved for now that it would be best not to accept food in this place, in case the stories of abduction, loss, and capture found in the old books were true.

The person's expression was unknowable beneath their mask. All that might have been seen were their eyes, but those were lost in the blackness of the shadow cast between the overhanging brow and the curved, pointed beak. The person only closed their hands over the fruit and withdrew it, before holding out an apple in the same manner.

Elsinore shook her head and backed away. Even if she were willing to accept food from the fae, she didn't know what this person wanted in return, and thought it better not to ask.

"I'm afraid I have nothing to offer," she said to the silent figure. "I have nothing to trade or barter. This is lovely, but I'm sorry, I cannot accept it."

She wanted to ask more about the domed building, but a doubt engendered by the others' refusal to respond to her overtures or speak stayed her tongue. Instead, she turned to continue through the market.

Elsinore wandered from table to table and stall to stall. She saw medallions with strange sigils and statues with features she could not recognize. There were lidded boxes leaking mysterious perfumes and baskets filled with strange shapes for which she could discern no purpose. One table held stacks of books bound in silk cloth, and Elsinore gasped with delight until she flipped through one, then another, and found that all the books were blank, their vacant white pages as cryptic as everything and everyone else in this place.

The people remained faceless beneath their hoods, not uttering the slightest sound. They bowed, held their hands out over their wares, gestured at each other, and shook their heads in the still air of this curious land under the Mountain. But none spoke or showed so much as their eyes.

Elsinore stopped when she came to a stall displaying flowers. She had seen such loveliness in the wood only a day or so before, but here, deep in the earth and far from the surface, it felt like it had been sleepless months. The flowers at the table before her were gorgeous: hyacinths of such a vivid purple, they seemed almost to glow, and roses as red and smooth as a human heart.

She looked for her favorite flower, a white-and-silver eight-petaled star that she saw often on the banks or the river in the outside world and which the gallae tended in bowers at the temple. But there seemed to be no such thing here. Disappointed, she turned and nearly collided with someone standing by the end of the stall.

Though masked with a hood and beak like all the others in this market, this person was singularly striking, tall and dressed in a simple black dress with a draped skirt and a top that clung to full breasts. In her slender hands, the woman—an assumption that Elsinore was unsure of—held a bouquet of the very flowers Elsinore had been looking for, with eight white petals in the form of a star and leaves of the very blue green she dyed her hair.

Inclining their masked head with a subtle grace, the person drew a flower from the bouquet with one hand and offered it to Elsinore with a slight bow.

Elsinore blushed, feeling an unplaceable attraction to this person despite not being able to see them behind the mask, and the thought of being obligated to return or repay the gift fled Elsinore's mind entirely. She took the flower and held it to her breast, then hesitated, unable to speak.

The figure turned away with the same grace they had

evinced in all their movements and began to walk away into the crowd. As Elsinore struggled to make a sound, the figure look back over their shoulder, the beak of the mask showing only slightly, and the young woman found herself wishing desperately that it was to steal a glance back at her. She could not fully articulate why.

As she watched them walk away, she heard the last thing she expected: the clearing of a throat and then a voice speaking the first words she had heard from another person since her encounter with the gatekeeper the previous night.

"Well! It isn't every day I see such a lovely new face here in the square. Failing to find what she's looking for in such a varied market, I'm guessing, from the disappointment in her bright eyes."

The voice was fluid and melodious, almost on the verge of singing the words. A few figures in the crowd stepped aside as a man approached the flower stall.

A man, Elsinore immediately took note, of unusual style compared to the others. His face was obscured by a mask of black feathers styled like a raven, and he wore a long fine coat of crimson, with a high collar, decorated with gold buttons and trim. Beneath the coat, he wore matching red trousers and shiny black boots with heels but no shirt. His muscles were remarkably toned. Stopping before Elsinore, he bowed with a practiced grace that she struggled very hard to find suspicious.

"You speak?" Elsinore asked. "I was beginning to wonder if that was possible here or subject to some taboo I didn't understand. It's hard to know how to act when you've come to someplace new and the customs are unfamiliar."

She smiled, then hoped it didn't make her seem too naive. She suddenly felt like some innocent country girl, an easy mark for this smooth talker who'd have been fashionable even in the cities in the surface world above. She stepped back as the man stood from his bow and closed her hands into fists.

Taking his feathered raven hood in one hand, the man drew it from his head. Elsinore gasped a little, at first in surprise, that any of the people here would take off their mask, and then at the man's face itself. His features were smooth and fine, and though his face was noticeably masculine, it had a tinge of femininity that showed in his lashes and in the angle of his lips. He had shaggy black hair that hung around his ears, which—much like Elsinore's—ended in noticeable points.

His beauty caught her off guard, and blushing, she put her hand to her mouth. Her doubts about her own sophistication fled involuntarily under this stranger's eyes; she was practically swoon. She hated it.

"I suppose one must wonder where she came from, how she found her way here, and with such a silly-looking cat." The man smiled, his full, fine lips parting to show teeth that flashed in the dim light.

"I come here with my own purposes," Elsinore said, not lying but careful not to speak any details. "I found my way here as any would, I suppose. Through the way in. The cat has done likewise, I suppose, as far as I know. They keep their intentions secret from others, as all cats do."

The man laughed sharply, his eyes twinkling, and he clapped his hands together, once, in front of his face. He grinned again.

"She is a natural at conversing in our particular idiom, I see. You could have been born and raised here, taught the words to the songs we sing in the circles cast where the mushrooms grow, taught how to treat intruders who wander in from the outside world seeking color and adventure. But I think really you are one of those outsiders, are you not?"

Elsinore didn't answer the question. Instead, she look at the feathered hood the man had cast aside onto a market table. "The masks?"

"A custom. Of the people of this place. Any from the outside must needs wear such a thing to breathe the air here, to survive—but to the dwellers of this place, it is only a fashion. And I am always one to discard fashions that no longer suit my nature. As you seem to do as well, my dear? My lady must have some affinity for this place, else one would expect her to take such a precaution. In any case, it stands in the way of us knowing each other, does it not?"

The man reached for Elsinore's hand and took the star flower without asking. He smoothed back the long hair unshaven on the right side of her head and delicately slid the flower behind her ear, and she allowed him to do so. She had forgotten, for the moment, the woman with the bouquet; now she only wanted this man's hands to touch her more, to slide over her skin, barely making contact, as she took his lips in hers.

The thought made her laugh sardonically, at herself more than at him, but he drew back at once, his hands in the air.

"Forgive me my forwardness, my dear. Allow me to begin the introductions? I am called Canter."

The man bowed again, never breaking eye contact with the lady before him. Rising to his full height, he towered over her, as did most of the masculine people in this market; Elsinore had never grown much taller than most other women—certainly closer to Milanda than to Glamis.

As Canter stood looking down at her with a guile that showed he knew what she was feeling, she blushed again.

Goddess, what is wrong with me?

"I dearly hope that you will tell me your name, Miss . . . ?" He trailed off expectantly.

"My name—"

Elsinore caught herself. Had she been so cautious with the gatekeeper the night before to be so easily led now? She knew better than to give up her name in a place like this, even if she hadn't been warned by the gatekeeper against that very mistake. Elsinore shook her head, more alert now and cautious of any fae tricks the man might be trying to pull. He seemed so sincere, and his eyes threatened to make her swoon again. And yet . . .

She felt the flower behind her ear with her fingers and smiled. "Call me Blue Leaf." She curtsied.

Canter held out his hand, and when Elsinore laid hers delicately in his palm, he kissed it.

"Perhaps the Lady Blue Leaf has grown tired of this crowd? Would it be too forward of me to invite you inside for a more private atmosphere and some conversation away from all these prying ears? They're not all as much for speaking as I am, but you can be assured they're all listening to those of us who give them something to listen to!"

Elsinore considered the offer. Curious, perhaps, but not unwelcome. She had been thinking much the same, wondering if there was anywhere they could go to get away from these hooded people, who unnerved her, more than even a normal crowd. And Canter's voice was so silken, the space between his open lips as dark as his eyes were bright. Elsinore thought she could listen to him talk for days.

Smiling, she nodded, unable to find the words to

vocalize her assent but communicating with her face and body as eloquently as she knew how. Were this place's customs beginning to affect her? Maybe she really did need to get away from the marketplace.

"My house is nearby, only a brief walk around the square. Come, just a little way off the road."

The houses of this little town stood all around them, along the spiral path that led out and away from the square and the market. They were built of clay and stone, with flat roofs of wood.

The two of them strolled gently, Elsinore listening to Canter talk about nothing of consequence. She couldn't focus on anything he really said; rather, she felt carried by his voice along the path, off the square, down an alley between stone and brick houses, then around a corner and a wall, through a gate and another alley.

Elsinore was entirely unsure where they had gone.

They stood before a little wooden door with a knob of brass in the center. Set above the know was a face, with a grotesque mouth and furious eyes that glared a dreadful welcome. Elsinore glanced back as Canter led the way into the house, trying to remember the route back.

Unsure of the way, but tired and confused, she followed her host inside.

Elsinore found herself in what looked like a peaceful sitting room, cozy and well-furnished with shelves of mugs and wooden tables bearing simple pots with flowers like the ones at the stalls in the marketplace. A warm fire burned in the hearth, and thick blankets sat nearby.

The cat dashed through the door, startling her as they brushed against her leg possessively. Elsinore had once again forgotten them, rudely neglecting them in her focus on this enticing man, and she made a note to ask their forgiveness. Apparently unconcerned, they walked directly to the fire and curled up on the blankets, warming themself by the hearth.

Canter took two mugs from a shelf. "Please do the same as your friend and warm yourself by the fire while I prepare us some wine. I'm sure you must be cold after the chill in the air outside." He disappeared into a pantry farther in.

Laying her scabbard and bag on a chair at one end of the hearth by the fireplace pokers, Elsinore walked over to sit on the blankets beside the cat. As she stroked their soft fur, they opened one eye, very slightly, then squeezed both shut again and began to snore quite heavily for such a tiny creature.

Elsinore let her mind drift as she stared into the fire. Oddly, it had already been burning when they arrived, but perhaps Canter had only come away from the house for a moment. It clearly wasn't very far, but something about the situation made Elsinore a little uneasy.

"I mean," she said to the cat, "everything seemed fine in the bedroom last night. Something about this seems different, though. I wish I had the Warding spell prepared to cast again; since I don't, we'd better stay on the lookout."

She yawned and stretched, feeling almost like a cat herself. "I should be well rested, but I feel so tired all of a sudden. Perhaps the market wore me out? And the wind in that strange, dark place was very cold, now that I think of it." She yawned again. "We can rest and warm up a bit, can't we?"

The cat only responded by curling up tighter on the blankets and leaning their head into Elsinore's fingers as she scratched behind their ear.

She had no intention of falling asleep—and no recollection of doing so—yet she was startled awake by the click of a doorknob and the squeak of its hinges. Whipping her head around, she saw Canter returning from the pantry with the two mugs. He sauntered over to the fire and settled himself on the rug beside Elsinore, setting the drinks on the floor. Steam wafted up from the mugs, and the aroma of mulled wine roused her a little more.

Just enough, in fact, to realize that Canter had seated himself between her and her bag.

More importantly, between her and her sword.

Neck tingling, she picked up the mug he'd placed beside her as he drank from the other. Remembering her commitment to not accept food or drink from this place, she brought it to her lips and inhaled the spicy steam, then set it down on the stone floor without drinking.

"Where do you come from?" Elsinore asked, starting a conversation partly to distract him from her decision not to drink from the mug. "How did you come to this place?"

"Come here?" the man responded, showing a little surprise. "I came in to warm up from the chill of death outside. The fellows outside in the town square would do well to do the same in their own homes! I don't know how much attention you paid to them out there, ambling about under the dark sky wearing little more than hoods and kilts, but they looked chilled to the very bone!"

He smiled charmingly as he spoke, and the music of his voice echoed in Elsinore's mind. She was nearly overwhelmed by a deep urge to sink back into the blankets and listen as he spoke about nothing while the fire glowed warmly. Fighting it back, she pulled her mind forward into the conversation.

"I meant this whole place," Elsinore said. "This market, this village, the country under the Mountain. How did you come here?"

"I live here. I belong here. Don't you? You look like someone who would, though I took you for an outsider before. Have I not met you once? Don't I recognize you from somewhere? Surely you're coming to the banquet this evening?"

"Banquet?" Elsinore shook her head. "What is the banquet for? Is it in the market?"

Canter laughed condescendingly.

"Why, my dear, it is in Her honor. It is at Her house. I would have thought you would at least know that much." The way the man said the pronoun made it clear it was spoken with emphasis, respect, and a little fear. "It is always held in the same place. I would have thought you knew."

The beautiful man reached into the pocket of his scarlet coat and produced a roll of cannabis. He searched his other pockets and laughed apologetically.

"I'm afraid I've forgotten my matches. May I impose on you to put a taper to the fire and light this for me, Lady Blue Leaf?"

Something in her felt hurt and ashamed, and she didn't quite know why. Rather than take one of the tapers leaning by the side of the hearth, the witch kept steady eye contact with the man and cast her fire spell. A luminous orb of magic fire hovered over her palm and gripping fingers, and she held it out to him.

Canter showed no apparent surprise, only leaning in and lighting the weed in the flame. As he leaned back and exhaled, Elsinore threw the fireball into the hearth, where it scorched the brick of the back wall and made the fire blaze. She couldn't do much harm with the little cantrip if she threw it at someone, but she hoped the display was intimidating enough for him to believe she could do it to him if it came to that. She was beginning to grow wary and wanted to pacify her own fears as best she could.

Meanwhile, Canter pointedly took a drag, propped his elbow on the blankets, and offered her the cannabis.

On the list of all the things I shouldn't do, Elsinore thought, *getting high with this fae has to be near the top.*

The ease of his smile and his flashing eyes were very enticing, and as she looked into his face, she accepted the roll. Instead of taking a drag, she threw it into the fire and grabbed his muscular shoulders, kissing him and trying to tug his coat off.

His hands met hers and slid the coat off, guiding her hands down from his shoulders and across his arms. All the while, he kissed her ever more passionately. Elsinore slipped out of her hood and jacket and fell back as he slid his hand under the skirt of her dress, caressing her thigh as he gently pushed her down to the blankets with his other hand.

"So you like to be on top, huh?" Elsinore said into his lips as she reached up with her mouth to kiss him.

"You don't want me to be?" Canter asked playfully.

"I like to trade off," Elsinore murmured. "We can each take a turn, if you like." She grinned, sliding her hands up his thighs and around to his backside. He took her hands in his again and gently led them back around to his chest.

"Why don't I stay on top," he stated, not asking.

Elsinore kissed his mouth, his throat, his chest. "Why don't I get something from my bag," she said in a similar manner—stating, not asking.

Pulling away, she rolled to her knees and started to crawl around him to her bag. But Canter turned with her, standing and stepping in front of her, unwilling to take his eyes off her body or let her move forward. Fear rose in Elsinore's heart at once; this wasn't right, and the look on Canter's face showed that he knew it.

The cat, who had until this point been dozing peacefully, forgotten beside the hearth, woke suddenly and began to hiss and yowl. Leaping to their feet, they arched their back and bared their tiny fangs, glaring up at the man, who had turned his back on them when he stood to block Elsinore.

"What is it, baby?" Elsinore asked, suspicious. "What do you see?"

Canter glanced over his shoulder at the cat, then turned back to Elsinore, scoffing dismissively. He never turned his back fully to her, she realized.

"This is silly," he said. "Your cat is just misbehaved. Probably bothered by a stray ember from the fire. Come here, Miss Blue Leaf, where were we?"

Elsinore stood as well, her arms at her side, staying away. "No, I think they have something they want to bring to our attention. Isn't that right, kitty? Don't you have something you want to show me?"

Yowling once more, the cat leaped at the man, claws open, and slashed across the man's head as they fell to the floor. The man doubled over in shock and pain from the cat's sharp claws. Shaking, he turned instinctively to kick at the cat, but they jumped away from his foot and onto the mantelpiece.

The moment his back turned to Elsinore, she quickly ducked away and drew one of the sharp iron pokers from beside the fire, holding it out in front of her.

Though the man's face and front were beautiful and enticing, his whole backside, from his neck to his buttocks, was hollow and rotten. Insects and spiders crawled within, as if he were the desiccated husk of an old tree.

Great worms with pincers on their faces waved outward like horrible little arms.

Turning back to face Elsinore, he bent down and swept his coat back on, covering himself up. He stood watching her and the sharp poker in her hands, tapping the toe of one shiny black boot on the stone floor.

He laughed discourteously. "I suppose our fun is finished for now. I rather regret you having to see that, but what's done is done." He smiled, and a beetle of some kind scurried from his open mouth and into his hair.

"I don't much like spiders and centipedes," Elsinore said. "You should keep yourself a little tidier and cleaner, wash a little more often, and you can avoid situations like this in the future."

"If you don't care for such things, then I admit you wouldn't have liked it when they covered your smooth, clean body and stripped the flesh from your beautiful breasts and soft little penis."

Elsinore stood behind the iron, shamefully aware of her body, of her vulnerability. She cursed internally for allowing herself to be romanced by the fae's sweet voice.

But that wasn't what had happened, was it? She had been manipulated . . . and somehow, in some way she couldn't identify yet, she was still being manipulated. She tightened her grip on the poker.

"I think you don't really belong here after all, Miss Blue Leaf." Canter stepped forward despite the sharp iron point aimed at his chest.

"If you did, you would realize, wouldn't you?" He reached out before Elsinore could react and grabbed the iron, snapping it like a twig.

Which was exactly what it was. The fire poker had only been a thin, dry tree branch in Elsinore's hand, and it snapped as easily as any other fallen branch left drying in the dirt. It had only been an illusion, a glamour that Elsinore had fallen for despite her knowledge of witchcraft.

She'd have felt like a fool if she weren't so afraid.

The man grinned, revealing teeth that were long and sharp. His eyes were dark, sunken deep in his skull. The pincers of worms reached out from the collar of his coat, even as he reached for her with hands bearing twisted fingers tipped with hooked nails like talons.

Elsinore despaired.

A yowl cut through the house, easing her fear, and the cat leaped from the mantel, raking their claws across the fae's neck. The creature snarled, his attention diverted by the cat, though only for a moment before he turned back to Elsinore.

The distraction, however, had bought her time, and she ran to her bag, drawing the dagger she had brought from her altar rather than the sword given to her by Glamis. The dagger flashed in the dim firelight as Elsinore struck out, slicing the palm of Canter's outstretched hand.

He released a piercing cry utterly unlike the entrancing voice he had used to seduce the young woman. Smoke, or steam, rose out of the wound, and even after his scream died away, he continued to hiss like a serpent.

Elsinore held the dagger before her, and this time, the man shrank away in honest fear. The dagger, which she kept for ritual use, was made of rare iron, which she knew from her studies was a powerful charm to repel fae, but seeing its effect was startling.

Clutching his wounded hand, Canter retreated to the front door. "I ask the lady's permission to take my leave." He waited until Elsinore nodded to take the knob in his good hand. "I look forward to seeing you at the banquet in the Ganzir." He smiled, his teeth and eyes returning to their previous beauty, and opened the door. "If we meet then, I would be most honored to dance with you, if you would be so courteous. You can leave the knife aside, if you would."

With that, he withdrew and shut the door.

Elsinore waited at least five minutes after he left before sheathing her knife and returning it to her bag. The cat, likewise, kept watch by the door for ages before returning to their mistress's side and rubbing against her leg.

Putting her jacket back on, she pulled her hood up and gathered her things. Having had more than enough of her recovery from the cold outside, she and the cat set out to return to the market and decide how to progress.

* 14 *

THE CATACOMBS

Opening the door, Elsinore stopped on the threshold and stood in silence. Where she had expected to find the town, with its alleys and spiral path to the market, there were now only piles of rubble; fallen stone figures, the original forms of which were impossible to determine; and coatings of mushrooms, white fungus, and mold. What had once been pretty stone houses were now ruined old hovels, barely showing the shape they'd once held.

When Elsinore turned back to the house she had just come from, she found only an empty ruin, devoid of shelves or pantry, with only an old burned-out chimney to remind her of what she had seen inside.

The market—the entire town—had been a glamour.

Feeling in her hair behind her ear for the flower the lady had given her, she found only a dry, dead brown weed that crumbled in her fingers.

Elsinore couldn't even recognize the house she had entered town from, where she had rested in the bath. Had that been an illusion as well? It was unlikely, persisting as it had overnight while she slept, but she feared she wouldn't be able to tell, and if so, that she couldn't return.

The dim light in this unwelcoming place was worse than before, now clearly emanating from luminescent fungus growing visibly in the high cavern ceiling and walls. There wasn't a dark sky or distant horizon at all. She truly was under the Mountain and knew now to better keep up her guard.

The one part of the town she now saw truly existed was the domed building, which stood as squat among the rubble and ruined houses as ever. It looked the same as before, the doorless and windowless facade hiding the secrets within. After a final glance around to make sure she wasn't being watched, by Canter or anything else as sinister, Elsinore set off from the hovel, the cat staying close by her side.

"I'm glad you're here," Elsinore said aloud to her new friend. "You give me one thing to be comfortable with, at least, in a place of such mysterious risks. Thank you also for your attempts to protect me from that ogreish creature; it's appreciated. But you're only a little cat, and I should probably be the one protecting you.

"I don't even know what to call you to thank you. Do you have a name?" Elsinore considered what she was saying. "I suppose it's inappropriate of me to ask that of anyone in this place. I of all people should know that by now. But maybe I can come up with something to call you for the sake of my own convenience?"

Picking up the cat, she held them out in front of her, and they dangled there in annoyance. Did they understand the sharp discrepancy between her internal worries and her attempts to distract herself? Or did they only dislike being handled, in the same way all cats did?

"Let's see, first of all, are you a girl cat, a boy cat, or neither? I can never tell with cats. I know you're adorable, though!"

She brought the cat back in and snuggled her face in their dark fur. Clearly deciding they'd had enough affection for the moment, the cat jumped out of her arms, landed on the ground, and tail in the air, began to walk over and around the fallen stones of the ruined mold-ridden field in the direction of the dome.

With nowhere else to go, and no other leads, Elsinore followed.

"In the brief time I've known you, you've done quite a lot to put yourself in great danger coming to my aid. I think I'll call you Risky. Unless you tell me you've got a better name?"

The cat looked up at her and meowed.

"No? Risky it is, then! Now, do you have any advice about where we're going?"

The cat stopped to lick themself.

"Yeah, you're a regular cat, I think."

The cat didn't give any indication they were listening and merely began to walk again, leading Elsinore to stand before the face of the great structure.

As Elsinore had feared, there seemed to be no manner of ingress. The cat sat contentedly by her side as she felt the curved wall of the dome, finding only smooth stone all the way around; not a joint or crack appeared in the surface beneath her hand. She slumped down against the wall, trying to think of what to do or where to go.

In the silence of the cavern, the light from the fungus glowed faintly, never changing or flickering. Her slightest motion echoed all around, and Elsinore began to grow uneasy. Any other person or entity like Canter would be able to see or hear her, and she suddenly felt a great urge to keep still and silent. So great was her focus on remaining unseen that she almost took for granted that there was something out there watching. Yet she still almost gasped when an echo rattled out from the movement of rubble in the field.

Straining her eyes to see in the dimness, Elsinore could just make out a figure, small and hunched, pushing aside stones and fallen statues with great effort, hunting through the rubble. There was another sound coming from the figure, a muttering or babble, magnified by the echo but still indistinct and muffled. Elsinore silently glided along the side of the wall and crouched down beneath a boulder, keeping just enough of herself over the edge to keep sight on the entity. Risky, she realized, didn't move from their resting spot but seemed hardly noticeable.

The figure rooted around in the field for some time; Elsinore was unsure how long they had been doing so before she noticed their presence. It was hard to see from her vantage point, but the person appeared to be doubled over, dressed in torn rags, with long scraggly gray hair or a hood. Like Canter and the illusory people of the marketplace, they wore a mask with shadowed dark eyes and a long, curved beak like a bird. They continued talking to themself inaudibly and incoherently.

Finally, after rummaging in the ruins for a long time, they made a loud exclamation, a yell of triumph or excitement, and they dove down beneath a boulder and vanished.

Elsinore remained where she was for another moment, then rose from her hiding spot and made her way carefully to the place where the figure had been digging. Standing as well, Risky stretched and followed her.

Taking a moment to get her bearings, Elsinore found

the place the person had been searching and what they'd found: in a gap between two large stones leaning against each other, a staircase went down into the earth, much like the one opened by the gatekeeper. Looking around to make sure she hadn't been seen, Elsinore steadied herself against the boulders, confirmed they wouldn't fall and entrap her, and slid into the hole, followed by the cat, who she supposed had an easier time of it.

She descended slowly, trying not to make any sound that could alert whoever she was following. The path below was wide open, seemingly stable and safe, so Elsinore was confident someone had gone before her—as confident as she could be of anything in this place of tricks and illusions. Quietly moving, step by step, keeping a close eye on her surroundings in case of an ambush or a surprise, she descended, Risky following close behind.

Elsinore came at last to the landing, and still there was no sign of the mysterious robed figure. It was only a narrow hallway space carved out of the mountain stone, with nowhere to hide or flee except back up the stairs. At the end of the hall, tall wooden double doors stood thick and barred with metal bands. An arch over the door was supported on pillars, and the whole edifice seemed solid and impenetrable, and silent as the hooded illusions in the market.

Elsinore tried to push the door open, but it wouldn't give even a finger's width. She pushed with her shoulder, gave it her all with what little strength she had, but the door remained shut, as it seemed it ever had. Had the person she was following passed through? There seemed to be nowhere else they could have gone, leaving Elsinore puzzled.

"Well, what do you think we should do now?" she asked the cat, who sat by her feet, licking their paw in disinterest. After cleaning themself to their satisfaction, Risky walked past her leg, looked up and pawed at the door, then walked right through it as if it were an illusion, a phantom of mist distorting the air.

Elsinore stared at where they had disappeared, her brow furrowed and mouth open ever so slightly, holding a question she felt she needn't ask. Perturbed, she raised her hand to the door again and pushed it halfheartedly.

This time, the door slid heavily but easily in an arc along the floor. Elsinore stood back, wary. After a moment, she heard a meow call from within. Standing on the other side of the threshold, the cat looked up at her, meowed again, and hurried inside.

"Did you . . . ? How did you do that?" she called after Risky.

Thinking for a moment, she reasoned this place held secrets she had no immediate need to understand. She followed the cat inside to an antechamber before another arch and through it into the wide body of a temple. It appeared she had entered the dome from the passage underground.

The interior was dim but lit by a pale-green light falling from glass panes set along the domed ceiling. They were almost like windows to a landscape and sky of dim glowing fog, but Elsinore had seen no windows set in the dome from the outside. The green light they cast was like that from the crystals in the place of the gatekeeper. It tinted the skin of her hands an unnatural deathly pallor; she imagined if she looked in a mirror, it would look even more ghastly, that the light would cast dark circles under her eyes and exaggerate every flaw.

She was glad she saw nothing here that would show her reflection.

The place she was in now was one wide circular

room beneath the dome. Rows of stone benches or pews—some fallen over, some broken—radiated from the far side of the chamber around a raised stage-like platform against the far wall.

In the center of the stage sat a long, flat-topped block of what appeared to be solid stone, possibly an altar, though that was unclear. It was large enough, at least, to be a coffin.

The thought chilled Elsinore but didn't deter her from stepping forward. She thought the chamber seemed like a shrine, some sacred place long abandoned but still resonant with an aura of the divine.

Risky was looking around, sniffing underneath and climbing on top of benches, and seemed generally curious. Elsinore, too, looked around as she walked down an aisle that cut through the rows. Pillars near the wall held up the edges of the dome, and the strange green glass panels were set in the dome above and alongside them. Set into the wall behind the stage was an alcove, shadowed in darkness from the angle of the green lights. There appeared to be something in it—a statue, maybe—and Elsinore cast her light spell to see more clearly.

The light spell revealed a twice-life-size statue of a woman—rather, a goddess. It was very simple and roughly carved, a column in the basic shape of a human form, as if it had been made to fit a person inside. Elsinore wondered, briefly and with fear, if it was a sarcophagus. The face was intense and severe, the eyes hollow and black with shadow, as if the sculptor had simply chiseled deep holes into the head. Surrounding the face was a hood or hair—the ancient style made it difficult to tell—and on the head sat a crown, unadorned but crenelated, like the battlements of city walls. In the front, the crown came to a pointed crest, like the peak of a mountain.

The goddess's hands rested on the heads of lions that sat upright on either side of her, looking ready to leap at her command. The lions were as simply carved as the goddess, and like her, their eyes were black hollow holes, sinking into darkness but staring ceaselessly at nothing and everything. Though tame faced, their expressions filled Elsinore with disquiet.

The three figures stared down at her from the dark alcove, making her feel very small and uneasy. She felt not only as if she were being watched but as if there were some secret—the answer to some gravely important question she had forgotten long ago—that these figures knew, hidden in the shadows of their eyes, and they glared at Elsinore in disapproval for not remembering.

If only she could see what was behind their eyes.

Elsinore gazed up into the dark, staring eyes for a moment longer, then dismissed her light spell, shrouding the alcove again in darkness. She felt a little more comfortable now that she couldn't see the figures gazing down at her, though she knew they were still there, watching.

Turning from the alcove, Elsinore looked back at the altar below. With the light grown dimmer, her other senses seemed to have grown keener, and something seemed out of place. Examining a spot at the edge of the great stone block, she had to step back and then return to determine whether it was only her imagination.

Finally, she was certain it wasn't. There was indeed a draft, faint but noticeable, coming from a gap at the edge of what she now realized was a heavy metal slab on top of the block. It was a lid, and the stone a hollow box; was it a coffin after all?

No, Elsinore thought, dismissing the gruesome speculation. *Why would a draft be blowing from a coffin?*

The cat called loudly from the side of the stone, reaching up and pawing at the lid.

"Please, kitty, I'm trying to figure this out."

Could Risky even understand her? She still didn't know whether she could trust this cat, if that was even what they really were. In this strange place of fae magic, should she have followed the first trustworthy-looking entity she encountered into the entrance of the Mountain, despite the explicit warning? She shouldn't have followed the voices in the wood, and she'd refused to follow the lights of the will-o'-the-wisps. So why, then, had she followed the cat, and why did she continue to follow them?

They helped me fend off Canter and defend myself from his deadly trick. I owe them for that, if nothing else.

Risky meowed again.

"All right, I suppose you know what this is?" Elsinore replied apologetically. She lost nothing by acting as if the cat understood.

Giving one more plaintive meow, the little creature hopped onto the edge of the altar by the source of the draft. Elsinore scratched them behind the ear, then examined the lid again.

Determined to figure it out, Elsinore leaned as hard as she could against the edge of the lid where the cat stood, trying to dislodge the metal and reveal whatever lay beneath. She was hardly surprised when she couldn't make it budge. The cat, still standing on top, looked at her curiously, head cocked, and meowed once again.

"I think you must be weighing it down," she said sardonically. "Otherwise, I'm sure I would have been able to lift it." She rolled her eyes at herself and sank to the floor against the altar.

Twirling the ring on her finger, she considered the spells she had studied to aid her on her way through the

Mountain. Though most were given more artful, theatrical names—the typical bravado of mages who discovered and recorded such startling and magnificent spells—some were merely utilitarian, in both name and function. Elsinore had prepared a simple spell, one mundane enough that she could cast it at least twice before studying it again. It was a powerful force that had been named simply Push.

The sorceress looked around at the wide chamber. The box was close to the wall with the statue; she had enough sense not to face the near wall, so she positioned herself between the wall and the box, her back to the statue of the Goddess above. Elsinore picked Risky up off the box and set them safely on the floor between her feet. Then she laid her ringed hand flat against the side of the box, braced her feet against the stone floor, and whispered the word of power.

The effect was instant and kinetic; the spell was cast. Elsinore drew her hand back in fear as a wave of force pushed forward from her palm, an invisible typhonic movement like the wind, striking with the might of a hammer of the gods. The once-immovable metal lid flew through the air as if carried by a hurricane or hurled by a giant, spinning rapidly end over end. It slammed against the far wall above the portal to the antechamber from which Elsinore had entered the room.

The whole chamber fell still, and Elsinore let her tensed muscles relax. She sighed.

Too soon.

Shaken loose by the impact of the heavy lid, a massive stone slab slid down from the ceiling, hitting the floor with a tremendous impact that shook the chamber with a thunderous boom. Despite her solid stance, the light-footed dancer lost her balance and fell to her knees. Several of the light panels in the ceiling flickered and gave out, shading more of the room in darkness and leaving only a little of the pallid green light.

The slab had shut the portal to the antechamber, totally blocking the only path in or out of the shrine that Elsinore knew. She looked around, but in the remaining light, the room was shadier still, and the circles of pews stood squat and dark against the floor.

"Fuck," Elsinore muttered. "Okay . . . fuck."

Looking up at her, Risky mewed.

"Yeah, I don't know. I'm sorry."

The cat leaped up on the edge of the now-uncovered block and stuck their head into the newly revealed dark hollow within.

The way back had been closed off, but the way forward, at least, had been opened.

The pit was not merely the depth of the box; the darkness went down farther than Elsinore could see. A cold draft rose from within, chilling her skin and spirit. Undeterred, the witch cast her fire spell again, held it over the pit, and dropped it down to see how far it fell.

The drop wasn't that deep, and only a short depth from the top was a flight of stone steps leading down through the altar. The steps descended far, however, and deep into a room she could not see from outside of the box. The fireball cast light as it rolled down the steps and into the room.

Elsinore was considering the wisdom of climbing in and descending the stairs when the orb of light went out.

The fire spell should have remained illuminated as long as Elsinore willed, only going out once she dismissed it. Yet darkness fell over the pit, the shadow stronger than before, seeming to reach up and out of the altar passage to darken the space around her.

She could no longer see into the altar.

A chill ran over her whole body, as if the darkness rising from the pit gripped her. She struggled to keep her feet and not let it pull her down.

Yet where else did she have to go?

She looked around the shrine one last time, considering her lack of options for escape. When nothing new revealed itself, she turned to the edge of the altar, cast her light spell again, and decisively vaulted over the edge, landing at the top of the stairs. The cat jumped in after her.

"Yes, I know, but if you didn't want me delving into ominous tombs, you should have helped me find another way to go," Elsinore chided the cat, though Risky didn't meow or otherwise protest. They just followed her down the stairs and into whatever was beyond.

The chamber below felt cramped and dark. As Elsinore stepped off the stairs, she held up the orb of light hovering above her palm and looked carefully around. It was a wide antechamber lined with dull, faintly reflective metal panels on the walls and some manner of crystal or frosted glass panels in the ceiling. As Elsinore and Risky stepped forward, a ghostly light flickered to life from behind the glass panels, coloring the room an uneasy blue. The witch dismissed her light spell and looked around the sad, undecorated room.

On the far side, a single door blocked the way forward. It was the same dull metal as the walls, a flat gray slab that was barely reflective, in which no doorknob or locking mechanism was visible, nor even hinges. The door seemed to have been built to slide into the wall on either side, away from the slit in the center.

Risky stopped and looked around. Having apparently made a decision, they walked straight up to the solid metal of the door and pressed their head against it. Sliding down, they rolled over and laid down on the ground, looking up at Elsinore.

She smiled. "What's wrong, Risky? Can't you walk through it like the last one?"

Elsinore examined the door, pressing the sides and the slit in the center, but still she found it stood solid and would not open.

"A lot of good the gatekeeper's promise turned out to be," Elsinore muttered.

Risky looked up at her curiously.

"The gatekeeper told me 'the barriers wouldn't be barriers to me,' or something like that. I don't know if you were there watching from somewhere at the time? Or if you know what I'm talking about? Or if you can understand me at all?

"The gatekeeper told me a few things. Strange things. It also said to keep my . . ."

Elsinore looked from the cat to the door.

"It told me to keep my deep name a secret. Or the power to destroy me would follow." She ran her hand along the edge of the door once again, thinking.

"But maybe that only matters if I'm talking to somebody? The gatekeeper also said, 'the way will open for me.' Maybe if I identify myself . . ."

The witch leaned her head in close to the slit in the middle between the two sides of the door. She whispered—breathed, almost inaudibly—the name she had been given by the creature at the entrance. She enunciated each syllable, her lips and tongue feeling them form in her mouth from the secret held in her heart.

"EN.SIN.NU.UR.MA."

The door responded as if she had spoken a word of power to cast a spell. It opened at once, the slit widening into a doorway as the two panels slid into either side of the wall, accompanied by a hiss like the voice of a serpent.

Risky mewled, then leaped to their feet and dashed forward into the shadows of an unlit hall. "Kitty! Wait for me!" Elsinore yelled, quickly setting off after them.

Light flickered on in the ceiling—the same shallow blue light behind frosted glass as the previous room had. The light followed the girl, flickering on as if sensing her presence, leaving the space only a few yards ahead obscured in darkness. The walls of the passage were narrow, built of the same composite cement she had seen before, outside the entrance to the Mountain.

At the end of the passage, Elsinore found the plain arch of a doorway standing firm in the wall ahead. Decorated with unguided spiral carvings, the frame seemed thick and imposing. Elsinore ran her fingers along the edges, and they came away filmed with ancient dirt and grime. She wrinkled her nose and wiped her hand off on her skirt.

As she passed through the doorway, lights weakly flickered ahead, and Elsinore found herself in another chamber, this one wide and tall, rectangular with a high arching ceiling, and dimly lit by blue frosted glass at regular intervals from each wall. Inset in the walls were row upon row of rectangular metal slabs, though some had fallen to the ground, revealing deep, low, narrow recesses that plunged into shadow. These spaces and alcoves covered the length and height of the great walls, vanishing into the far dark distance of the chamber, deeper than the sorceress could tell.

Elsinore was disturbed to see a figure, hooded and silent, lightly swaying from side to side in the middle of the floor in front of her. Its head hung low over its chest, and she could see no part of its body beneath the pale, tattered robes, which hung to the floor.

There was no one and nothing else in sight, and no doors that she could see.

As she approached, the figure showed no reaction; it remained silently swaying, its shadow passing to and fro in the flickering light of the glass.

"Excuse me, friend. I'm looking for my cat? Well, *a* cat. A cat I'm with, really more of an acquaintance? I named them Risky, but you probably wouldn't have heard about that yet? If you know them at all, I mean."

The figure did not respond, nor did it cease swaying ever so gently.

"Did you see a cat go by through here? That's really all I'm trying to ask you. I don't see how you could miss them. But then Risky can just walk through walls, apparently, so you could have missed them, come to think of it. They could have passed through the—are you listening to me?"

At last, the figure stopped moving and stood stone still, lifting its head to look at Elsinore. The hood still hung low, hiding much of its face, but Elsinore could see its mouth—the teeth and jawbone of a skull—and the back of the hood beyond the vertebrae behind it. This time, the skeleton seemed human, not the bird-headed ghoul of the gatekeeper she had met the night before, but the fact did little to comfort the witch.

The figure turned to face an unlit space of the hall to Elsinore's left and waved its arms forward, revealing dry, skeletal hands.

Elsinore looked to the dark wall and back to the figure. "Thank you? I guess?" She pointed in the same direction. "Should I . . . ?"

She trailed off as the hooded figure resumed its swaying. Slowly and cautiously, she turned from the figure and walked into the darkness, casting her lantern spell to see more clearly. She approached an alcove whose door was broken off, the shadow within too deep to be lit by the lantern spell until she came closer.

Drawing near, Elsinore bent and looked first at the fallen metal lid. The cold, dull gray barely reflected the fire of her spell, and she realized it was made of lead. All these lids, the dull metal of the walls and door in the previous room, the lid that flew away under the power of her spell in the shrine above—much of this place was lined in lead.

Bending over, she peered into the open alcove. She was hardly surprised to find a reclining skeleton within; these were burial places, and the chamber itself was a crypt. Elsinore went to another a few spaces down the hall and found it was much the same. Each alcove held a full skeleton dressed in tattered rags, all that remained of the clothes they'd worn in life.

Drawing closer to one alcove, she looked more carefully. Suddenly, she gasped and jumped back.

The skeleton had moved.

In only a second, Elsinore realized it was just the arm, which had dropped a few inches with a loud, brittle crack. She sighed, relieved; she had only disturbed the ancient, precarious remains, dusty with decay. She had no idea how many decades—or centuries, even—these tombs had lain undisturbed.

She was slowly standing up, thoughts unfocused, when the dim blue lights flickered and went out, leaving her in total darkness.

From farther down the hall, there came a buzzing sound, like the wings of countless flies passing through the air and filling the room. Elsinore's skin crawled, though a moment later, she tensed in fear. The buzzing had stopped suddenly, replaced by heavy scraping sounds that echoed and filled the dark.

Instinctively, Elsinore backed away from the wall, halting only when she thought she must be near the center of the floor. The sounds seemed to come from within the walls and the shallow graves of the crypt.

Following the scraping came a discordant chorus of rattles, dry and empty, carried up on a chill draft. The rattling grew louder as her hands trembled, and louder still from every direction, and there was an audible sound of whispering, some voice at once in the room but also, surely, only in her mind.

At once, Elsinore was seized by the urgent need to flee, to rush out, but she had gotten turned around in the dark. She backed up, but the rattling before her grew terribly close.

Abruptly, the ghostly light from the glass flared up, brightly illuminating the room. The tombs were open, and out of them climbed a horde of terrible underworld creatures the likes of which Elsinore had never imagined.

They were animated skeletons, barren of any flesh, their yawning skulls dusty and silent, their clattering femurs, fingers, and ribs a cacophony of scraping, scuttling bone. They seemed to have started from farther down the hall, but those closer to Elsinore also began to rise and approach. The nearest fiercely gripped the metal frame around its alcove-tomb with terrible claws, pulling itself into the room, and more climbed out from their own resting places, following it.

Snapping her fingers, Elsinore cast her light spell and hurled the fireball at the approaching things. She struck the nearest one; the skeleton broke apart and charred as the rags it wore burned away.

But it was only one, and there were so many more—too many for her to fight off individually.

Turning, she dashed away across the chamber, back the way she had come. The skeletons followed, but slowly. Less trained in gymnastics than the dancer and more naturally shambling, they struggled out of their narrow tombs and clambered over the fallen lids, slowed by climbing down from the walls and stumbling over their own undead bodies.

With her head turned to keep track of the skeletons, she collided face first with the pallid, hooded figure near the door to the crypt, and screamed. Fearfully, frantically, Elsinore cried to it.

"Help me! How do I escape?"

She knew the way back out of the temple above was blocked by the great stone door, fallen behind her as she went deeper in. She had nowhere to run.

The figure did not respond, silent as ever, but it ceased its lurching and stood still, grinning with ancient rotten teeth within its fleshless jaw. From the shadow of the hood, Elsinore could feel an intelligence, an essence deeply inhuman, watching and judging her in her fear with vicious silence.

"I'm shut in! How can I escape? Answer me!" Elsinore shrieked. She shoved the figure, expecting it to step back, fall, collapse, or perhaps crumble in a heap of bones and rags. But it stood solidly, moved not at all, only resuming its endless, repetitive swaying.

Though she'd seen the skull beneath the hood and the bony hands in the sleeves, what she felt beneath the robe did not feel like ribs. It felt solid, sturdy, living.

The figure suddenly flailed beneath the robe, jangled,

and rose off the ground. The room shook and rumbled, stone and dust falling from the ceiling. In the floor beneath the figure was a pit, which had been hidden by the robe, and rising out of it was a long white body, a column like the trunk of a huge tree. The skull and arms fell away, along with the rags, a tattered puppet now discarded, revealing the head of an enormous serpent. Its veins ran pink beneath its translucent white scales, its eyes glowed red, and its bared fangs were as long and sharp as swords.

Elsinore froze in astonishment and fear.

Its veil of bones cast aside, the serpent reared up before the young witch; it swayed yet, back and forth, the movement of a snake judging its prey, measuring the distance between them, studying her movements, preparing to strike. Its head was the size of Elsinore's entire body. It could swallow her whole, though not before slashing her with its terrible fangs.

All at once, it opened its mouth, jaws wide, fangs extended, and darted toward its prey like a spear.

Elsinore dove forward over the serpent's head and somersaulted across, landing on her feet behind its great body. The snake fell through the shambling skeletons, reducing them to broken bones and scattering those that remained.

She didn't wait to see how the rest reacted; she ran as fast as she could back down the narrow hall by which she had arrived, instinctively hoping the massive creature couldn't fit. She instantly regretted her choice of direction; she could continue for a little while but had nowhere to escape. She could flee a little farther, back up the stairs through the altar to the shrine chamber, but the exit would still lay blocked. But for a corner behind a pillar here and there, there was nowhere to hide or escape in the domed chamber with this creature in pursuit.

She was only partway down the tunnel when she realized she could hear the serpent close behind, squeezing rapidly through the narrow hall. It followed desperately, furiously, and Elsinore's heart raced with fear. When she reached the end of the tunnel, the automatic lead door opened for her, but the small size of the room beyond deepened her already considerable panic.

Once she was farther into the chamber, she turned and stood facing the portal, cursing herself for knowing no magic strong enough to really kill a creature like this— if the underworld monster was truly alive and could even be killed.

I may be able to hurt it, though.

The serpent slammed against the metal doorframe, its head and body too wide to pass through. The metal bent and twisted, widening the opening, but that only angered the beast further as huge fragments of cement from inside the thick walls fell upon its head. Elsinore watched it struggle and gradually squeeze through, but she was ready to meet it. If her Push spell had been able to cast the heavy lead coffin lid across the shrine and loosen the huge stone slab, then perhaps . . .

She laid her ringed hand flat on the ground before her with a flourish and spoke the word of power. The wave of magic tore through the floor in front of her, met the serpent at the door, and split the wall. Huge chunks of ancient cement blocks collapsed into the portal and onto the giant's body, bringing it to a halt. Flipping its head, the serpent writhed, trying to wrestle its way out of the fallen stone in the collapsed doorway.

Elsinore had bought herself a moment again, and whipped around to look—where? The domed chamber above? The word of power for Push had entirely fled the sorceress's memory; she could not cast it again for some time and free herself from the closed-off chamber above. And even if she could find a way out through the sealed door of the shrine, where could she go in the strange empty field of fungus around the shrine? Or should she approach the creature now trapped and try to put an end to it with her sword while she had the slightest chance?

Her considerations were cut short as the serpent threw a great stone from its neck and slithered farther into the chamber. Caught off guard and unable to summon the concentration to cast another spell, Elsinore braced herself for the monster's terrible strike.

As the serpent fell forward, a yowl and a hiss echoed in the tight antechamber, and Risky darted between the witch and her foe, dashing to the side and drawing the creature's attention away.

Diving after the little cat, the serpent crashed into the wall.

"No!" Elsinore screamed.

Risky dodged away only barely.

Cracks created by the spell grew wider as the snake dragged itself upright across the ruined metal and stone of the floor. The earth shook violently, the floor and walls slid toward the center, and the whole room split apart and fell in on itself.

The ground Elsinore stood on gave way beneath her feet, and with what little balance she could maintain, she leaped after the cat, catching them in midair and holding them in her arms as she fell through the open air below, stone and tile debris cascading all around her.

✳ 15 ✳

THE EMPTY CITY

lsinore found enough presence of mind not to panic, and in the bare second she had, she recalled and cast her levitation cantrip. It wasn't meant to allow her to fly, only to make curtains hover or pull an object from across a room; at most, she had only ever used it to allow her body to hover inches from a floor. But it was enough to slow her fall to a rapid but hopefully survivable descent.

Meanwhile, the rubble crashed and shattered on the cavern floor below. The fall was many stories, and Elsinore still feared she would be dashed apart on the rocks, but under her spell, she floated down easily, her clothes and hair blowing around her. At last, she came to the floor and managed to alight on an even spot in the fallen rock, keeping her footing.

Chafing in her tight, panicked grip, the cat jumped to the ground beside her.

Feeling safe for the moment, Elsinore looked around as her heartbeat slowed and took account of her surroundings. She was now in a huge cavern. Above, she saw nothing; the high ceiling of the cavern was too dark to see, and she could not tell where she had fallen from. In her mind's eye, a shadow passed—the freed body of the enormous serpent. She hoped it forgot about her, slithered back to its room, and continued its enigmatic business in the catacombs on the level above. Perhaps it was satisfied that the intruder was gone.

The new cavern was lit faintly by a weird blue-green illumination that seemed to emanate from the walls themselves. It was at least warmer, more peaceful, and more comfortable than the light of the glass in the rooms above. She knew not whether it was the light of a fungus, the ambient magic of this place, or some antique system of the Old Ones. Or something deeper, some unknowable radiance of the earth, a fire from before everything.

A loud meow rang out, magnified by the cavern. Elsinore looked around at the echo, but the voice came from right at her feet.

"Risky!" She scooped the cat up again, cradled them, and kissed the soft fur of their neck. She held them with one arm under their front legs, supporting their back end in the crook of her other arm. She was a little surprised the cat allowed it. Meowing again, the cat started licking Elsinore's cheek as if cleaning it with their tongue.

"I was so worried about you, baby! I thought the snake would crush or eat you, or . . . I don't know. Don't scare me like that, okay?" Elsinore kissed the cat on the head.

The cat looked up at her, ears cocked, and meowed.

"You didn't have to put yourself in danger to help me up there again, you know. If that's what you were intentionally doing. Why are you staying with me, I wonder?" She scratched behind their ear, and they purred a little, squinting.

"I'm beginning to realize I don't really know where

I'm going down here," Elsinore admitted to Risky. The cat, who had clearly grown uncomfortable again, skittered down to the floor. "I thought things would be clearer when I made it to the Mountain. I thought I would know where to go, what to do, what I am. But . . . I don't. I'm as lost as ever. At least I can follow a cat who only seems half interested in me."

Risky meowed at her, then started walking, padding softly along the naturally uneven stone floor to a tall, curved wall. Following the curve of the wall, they wandered into what might have been another chamber.

"Thank you? For reassuring me? I think?"

As they came around a bend of rock, their destination was made clear to Elsinore. She gasped at the sight that rose before her, so immediately different from the rough stone of the cave.

It was a temple or a palace or a city. Stone buildings, rooms, and shrines were hewed from all colors of pale marble, standing free or built into and out of the walls of the vast cavern chamber. This place was huge, filling a space that seemed somehow larger than the other chamber.

The centerpiece of the city was an amazing edifice, at once a tower and a colossus. It was the figure of a goddess the size of a small mountain, platforms and balconies and walkways built around it at various intervals. Around it, other buildings reached and spread, each their own structure but, at the same time, seemingly part of a singular complex that made up this fantastic subterranean city.

The whole of the place was visible via the same luminescence as the rest of the cavern. Though the marble was smooth and clean, the entire complex looked abandoned. All the doors and windows were dark, and signs of disuse lay all around—a fallen pillar here, a caved-in roof there. In a pavilion before the colossal goddess, a wide empty fountain was rimmed with waterspouts in the form of stone figures facing into the pool, gargoyles and grotesques carved in the images of fabulous animals. A dragon with wings and talons, a griffin with a beak and three horns, a unicorn, and a lion with the face of a human within its braided mane—a sphinx, like the one she encountered among the mounds before the Mountain.

Padding over to the fountain, Risky sat by the sphinx and curled up.

Elsinore looked into the pool. It was an empty cistern, though how deep she could not tell. It plunged very far, the walls creeping down into darkness. Nor could she tell how long it had lain dry, how long the whole city had been like this.

She looked up, up to the colossus, to the ceiling of the cavern now visible in the strange light. High above, near the top of the goddess's head, there was a hole through which she could see the strange glow of a blue light, sicklier than the light surrounding her in the city.

"I wonder . . . is that where we just came from? The hall of catacombs, with the snake?"

Elsinore wasn't surprised when Risky meowed, as if in confirmation.

She looked all along the body of the colossus; some of the platforms and ledges looked worn and broken. She supposed the snake had been coiled around it, its head poked through the hole above as it mimicked the form of a hooded figure. The city was scattered in places with statues, broken and cast aside; had these been toppled by the body of the serpent passing by? Had the inhabitants long ago given their lives to feed that creature? Or had this uncanny underworld city ever been populated at all?

Straying from the fountain, Elsinore approached the

door of a smaller building—slowly, tentatively, suppressing the fear that rose in the back of her mind that some terrible thing would be sitting quietly in the shadows, staring back. Inside, the rooms were no less unsettling for their emptiness, and the sad, dim rays of blue light cast long, dull-edged shadows of perpetual twilight that lay cold on the bare floors and walls. The structures themselves did not glow like the walls of the cavern, and the eerie light crept in through the windows and open doorways of the dwellings—if that's what they had even been.

As she passed through, looking from room to room, Elsinore tried to ascertain the purpose of this complex. But how could she when she had the same questions about the purpose of everything she had encountered in the whole of the realm under the Mountain? All the windows were empty, and the buildings looked to have lain that way for long, slow ages.

Elsinore jumped with a start when she realized something was silently following her, and she whipped around at once. It was Risky, padding softly on the stone floor behind her. The cat mewled questioningly, as if she should have realized, and Elsinore laughed.

"This place makes me uneasy. Please stay close to me, okay?" The cat walked forward without her, and the witch shook her head and moved on.

Elsinore stopped before a tall, narrow archway that fed into the dark depths of the interior of a larger building, rising above the others but crouching in the shadow of the goddess. The pillars to each side were chipped and cracked but stable, the arch above delicate but sharply curved over the narrow door. The keystone was decorated with a face, monstrous and deformed, tusks hanging out of its jaw, its hair twisting around in wild wandering spirals. Its eyes were wide and gray, and seemed to flash and follow the weird blue light of the cavern. Within the archway was a dark, shaded terrace before a tightly shut door of lead like the one she had encountered above. Elsinore eyed it cautiously, unsure of the purpose of this place and wary of where it might lead.

All of a sudden, Risky began to hiss, focusing on the corner of the terrace, the sound creeping along Elsinore's spine and chilling her heart. There was something terribly wrong, and she knew she was right; right about . . .

She drew her sword and swung it to the side, pointing it into the corner Risky faced, in a shadow below the dim blue light spilling in from a front-facing window. A muffled gasp responded from the darkness, and as her eyes adjusted, Elsinore thought she could see a tiny figure, a person hunched in the corner, cowering from the blade.

"Have mercy, please!" the muffled voice cried out.

Elsinore refused to lower her sword until she could see more of what was before her. Nodding, she gestured with the blade for the person before her to stand, and after a hesitant pause, they did. They were shorter than Elsinore by a full head, though the young sorceress herself was hardly much in height.

It was the person from the field of ruin, where the market had been. A bent figure, clad in torn robes and a hood covering scraggly, knotted gray hair, wearing a face mask with dark lenses over the eyes and a long, curved beak like a bird, though simpler and less lifelike than the masks of the illusory people in the marketplace. The person held their arms out, palms open in a gesture of peace.

"Please put away your sword. I mean you no harm. I swear on my life and the life of my son, who was worth my leaving everything to follow him and find him and speak to him." The voice sounded old and weak—the more so for being muffled by the mask—and seemed to Elsinore to be the voice of a woman.

"Why do you hide from me?" Elsinore demanded. "Who are you? What are you doing in this place?"

"I hide from you because you have the air of a mage, at least, or more—one of the People, the dwellers of this place, whose whims and passions are a danger to outsiders like myself." The woman said this without apology, matter-of-fact, and Elsinore was unsure how to take it. She finally sheathed her sword and motioned for the woman to go on.

"I'm a seeker," the person continued. "Only trying to find him who I lost long ago. And I was following you, someone I hoped would at last show me the way."

"Following me?" Elsinore said, more baffled than ever. "How? I was following you, after you descended into the stairs in the field of ruins. How were you following me?"

"I hid behind a stone in the ruined field outside the dome, after digging in the place where the tunnel was found. I'd been there—many times indeed—but it took me ages, ages indeed, to find a way into the doors barred so tightly at the end of the hall."

She paused to laugh, smug at her ingenuity, smirking that she had hidden herself from Elsinore so well despite the witch's diligence.

"I followed someone—a fairy, or a resourceful spellcaster, perhaps you, who walked this place unmasked, or perhaps someone else long ago—I can't remember! Whoever I followed, they passed through the door, and the way slammed shut behind me. I hid among the pews as my guide descended to the next hall, and while they were distracted by the dead and the monster in the pit, I climbed through the hole it had been guarding and descended by the steps and landings of the towers and colossus above us. I searched and searched this dismal place and found this door shut tight. Now we are here, and I for one am ready to open the way at long last."

"Who are you looking for?" Elsinore asked doubtfully. "Do they live in this city? You still haven't told me who you are—not really." She squinted suspiciously at the person, who shuffled and paced.

"No one lives here—no one in this whole place lives. Don't you know where we are? In any case, no one's dwelled in these ruins for a long time. Such a very long time. No one at all," the old person said, not ceasing to move. "I've been trying to find my way in, but I was lost till you arrived. There's a door here—this must be it. A way farther down—a passage deeper, to the heart of the Mountain—to the city."

"We seem to be in a city now," Elsinore said, growing impatient with the woman's dissembling.

"No, no," the old woman said. "This is a tomb, a necropolis for the dead who don't live. The city I search for is where he is—my son, Kern, my own blood. He was taken from me by a fairy witch, and I wish to see him just one more time, feasting at Her table. The city is where She is as well. Kern is with Her there, I'm sure, in the city of Dis, with the fae who live eternally."

Elsinore felt herself grow colder still and looked around the darkness of the room.

"I've been searching down here for so long, so very long," the woman went on, almost paying no attention to Elsinore as ranted to herself. "Years, perhaps lifetimes, though here it is impossible to tell. I followed my son here; in the end, he went to the forest, his shameful lust leading him after that unearthly wench. When last I saw Kern, he was wan and wasted, hollowed out by hunger.

When he didn't return, I followed and found my way here. The guardian said only a true name would open the way, but I never knew mine—or I forgot it. I can't remember which!"

The old woman suddenly faced Elsinore, raising herself up to her full height as she stared through the dark lenses of the mask, directly into the young woman's eyes.

"Do you know what that's like? To not remember who you are?" She chuckled and sank back down into a hunch. "You do know, don't you? It's easy to tell."

Elsinore fought the urge to sink into her mind and get lost in her own ruminations. "You miss Kern," she said numbly, dragging herself out of her mournfulness, feeling herself soften at the old woman's plight.

"More I wish to punish him for his foolish lust! And more I wish to spit on Her, the horrid queen of Hell!" The old woman cackled, hardly muffled now by the mask. "Queen of mourning, ruler of the mountain of stinking waste, where there is perpetual wailing and gnashing, weeping forever in the city of Dis! Where they feast eternally, but only on illusions—for the only food in this place is ash and smoke! Where She is surrounded by Her people, the kurgarra, the people of the mounds—the piles of shit! The aos sidhe, aos shit, the fae of faeces! Like flies to shit, they flock to Her! They took my boy, take all those who dare wander too close or heed their call and follow their lights. It's only my wits that kept them from taking me, and I'll tell them what I think—I'll tell Her to Her great gorgon face!"

Elsinore backed away. She wanted to run, to run from this woman, run from this place, but she knew not where to. She looked over her shoulder, to the door back out to the square. The woman laughed again and ripped the mask from her face.

She was wan and wasted from untold time in these caverns, far from the moon and the sun. Her hair beneath the fallen hood was thin and wild, her eyes wide, white, and staring, her teeth crooked and broken, grinning evilly.

"Perhaps I'll suffocate unmasked from the toxic air under the Mountain and be brought weeping before the feast of the queen! Or perhaps my corpse will be interred in the crypt, to waste, watched over by the serpent's unwavering gaze." She cackled.

Suddenly, she frowned, serious. "But you'll find them for me, won't you? You will open the way with your true name, and we'll come before Her at last."

Elsinore shrank away, repulsed by the woman's madness, then felt shameful and reproached herself. Was she not, in a way, looking for the same thing? Would it be her fate to waste away in this ghostly land as well? She bit her lip and clenched her fists at her side.

"I will open the door, but not with you," Elsinore said. "Wait here or by the empty fountain and don your mask. There's no sense exposing yourself to the risk. If I find something, I'll return to you."

"And if you find nothing? If nothing finds you wandering the halls and you never return?"

The old woman chuckled, shook, and convulsed wildly, her laughter carrying far and echoing off the pale stone of the city of the cavern. She laughed, and Elsinore drew back again in fear, her eyes widening at last in awe as the old woman faded and vanished, until only the echo of her horrible laughter remained.

Elsinore breathed tightly and heavily. The light from the walls of the cavern outside fell only thinly on the terrace, and the sorceress cast her light spell to look into the corner by the door.

There, curled tightly in on itself and wrapped in its own rags, was the body of the old woman, its skeletal hands raised to its masked head, dead and decaying for more ages than Elsinore could tell.

Sighing heavily, the girl shut her eyes. She dismissed her light spell and knelt before the body. In silence, she focused her energy, breathing into her surroundings a spirit of peace and rest. The uneasiness of this space, the fear that crouched in the shadows by the door—they swirled just beneath Elsinore's consciousness and then, in an instant, were gone.

Elsinore rose and turned to the door.

With a cautious glance around for anyone listening, living or otherwise, Elsinore leaned into the portal and once again whispered her name—her deep name. The door slid open with a terrible rusty sound, fighting against the age of its own mechanisms. The girl and her cat stepped in, and the door, almost reluctantly, snapped shut behind them.

Elsinore stopped and stood shivering in the dark.

A flash of green light low to the ground surprised her. Risky rubbed their body around Elsinore's boots, glowing as they had when she first encountered them in the fissure at the entrance. Kneeling, she scratched the cat's ears, still tense from the anticipation of some lurking peril.

As they sat together, the light of the cat's body faded, and the darkness closed in around them. A steady purr assured Elsinore that the cat remained nearby.

"I don't suppose I can rely on that trick of yours for getting us through this place?"

Unwilling to remain in the darkness or await a reply that might never come from the fickle little creature, Elsinore cast her light spell in one hand, throwing a light warmer, more peaceful, and less unsettling than both the blue luminescence of the cavern and the green of her companion. She stood, and Risky followed, and together they moved on, wandering for some time deeper inward.

It was a building of many rooms, and Elsinore quickly became overwhelmed. The outer chambers near the entrance were empty, merely stone rooms with sparse decoration and only a rosette or filigreed corner here and there. But as they moved deeper through the complex, to dark inner rooms lit only dimly by Elsinore's witch light, she found more to see, though all the objects were obscured with ages of dust and mostly broken.

Many of the rooms were scattered with strange objects, tablets set in the walls or against shelves, and pottery crouching in corners and on pedestals set in the center of the grim old rooms. Many of these objects were pressed with some form of strange symbols Elsinore did not recognize.

At first, she thought the symbols were only decoration, but something about the way patterns repeated made her think the symbols were less stylization and more likely a form of writing using characters she had never seen. It had the form of dots, or nodes, connected in various ways by lines.

Picking up a few fragments of tablets bearing this node-shaped writing, she dusted them off as best she could. She tried fitting them together, playing with them like a puzzle, but her inability to read the unknowably ancient script made the game tedious and, somehow, a little unsettling. Something about the form of the sigils and characters made Elsinore uneasy, as if in some corner of her mind, hidden from her waking consciousness, she could really read it and all that was translatable to her was an ominous, threatening mood.

Tucking two seemingly unbroken tablets bearing the

script in among the spare clothes in her bag, she followed her light deeper into the nesting complex of rooms.

Each door she took led to many more. Elsinore's sense of direction without the guidance of the stars had never been well-trained, but somehow, she felt confident in her ability to find her way back. Or else . . . some intuition in her heart told her to trust the path she took, that she moved forward in whatever way she was meant to. Door led to door, turn after turn, and though the architecture of all the rooms was much the same, the decor of each distinguished them enough to reassure her. Some bore more carvings, others pottery, and some abstract mosaics of faded spiral landscapes, maps of an unfamiliar land Elsinore never knew. A few housed strange statues, in form like humans in overall shape but misshapen, with long, narrow limbs; exaggerated shoulders and hips; inhuman faces with protruding snouts or beaks like snakes or birds; and wide, staring, bulging eyes. Whether she was being watched or these figures spoke only of a long-vanished legacy, the message of which the sorceress could not guess, they made her uneasy.

Risky made a straight line for one of these statues, and Elsinore followed for fear of losing her companion. The cat squeezed behind the figure, and as Elsinore followed, she found a damaged wall, the opening narrow but just wide enough for the girl to squeeze through. Wrinkling her nose, she peered into the shadow.

The ancient statue was bent and precarious; it took little effort to push away from the wall, and it fell to the floor with a dull but heavy clang. In the wall behind, the opening through which Risky had disappeared led to a path into darkness.

Once through the broken wall, Elsinore held her light spell up before her, lighting up a long hallway. Risky gingerly walked along some ways ahead, and Elsinore followed.

Once she had caught up, the two walked for seeming ages through more hallways and corridors. Elsinore could barely manage to remember which way they had come, and she began to fear for her ability to find her way back out to the cavern, to the plaza of the city and the great statue of the goddess. She didn't know how deep the rooms of this maze led into the mountainside, and she wasn't even sure how far in she could be or where in the facades and windows of the city the pair might have led themselves. It didn't seem as if Risky was leading the way, but rather Elsinore felt as if there was something she was looking for, that she hadn't found, that could be around any of the turns they took or beyond any of the thresholds they crossed. The floors and walls were finished stone, not like a cavern but more like those of a castle or a temple, though very bare. The light from her spell cast deep shadows in each turn and door, making all a venture into unknown darkness until they turned the corner.

Finally, Risky ran ahead, stopped, and meowed for Elsinore to follow. On one side of the hall was a closed wooden double door, and the cat pawed at it, not trying to pass through as they had before. The handles were curved brass, and as Elsinore turned one, the door clicked and opened, and Risky squeezed through at the first crack.

The room beyond was tall and wide, dark but for the light of Elsinore's spell. Rows of wooden tables lined the place, and its walls were set with shelves. On them, to Elsinore's surprise and delight, were many tablets, scrolls, and bound books of paper and parchment. Old wax candles stood in candelabra on the tables.

Lighting a few candles so she could dismiss her spell,

Elsinore spun around, looking up at the shelves in astonishment. She turned to the closest wall and blew unknown ages of accumulated dust off the books.

She took a scroll from the shelf but was disappointed to find it was written in an inked version of the strange node-shaped script that had been pressed into the tablets. It was unreadable, but at least it confirmed her assessment that it was an ancient, unfamiliar writing system.

Most of the other scrolls and books nearby were the same. A few volumes she found at the next shelf were in different scripts, though still the witch could not read them, literate though she was. If she remembered correctly, if the monument was real, she thought some of these could have been among the languages represented in the message of warning at the entrance to the Mountain.

Elsinore found a shelf farther in with a few bound books and no scrolls. These were written mostly in an archaic script, but finally it was one she recognized. The same script she had read—or imagined she read—on the monolith the previous night. To her disappointment, though, she found that most of these, while written in a script she could read, were in a language she didn't know, so it proved little use.

The final books she looked at on the shelf, however, at last had titles she could recognize, read, and understand, written in the script she knew. Giggling with excitement, Elsinore combed the shelf for anything enticing.

Opening one, she flipped through it. The title was *A Critique of Capital.* Though she could read the language and understand the words, the topic was completely impenetrable to her. It seemed to be about trade using an ancient and obsolete mode of economics and production to generate profit; it was something Elsinore couldn't bring herself to muster the least interest in, and as far as she could understand, something about it seemed cold, tedious, and inhumane.

Uneasy, she put it to the side of the shelf, unsure she had the patience to search for another.

As she turned to consider the books around her, she noticed something that nearly made her gasp, though she swallowed it soundlessly. Around the corner of the shelf, a dim, wavering yellow light glowed from a far wall. She had not lit any lanterns in that part of the room, and she felt sure the room had been dark when she and Risky entered.

Instead of drawing Moonstar, Elsinore reached into her bag and found her dagger, its iron reflecting the mysterious light dully and quietly. She held it at her side, trying to conceal it but ready to use it to defend herself if necessary. Trying to keep silent, she moved gently along the edge of the shelf, looked carefully around the corner, and saw a door to a side room, slightly ajar. The light spilled out through the crack, looking very much like that of a candle.

Steeling herself, Elsinore moved forward, carefully and cautiously, her heart racing as she set her hand tentatively on the door and pushed it slowly. It slid silently along its hinges.

She seemed to have attracted no attention, and the room within was peaceful. It was a small study, lined with yet more shelves. Cushioned chairs and a lounge crouched between a table and a desk, and on the desk, the flames of a candelabrum flickered and sputtered, filling the room with natural orange light.

The room was so cozy and mundane, it seemed almost proper that a woman sat in a high cushioned chair, silently reading a heavy old book that rested open on the desk before her. She seemed entirely unaware of Elsinore's presence, her back turned to the door, fingers flipping the yellowed pages, absorbed fully in her study.

On the desk beside the book sat a black feathered mask bearing the same dark eyeholes and long, curved beak Elsinore had seen on the entrancing woman in the marketplace. This woman wore a simple black dress, and her hair, tied loosely behind her head to keep it out of her eyes, nevertheless fell forward, escaping the bun and forcing her to brush her hair back from her eyes every few seconds as she read. Elsinore could not see her face, but some instinct, some memory she could not place, irresistibly drove her to make the woman's acquaintance.

Timidly the sorceress cleared her throat and attempted an introduction. "Excuse me," she said, quieter than she had intended. "I don't mean to bother you, but may I ask what you're reading?"

The woman looked up slowly, turning over her shoulder to look at the girl in the doorway. Her hair and the dim candlelight hid her face still from Elsinore, whose heart raced with anticipation. The witch found herself more frightened, somehow, than she had been when surrounded by the undead in the crypt, for reasons she couldn't articulate—something kept from her conscious mind but which she suspected, somewhere in her heart, she knew.

This tension, this foreboding, brought Elsinore's voice out in a brief scream of fright when the candles on the tables, all at once, suddenly flickered out, as if an intangible wind swept through the room and carried the flames away into oblivion. The room fell into total darkness, and Elsinore, fearful, instinctively snapped her fingers immediately and sparked her light cantrip, hoping to see the woman's face at last.

But the woman at the desk was gone, the chair she had occupied seconds before empty, and no noise whatsoever had betrayed her retreat. It was as if she had vanished with the light, sunk away in the darkness, and Elsinore was alone.

Hurriedly, the witch used her cantrip to light the candles again, letting each flicker with warm, natural ambience. When the room was lit, Elsinore tentatively approached the chair and desk where the woman had been reading, tested the seat with her hand to make sure it was safe, and sat before the book, holding the page as she turned it to look at the title. On the cover was an embossed metal icon that glittered in the dim light of the candles. It depicted a humanoid form, highly stylized, but something about the expression on its face gave Elsinore the impression of an artificial creation or automaton. The title was *On the Anathema of Iron.*

This one was more transparent than the last she had tried to read, but the uneasiness that had risen in the back of Elsinore's mind while reading the other book took shape and grew stronger. This book held accounts of the avarice of a people long dead, whose pride had misled them to think they could enclose and claim ownership over the earth itself, exterminating those who had lived in the land before, displacing the survivors, and keeping them away with further threats of imprisonment, starvation, and death. As if the land were something one jealous person could claim and not the body of all peoples.

These people had mined the earth at a frightening scale, stripping the surface of entire landscapes using terrible metal engines, so forests and fields became deserts of gravel and ruin, until the mountains themselves shook and slid and poison ran over the stone and into the sea. They mined for paltry handfuls of gold, each worth more in the delusions of those who boasted to own the mountains than the lives of the entire communities they had murdered.

Elsinore read that in the early days of these people, before the use of iron spread among them, there had been herbs, beautiful stalks grown by the goddess of love with yellow flowers and special fruits or seeds that could cure all manner of ailments and allow women to control their bodies. Those capable of pregnancy could prevent conception or miscarry at will, and others—women like Elsinore—could bring the form of their bodies closer to the shape of their hearts.

But the greed of the kings of the Old Ones could not be sated even in those days. With their iron tools, they overharvested the earth. The herbs were driven to extinction, and the lands where they grew were reduced to barren desert.

As she pushed on through this dumbfounding story, even in the brief excerpts she thumbed through, Elsinore read that these economies of mining and extraction relied on the forced labor of enslaved and forcibly displaced peoples, as well as large-scale conflicts the enormity of which the young sorceress could scarcely imagine. These wars were fought using terrible weapons of iron that cast eruptions of fire and lead that could kill in an instant, and others more terrible that could level entire cities. They burned and ground their way through more lives than Elsinore could believe, wars of territorial conquest to steal even more land and strip it of more gold, gems, trees, and fuel once the people who tried only to live in peace had been killed.

The iron engines and economies that were built to perpetuate these cyclopean wars clawed further on, shearing forests, leveling mountains, and choking the air with ash. All the while, people were taken, killed, or bound in chains of iron and forced to work for this bloodthirsty engine, this military idol with a mouth and wide eyes that glowed red with the fires of the consumption of bodies fed into it. The survivors' names were taken from them, rewritten, or never allowed to be bestowed upon them at all, and their dreams were obscured from their sight by the smoke pouring from the guts of the engine.

Looking at her hand, Elsinore realized she still held the iron dagger she had drawn to protect herself as she crept into the room. She stared at it, her bright-gray eyes dully reflected in the blade from the dim candlelight. All at once, an image flashed behind Elsinore's eyes in her mind, unbidden—a memory of something she never knew, placed in her mind by the Goddess and lighting up only for an instant, before flickering away: many of these people, so many of these people, had been like her. So many people had been killed because they were like her.

Overcome with a wave of dizziness—whether from the effects of the momentary vision, the enormity of what she had read, or simply the tight quarters of this dark chamber in a subterranean cavern city—Elsinore staggered back out of the chair, knocking it over. The knife dropped from her hands, and the candelabrum fell, flickering out.

This place held books about the Old Ones, and though she could understand the text, Elsinore found she could bring herself to read it no more. The Old Ones, whose crimes at last awakened the vengeance of Lord Wind and who were punished in kind as they themselves had injured the earth.

And did the god have any choice in the matter? So many innocents suffered and died and were forgotten at the bloody hands of a tiny-few greed-addled would-be lords, more innocents than Elsinore could have believed. The oppressors among the Old Ones spared none who fell within their grasp, but neither did Lord Wind, and his grasp was wider, sharper, and even less particular. The Old Ones were gone, killers, victims, and survivors alike. But the gravity of the evil a few had perpetrated endured, hung deep in the earth, and gathered sorrow all around itself.

Pushing herself to her feet, the young witch rubbed her eye with the ball of her thumb and cast her light spell once more. Retrieving her dagger, she hurriedly tucked it away in the sheath in her bag, then stumbled back into the hall of shelves.

The hall was still and somber.

Remembering Risky, she saw them sitting nearby in the dim candlelight. They lifted their head and looked at Elsinore, squinting their eyes pleasantly. This brought her some comfort. The cat was familiar and grounded, by the standards of this place, and Elsinore thought once again of her gratitude for that in this lifeless, unnatural city.

Stretching, Risky rose and walked casually past the high shelves. Elsinore followed them to another door and through another narrow hall, at the end of which she at last dimly saw a weird blue light, like that of the cavern outside. She hurried ahead with Risky through the hall and an outer antechamber, where the blue twilight glow of the cavern walls fell slanted through tall, narrow windows, unchanged since she'd been here last.

Outside the complex once again, Elsinore found the maze had ultimately led her around to another side of the pavilion. She turned and looked at the structures above, then slumped against the statue at the fountain. Reaching in her bag, she pulled out one of the tablets bearing the shapes she described to herself as nodiform.

"Do you know what the writing says, Risky?" The cat squinted their eyes shut and looked away. "Me either," Elsinore said sadly. "But I think maybe if I work at it, I'll be able to figure it out."

Suddenly, the cat's mood changed; they opened their eyes wide, the hair on their back stood on end, and they hissed and yowled loudly, echoing across the square.

"Sorry! Do you not like tablets?" Elsinore asked. "Writing? You seemed fine in the maze. What is it?"

The ground began to rumble, and Risky stood, hissing, their back arched. The statue of the goddess above the town looked, in the weird light, as if it were undulating, shifting, and dancing. Standing, Elsinore stepped away in fear and amazement.

As her eyes grew used to the unnatural light, she saw the truth: the serpent slithered down from above, white scales flashing in the blue light, its face locked on the girl, eyes red and terrible.

"Risky, run!" Elsinore yelled. The cat darted away, disappearing through a wall. "Okay, good!"

The serpent missed not a moment and dove right for her, its jaws wide enough to swallow her body whole, its fangs long and sharp enough to impale her. Elsinore jumped away, using the creature's great size and momentum to her advantage. Though massive, the serpent was still lithe and quick, and its clashing fangs crossed close to its prey over and over, while it tried to constrict and close upon her with its coils.

Elsinore dodged as nimbly as she could, her skill as a dancer giving her an edge. At times, it was no more difficult than dodging rotten fruit thrown by hecklers on a bad night. The thought energized her as she danced out of reach of the creature, keeping away and trying to maintain her balance.

Elsinore dove under cover of a roofed terrace, hoping to escape back inside the buildings, but cursed herself when she saw there was no door. Ducking down out of reach of the massive serpent, she tried to catch her breath.

What do I do now?

Unsure of herself, that she could even survive, Elsinore thought of her mothers. Elsinore sighed between heavy breaths to think of Milanda and Glamis in this place now that she was so far away. The Mountain couldn't have been that distant from her home, physically, but something about the nature of this place made it feel farther away than she had ever been from the daylight.

Elsinore thought of Glamis, in the girl's adolescence, teaching her the use of the sword for self-defense and exercise. Glamis was a master swordswoman and practiced expert tricks for performances she put on while traveling with Milanda, but of course, she also knew simple, less showy techniques to be used for real combat. The girl had little patience for these lessons, and always tended to add her own flourishes as a dancer that made Glamis laugh, though she reminded her daughter that such frivolity would likely get her killed in a real battle.

Elsinore drew Moonstar, the sword her mother had given her, the same she had practiced with years before. It felt surprisingly light in her hand but seemed solid and effective. She swung it through the air a few times to test it. It cut the air smoothly, whistling as it flew. Glamis had rarely used this sword in her performances and never for practical purposes of self-defense; it was rather too small for her strong arms and incredible strength.

Elsinore found herself wondering why Glamis had brought this one with her when she followed with Milanda to stop her daughter from leaving Nin. She reached the only conclusion she could: that Glamis had meant to give it to her all along.

Rising from her hiding place, Elsinore turned to face the serpent.

As the monster's body and tail flicked by, Elsinore struck out, slashing with Moonstar, trying to wound it without lowering her defenses. She regained her footing from a near miss, but the serpent drew back and reared up, its eyes fixed on her.

The sorceress stood still and watched.

Swaying back and forth as it had before, its red eyes wide, its mouth shut tight, and its fangs retracted, the serpent measured her. Then, in a single motion, it halted and spat out a stream of white acrid poison.

Elsinore leaped to the side as it splashed where she had stood seconds before. The acid ate into the stone of the ground, steaming and stinking, a vile burning smell of death.

Coil, fang, and fiery acid—Elsinore danced from the sting of each of the serpent's attacks, running under its arching body, then up and along its scaly back to strike at its head. The serpent snapped its long body, throwing the dancer off and into a nearby pillar. She had no time to catch her breath as the giant hooked itself around the pillar, bringing the dome it held up crashing to the ground. She barely rolled out of the way of the falling rubble in time. The snake itself slithered quickly away, not to be trapped beneath a falling roof a second time.

Elsinore grew weary, though she fought for her life. A strike from the monster's fangs, and a parry with the sword. A swing of its coils, and a dodge. A duck and a roll away from the burning spray of poison that cut into the very stone where she had stood.

Finally, in a moment of calm as both she and the

giant regained their breath, Elsinore held Moonstar before her, and it flashed blue in the ambient light of the cavern. As the snake opened its jaws once more and fell upon her, the sorceress ducked and raised her sword above her head.

The snake impaled its throat upon the upright blade, and as it fell forward, it was slashed farther down its body to its core.

Withdrawing her sword, Elsinore stood and turned to face the serpent's head. It was wounded but not slain. It reared up, dripping blood from the long vertical wound, and motioned as if to once more spit burning white acid at its would-be-prey.

The acid did not come. Blood oozed from the gash, and the serpent lowered its head, resigned. It regarded the woman for a moment, unwilling to pursue her further, then lazily turned its bloodied head and began to slither away, through the city, up along the colossus, and back to the room above.

Elsinore could barely believe it was retreating. She felt exultant but was too exhausted to cheer or even move. Her sword hung at her side, dripping with gore from the serpent's wound, and she breathed deeply, watching its great body slither upward. It was so huge and long that its tail remained behind her.

As the last of it passed by, the tail flicked, smacking the winded woman in the side, throwing her off balance, and knocking her over. Falling, she tripped over the edge of the deep, empty cistern.

She grabbed for a gargoyle but missed, and she was too exhausted to cast any spells she might still have available. Unable to save herself, she plummeted into the darkness, Moonstar glittering at her side.

✴ 16 ✴

THE CIANZIR

The distinction between waking and dreaming was misty and indistinct at the best times. One might rise from the most terrible dream to find their fears past, then wake again to find the sufferings of their nightmares were the physical truth, the relief itself only a teasing hallucination. Sometimes, when one dreamed, they would glimpse for a moment who they really were, then in waking be compelled to perform a phantasmagorical fiction, and only the dreamer would be able to say which was the true travesty, if they could.

In this moment, Elsinore could not tell waking from dreaming. She had tumbled into the black pit of the cistern but had no memory of falling nor of landing, however far down it had been. She had been engulfed right away in complete darkness, which persisted now that she was on the ground. She looked up, but there was not even a distant light from the mouth of the fountain; there was darkness and her own echoing thought. She had blacked out totally sometime during the fall, of that she felt sure, but she could not really know. Was loss of memory a loss of consciousness? A loss of self? Was she the same person she had been before falling into the pit? The same person she had been before entering the Kur? The same person she had been when she was a little girl in her mother's arms, before she was left alone in the woods and called herself by a new name and lived a new life with her new mothers?

Was anyone the same person, moment to moment, blink to blink, sleep to sleep?

Elsinore lay in a very thin—perhaps finger's depth—layer of water, on a smooth, level surface of some cold, hard stone. Sitting up, she felt her neck, back, and hips. She was sore all over, but surely she would feel worse if she had fallen very far.

After a few moments of meditation, Elsinore concentrated and cast her light spell; the orb of magic fire floated over her palm, illuminating her body and the ground beneath her, but nothing else. The stone floor beneath the water was black, reflecting her body perfectly. But it continued indefinitely in all directions, with no identifiable end, destination, or change. The light illuminated at best twenty or thirty feet, and beyond that was simply more darkness. Except . . .

A glint on the ground a few yards away drew her attention. Seeing no reason to hurry, she walked over and found Moonstar sitting in the water, apparently washed clean of the serpent's blood. Elsinore took it up and swung it to dry it off a little before sliding it back into its sheath.

Her clothes were wet, of course, and her hair was a bit wet as well, but she had at least been lying with the shaved side of her head down. Her medicine, her spell book, and the doll made for her by her lost love in the temple of the Goddess had been spared by the thick canvas of her bag, which was a blessing.

She considered calling out in the dark, for Risky or anyone, then dismissed the idea as unwise. She could not see a destination, nor could she see a path, so she picked a direction and began walking, splashing lightly in the water, not even sure she was walking in a straight line.

She walked on, for perhaps an hour, but came to no wall, no structure, no change. It seemed to be an endless expanse of the same featureless, horizonless landscape. How long could she go on in this way? She had a perceptible, nagging sense that in the darkness, she was just missing what she needed to see, that if she turned and walked to the left she would come to something, but whenever she changed direction, the space always merely continued as before, with no end. Her light spell illuminated herself and nothing more.

Elsinore grew weary. She splashed and kicked the water, wishing there was anything, any marker or waypoint, but the blankness just went on. Her spells, her perseverance—all felt useless.

In her frustration, she drew her arm back and hurled the magic fire of the light spell, watching it fly into the distance, illuminating only the water below and reflecting itself as it went on.

Elsinore could not throw very far, nor with much strength. When she was a little girl, she and Glamis had played catch with a leather ball, and her mother had laughed gently when Elsie tossed so poorly. She had gotten a little better as she grew up but was never more than adequate.

The fireball cantrip had no magic to propel it across a distance; she only threw the light like a ball. Yet the light flew farther and farther, straight and even into the horizon, shrinking but never fading from her sight.

At last, it was a tiny pinpoint of light in the distance like a low-hanging evening star. Finally, it grew no dimmer; instead, it seemed to stop and hang at a point on the horizon, staying as Elsinore watched, perplexed. Looking around to make sure there were no other changes, she began walking, following the thin reflection of light cast along a line in the water.

She walked on, and the light grew very slowly larger and brighter as she came closer. After another hour or so, it appeared to be less a star and more the light of a structure, like the window of a faraway inn or tower.

Elsinore wondered once again where this was, this lowest depth of the Kur, of the country beneath the Mountain. Did this expanse of darkness lie only below the Mountain and the wasteland of mounds, or was it beneath the entire earth? Could this be the aquifer of Lady Water, where life was sustained after the Old Ones fell, the source from which all wells drew?

Or did she dream still, the vastness of the mirrored surface only the calm of her resting mind? Had her life ended in the fall through the cistern or the fight with the serpent, and her shade now wandered in the intermediate darkness of the after-death place? Was the light she approached the dawn of rebirth?

Did it even make a difference whether she had been slain by the serpent? For, willfully and deliberately, on her own feet, on her own hands and knees, on her own belly, she had entered the country of death. Was there a difference between her and the other ghouls in the graves above the city of the colossus, anything yet that separated her from the fae of this country?

Was this not where she suspected she was from? Where she might still belong?

Still longer she walked through the water in the darkness of the underworld toward the light. It grew closer, clearer—it was not the magic fireball she'd thrown away, but a structure. As Elsinore approached, the light resolved into a pyramid, set around with pillars or obelisks. Closer, and the pyramid was clearly stepped, a ziggurat with terraces, like the temple of Tiranna at Sanisa but so much grander.

The light that shone through the darkness and reflected in the water was the ziggurat itself, a place of radiant energy, constructed of solid gold that burned from within, driving away all shadows, casting none for there was nothing to cast them from, save the woman who, with every lightly splashing, step drew closer.

The ziggurat was complicated; there were smaller buildings, echoes of itself, built into the corners, and rather than a single staircase to the top, the stairs split apart at each level, continuing around grand doorways into the structure itself. The whole thing was incredibly vast, more a city built on a grand pyramidal scale than merely a building.

As she approached, it became harder to see from one end to the other, so wide was the base, though Elsinore was near the center, where a high ceremonial gate led to a flight of stairs up to the first level. The pyramid was of such a massive scale that she could scarcely believe it was possible, and it made it no clearer whether she truly yet lived or if she merely beheld a phantasm composed by her own mind in the moment of death.

It appeared to Elsinore as if all the gold ever cruelly plundered by the Old Ones from the body of the earth in all their catastrophic history had been taken here, melted down, and made into this place, into the pyramid, the walls, the stairs and gates and arches and obelisks. As if here, it had all been finally returned to the Mountain where it belonged, not in the veins of the earth where the gold had once been found but as a radiant, beating heart of the world.

Elsinore shaded her eyes at first from this luminous place, but the closer she came, the more her sight acclimated. She followed an avenue lined with pillars, the bricks beneath her feet similarly of luminous gold. It was, she felt, like walking inside a star. The avenue led to the steps up to the first level of the ziggurat, and Elsinore began to climb, though the way was steep and high.

Her ears rang with a droning hum, and her first thought was that she heard the buzzing of flies, countless insects swarming and filling her mind and every thought with the sound of their wings. But the higher she climbed, legs moving automatically, the clearer the sound became, no longer a hum but a tinkling, and Elsinore's mind was drawn to the thought of countless perpetually ringing bells.

The light shining off the walls of the pyramid glittered in time with the droning bells, and Elsinore realized at last that the sound was the gold itself, the walls of the ziggurat, shining, buzzing, and droning with a dull metallic song that surrounded her and pulled her ever deeper into the glittering city, until her conscious awareness of the sound faded and the witch was enveloped only in the cold light.

As she neared the landing of the stairs on the first level of the ziggurat, she could see that far across the terrace there was a building, a tower or gate, and steps on either side that led up over it to the next level. The huge double-doors of this gate were of darker, burning bronze, shut tight.

Echoing across the steps, there came a cacophony of voices, each drowned out by the others—and more, it seemed to Elsinore, by the audibly ringing light of the gold. As she crested the steps to the terrace with the gate, she saw a host of people dancing in the bright light, standing in groups watching the others, and sitting at tables all around the terrace, each of which seated dozens. The people gossiped and cavorted, and Elsinore was unable to clearly make out anything being said.

Elsinore was unsettled, but no longer surprised, to see each person wore a hooded mask like a bird, completely hiding their face, and most wore cloaks, coats, and capes of feathers to match. Some feathers were black, some red, some yellow, many a mixture of hues fading into rainbows. All had eyes hidden in shadow, as dark as the water of the unlit aquifer.

Other than the masks and cloaks, these people were dressed eclectically, in robes and gowns, capes and sandals and boots, bare-chested and kilted or coated and collared, with no distinction in dress on the chest between those with breasts or without. All sexes wore gold and silver jewelry, necklaces with gems, or else an obvious and somehow decadent lack of adornment. Their arms and chests were a variety of hues. They leaned into one another's ears, caressed their neighbors' cheeks and kissed their necks with the beaks of their masks in a feast of sensuality.

Drawn in by the spectacle of their merriment, Elsinore walked slowly across the terrace and into the crowd, dancers all around her as she looked from face to hidden face, trying to tell what she could of their manners. The people were so engaged with each other that Elsinore thought no one would notice her at all, until a mellifluous voice called out to her.

"Blue Leaf! I'm so delighted you could attend the banquet!"

The speaker called from a clutch of dancers nearby, and despite the black raven mask, Elsinore could see it was Canter, as fluid and charming as he had been when they first met, his chest shining gold in the ambient light. He wore his scarlet coat with gold buttons, the collar up around the edges of his mask, hiding the hungry insects that crawled through his hollow back.

"I'm so glad you've come to join the festivities after all." She could hear the smile beneath his mask in the sly shape of his voice. "You may dance with me, as I have no doubt you are eager to do."

Elsinore drew back as other fae watched and laughed at her hesitation. Canter strode forward, taking her hand in his right and putting his left in the small of her back, sweeping her into the center of the crowd and swinging about in a wild movement that, she supposed, was meant to be a dance.

The nerve he had to consider this dancing annoyed Elsinore almost more than the abrupt entitlement he displayed by touching her. She kicked him in the shin—not to stop him but to force him to move as she directed, taking the lead and turning the dance into one she found more familiar, more comfortable.

She led him across the terrace, swaying to what she now recognized as a mournful but rhythmic song ringing out from the golden vibration of the ziggurat. The fae all moved to it, in one way or another, whether dancing or talking in tune, and it made her uneasy, but she channeled that uneasiness into leading the dance with Canter.

"I'd not have taken you to be one to evince such grace," Canter sang. "Not after the mess you made of the poor serpent in the city plaza beneath the great statue. At least I, after I was finished with you, planned to throw your bones in the fire, to keep the place tidy." His voice was cheerful but sincere.

"I have a lot of shit on my mind right now," Elsinore said, not missing a step in the dance. "Sometimes I can be a little messy. It happens. I couldn't help but notice you had a lot of hygienic trouble when you took off your coat. So I guess we could both stand to clean up a little."

Canter's blithe replies fell silent, and Elsinore liked to imagine the grin beneath the mask turned into a scowl. Elsinore's face did the reverse.

"A lovely guest you've brought us, Kenkena," one of the fae teased as she stepped in, putting her arms around Canter and pulling him away from Elsinore by the collar of the coat.

Elsinore stopped moving to keep her footing as her dance partner was shoved off. The person who now stood before her seemed feminine, as far as the young woman could tell from the presentation of the fae around her. She was striking; taller than Elsinore, slender and elegant, with strong arms decorated in glittering bracelets, and a mask and gown of yellow feathers that shone out as brightly as the golden palace around them.

Though the eyes of the dancers were hidden in the shadows of the masks, Elsinore thought she could see pinpoints of golden light flashing from far back in this person's hood. Elsinore gasped a little to herself at how graceful she was and imagined her to be very beautiful. The young witch blushed, suddenly certain this fae was the woman she had met with the flowers in the market and reading the book in the maze of the dead city.

"You dance so well. Are you mortal?" The fae examined Elsinore. "You look mortal. Or are you like us? It can be so hard to tell."

"Her body is distinct and luxuriant," Canter—Kenkena—said from where he came to rest at the edge of the crowd. "I know that well."

Elsinore hated him and tried to direct the hate at him through sheer force of will.

"Without her glamour, she must be quite wretched to look at, indeed."

Another fae stalked over and peered closely at Elsinore, scrutinizing her all over, not laying a finger on her but combing her over with the dark, hollow eyeholes of the hood, the beak of a hawk barely an inch from her neck.

"You wear a most subtle glamour, sister," the hawk-beaked fae said. "I do wonder how you look underneath. How you really look. If only I could take a peek . . ."

The fae's fingers spread out with long, pointed nails like a hawk's talons, waving through the air around her, still not touching. Elsinore stood perfectly still, did not even turn her head to look at the people who surrounded her, afraid of what they wanted to do.

"She wears no glamour at all!" another hollered as they approached the one studying her, pushing them aside in anger. "I think she really looks how she looks! That's disgraceful!"

"She looks better than you do, you haggard old vulture!" said the hawklike fae.

"Haggard old vulture? Really?" said Kenkena, "Haggard and a vulture, now that really is too much."

"It doesn't matter!" said the angry one. "She doesn't wear a glamour! Not wearing a glamour is disgraceful, however she looks!"

"What need?" Kenkena asked. "Her beauty is marvelous all over, as much as her sweet face."

At last, he drew the hood off his face with one hand,

the first of the fae here to do so. He dragged a lazy, predatory eye up and down Elsinore's body as he spoke.

"Then she should put on a glamour and make herself uglier!" the angry one shouted.

The clique around them erupted in a wave of laughter. Elsinore flushed red and glared at Kenkena as he laughed. The vile, unwelcome desire in his eyes made the young woman shudder—until a realization struck her.

This lustful, hollowed-out creature; could it be . . . ?

"Kern." The fae turned to her with a smug smile, which faded when he realized what she had said. "Your mother is looking for you. To chastise you for your wickedness. You've acted very poorly. She's waiting for you at the door to the hall of the library in the empty necropolis, around the cistern."

Kenkena's eyes darkened with fury. More than that; his eyes, once bright, turned fully black, and his mouth opened in a snarl. His body twisted and convulsed, and in a cloud of smoke and feathers, he was distorted into the form of an ordinary raven. The city's gold light shone red off his glossy black feathers, and he took at once to the air, flying off into the distance, into the sky.

"Run back to mother!" screamed a voice from the crowd, and the fae broke out in laughter again. A few closed around Elsinore, tried to clap her on the back and shake her hand, but the girl just stood in astonishment.

One of the fae stood before her—the graceful one who had pulled Kenkena away from his dance with Elsinore. She remained silent and demure, her hands folded at her waist until she raised them to remove her yellow hood.

She was, as Elsinore had predicted, ferociously gorgeous in the golden light of the pyramid. She bore high cheekbones, a perfect chin, and soft hair tied back partly in a bun, leaving a few curls to tumble down to her breast. Her eyelids were painted black, and her eyes flashed gold, though with an unnatural magical light or merely reflecting the glow of the palace around them, Elsinore could not tell.

She took Elsinore by the hand and led her to a banquet table near the central tower gate, and Elsinore followed without hesitation. She started to tell herself it was for fear of making more of a scene but cut off the excuse in her own head. This person was madly attractive, and it practically pained Elsinore to look away from her beauty. She was led away from the crowd, followed by several of the other fae—including the one who had demanded the glamour—who sulked and glared at her as they all took their seats.

"Never mind the others. We can be quite particular here, but don't allow it to bother you," the lovely fae said. "I am called Delidua, She Who Walks Alone in the Halls of Waste. It is my pleasure to welcome you to Dis, capital city of Faerie—also known as Ganzir, the palace in the heart of Hell. You were called Blue Leaf by Kenkena; is that your name, really?"

The fae smiled knowingly.

"I told him to call me that," the young woman said. "Whyever should I not have done?" She looked at the fae curiously. There was something frightfully, dreadfully familiar about Delidua, but the luminous aura of the Ganzir and the flashing gold of her eyes distracted Elsinore until she lost hold of what she had tried so urgently to remember.

Consciously and awkwardly changing the subject, she said, "But really, I want to know why you hold this banquet. In whose honor do you celebrate?"

"It is in honor of the Queen of Faerie, the Far-

Reaching Ruler of the Great Earth, whose house is this Ganzir and whose guests we have the honor of calling ourselves. As a guest at Her banquet, you must not be ungracious; you must not refuse Her hospitality. Besides, you are famished after your journey. Will you eat? And drink?"

The fae passed Elsinore a tray like an overturned drum, bearing cakes set on beds of flower petals and sprinkled with pomegranate seeds. She gave her also a wide, shallow silver chalice with a deep purple-red liquid.

"Will you rest and dance here with us, with me, for as long as the stars burn or till the moon falls?" As if to demonstrate or share in the meal, Delidua took a cake from the tray and ate, then sipped from the chalice, before passing them both to her guest.

Elsinore was indeed hungry and thirsty after her long journey—through the forest, under the earth, in the halls of shadow, and the fight with the great serpent. She hadn't eaten, she realized, since she woke. Was it even the same day? The passage of time here made the young witch wonder.

In her weakened state, she was all the more dazzled by the beauty of the fae before her. To refuse the food she offered would be, as she herself had said, most ungracious. Elsinore despaired at the thought of disappointing Delidua.

She reached out automatically, took a few pomegranate seeds—six—and ate them, one by one, feeling their tartness sharply in her mouth. Reaching for the chalice, she brought it to her mouth and smelled the dark liquid, not surprised that it was pomegranate wine.

She sipped lightly, and as she did, she thought of the old stories. It was not good, she remembered, to take food or drink from Faerie. By the ancient laws, to do so made the guest the property of Faerie, damned them inescapably to dwell among the underworld hosts.

Suddenly regretting eating the seeds and drinking the wine, she lowered the chalice with some small sense of shame, set it on the table between her and Delidua, and frowned. She was unsure yet if this curse applied to her, if being a changeling would mean she was subject to the same laws as a mortal. But even if it did, wasn't this what she wanted? To be part of the world she had come from? Was it true that this was her real home?

"I have always heard," Elsinore said, speaking carefully, for she knew the danger this place held for her, regardless of her origin, "that the fae are a people of laws and oaths, fastidiously kept. Please excuse me for saying so, and perhaps it is my ignorance due to being raised in the mortal world that makes me ask, but it seems to me that this time and place is more given to misrule, to chaos, than to strict order?"

Had she been too specific? Too leading? She wanted to know if the rules the stories spoke of applied to her, but did they apply at all?

The fae called Delidua laughed brightly, joined by those around her. Soon, the whole table shook as the diners erupted in peals of laughter. Surely only those immediately next to Elsinore had heard what she said. The rest laughed only to join in—laughed because the others were laughing.

Elsinore blushed in shame, and Delidua fell silent suddenly.

"Why do you draw such a distinction, my dear?" the fae asked without a giggle. "It is a peculiar preoccupation they have in the mortal country, that of inventing and enforcing such solid boundaries between those things that are really from one point of view the same and from another only two of an infinite number of possible states. That which you call order—is it not the same state as what one might call chaos? Is chaos not simply an order that one does not understand? Order merely a chaos that one is familiar with? Are your 'order' and 'chaos' not merely degrees by which you class a multitude of observed states, which exist in total disregard for your attempts to apply these labels? The mortals draw a distinction between madness with a 'method' and madness without, but does not every madness follow its own respective method? Such arbitrary categories are beneath ones such as us, are they not, Blue Leaf?"

Elsinore thought of her dear Folia, who she once loved in seasons past. Folia, whose uncle had tried to impose his own kind of order on his poor niece. Folia, whose uncle decided her failure to conform to the strict sex roles imposed by the law of god the sun meant her life should be forfeit, by rights. By rules. To preserve the "order" of Lord Sun.

Elsinore thought of what Folia had told her once. *There's more to you than girl or boy, or woman or man. I think there is to many of us.*

Suddenly, a terrible thought took hold of Elsinore's mind. Her heart raced, and she could feel something, a warmth that overtook her as if she had drunk hot soup. She realized something was beginning to flow out of the seeds she had consumed—a magical energy, awakening her to the reality of this place.

She looked around at the banquet, and though most of the guests still wore their hoods, many had taken them off as they sat at the tables to feast. Their beauty faded away as the seeds worked their magic, drawing back the veil of their glamour from Elsinore's eyes.

They mostly all looked the same as before, but a

little stranger. Different. Queerer. She realized now—their glamour drawn away, their eyes sunken, their hearts hollow—it was so simple, made so much sense now. This was the heart of the Kur, in the city of Dis, in the house of Ganzir, the other realm beneath the earth from which no ordinary mortal could return.

At last, Elsinore realized the fae, the people who danced in this place, were all the dead.

She looked back at Delidua. She was still beautiful, but the familiar aura she emanated grew more solid to Elsinore.

"Are you male?" Elsinore asked Delidua suddenly, without elaboration. "Or female? Or . . . ?"

"Ah," Delidua sighed with delight. "You do understand, poor child." As the glamour fell away, acne scars dimpled Delidua's cheeks, and Elsinore gasped with recognition.

"Folia?"

Realization came quickly now. Elsinore recognized her lover at last, dead and passed and interred through the gateway beneath the mound long before. But she was here, dining at the banquet of Faerie in the palace of death and gold, practically presiding over the lovely, ghastly fae who surrounded them. Elsinore gazed deeply at the lost face of her phantom lover.

"Folia . . . is it really you? Is this a glamour still? Or are you here? Are you with me again?"

"I really don't understand you, sister," Delidua said, golden eyes vacant, oblivious. "I have always been of Faerie, for all my life. All of us—we are part of this place. We belong here. Don't you?"

Elsinore's heart sank in despair. How long had her love been here, in the time since her death? What had they done to make her forget her life and the time it had been? Was this the fate of a changeling, that which awaited Elsinore herself? To dance forever in the golden palace, to dance for a queen who hadn't even shown herself? Had this fate already begun?

Elsinore shook her head and reluctantly pulled her gaze from Delidua's mysterious eyes. She reached into her pack, quickly and decisively, and pulled out what she wanted after a moment of searching: the one thing she knew still contained part of Folia, the thing she needed to be herself. Elsinore held her rooster doll in both hands, hugged it tight to her breast, and then offered it to Delidua.

The beautiful fae took the doll without recognition, and her eyes locked on it for a long time. For Elsinore and Delidua, the chatter around them, the talk of the guests, the vibrant ambient hum of the palace of gold—all sound faded away, and an aura of silence fell over them both. Elsinore gazed at Delidua, and Delidua gazed at the doll.

Finally, a single tear stole down the dead woman's cheek from her black-lidded golden eye.

"Elsie?" Delidua—Folia—whispered at last.

But she said no more, as an eerie happening brought their reunion to a halt.

From inside the ziggurat, through the fiery towering doors of bronze, rose a low, deep moan that bore a note of otherworldly agony. At once both human and animal, the cry of throbbing pain shook the luminous golden floor of the city with resounding misery. The fae all around ceased their talking, their dancing, their merriment. Folia stood and burst into tears, her body shaking with sobs. Another fae fell over out of the chair in pain, clutching their belly. Elsinore stood from the table and drew away, looking around. All the guests began to wail, their voices finding each other, matching the waves and motions of the moan from the tower gate perfectly, offset by a mere half-second, following its depths and its peaks. The keening rang around the moan like a wreath around a bonfire, feeding it, flashing when it burst, rising and falling, the icy peak of the mountaintop and the dark sodden depth of the pit below.

The bronze doors flew open, ringing like a gong. From the darkness of the chamber within stepped a brilliant figure, huge and majestic, its full height obscured by its doubled-over agony. The figure stumbled, head in hands, their moaning filling the world with pain.

Elsinore tried to see them more clearly, to follow the form of the body, but her vision was blurred and indistinct. She tried to wonder aloud what was happening, but when she opened her mouth, her voice only echoed the awful lament, keening in unison with the cries around her.

The body that stepped through the towering gate shook as they wailed, tearing at their own dark eyes, clawing their breasts and neck. The fae in the crowd shook in ecstatic frenzy, matching the figure's suffering, mirroring them by gashing their own arms and breasts with their bird-talon fingernails, shaking as if covered in insects from out of the deep pits of the earth.

Elsinore was unable to see anything more, overcome as she now was with weeping. She felt, not in her mind but in her heart, an overwhelming avalanche of suffering. It was not her own, not her regret, not her loss or fear, but that of the world around her, of the body of the earth crying out in pain, of the innocents deprived and oppressed and subjugated by the wickedness of the Old Ones, who were the children of the earth and part of the earth, each person a divine spark composed of starlight but dragged, abused, and chained with iron by the greed of the privileged. Elsinore felt their suffering, felt every moment of it, and the force of it shook her body more than she feared she could endure. An ocean of tears, a wailing and keening like the sound a star would make when ripped apart by its own gravity—Elsinore felt the galaxy dying within her and struggling to be reborn.

"Ohhh! Oh! My insides!" cried the great moaning voice, as deep as the darkness of the sky behind the Mountain.

"Oh! Oh! Your insides!" the crowd cried with them.

"Ohhh! Oh! My skin!"

"Oh! Oh! Your skin!"

"Ohhh! Oh! My head!"

"Oh! Oh! Your head!"

"Ohhh! Oh! My heart!"

"Oh! Oh! Your heart!"

Finally, the figure fell silent, stood straight, and raised both hands, and the crowd fell silent with them.

No longer caught up in the empathetic frenzy, Elsinore breathed deeply and examined herself. Her arms, she was shocked to find, bore cuts and scrapes from her nails where she had torn at her own flesh. She looked back at the figure and nearly fell back into keening, this time from fear, but she kept it from gripping her heart and stood silent.

At full height, the figure stood twice as tall as the tallest person Elsinore had ever seen, or more. The figure had a clear crystal body the deep blue of lapis lazuli, within which was visible the black silhouette of a skeleton. Through the blue crystal of the face, the skull bore an expression of death. The body glowed faintly, not in reflection of the gold light of the Ganzir but with its own divine luminescence.

The body stood on teal-green feathered legs, with the

scaly clawed feet and terrible crescent-moon talons of a raptor, a bird of prey. From the figure's back spread four wings, one pair angled up, the other pair down. The feathers of the wings were a deep purple red. Crowning the head was a display of curved horns encasing a horizontal crescent, its points up, all glowing white with the light of the moon.

The figure's eight limbs—two wings up, two arms to the side, two wings down, and two legs—recalled to Elsinore the eight rays of the star on her necklace, the star of Tiranna. Elsinore knew that she stood before the Goddess Herself. The emanation of the Goddess as ruler of the underworld, the Queen of Faerie. This was the Goddess as queen of the Kur, at Her house the Ganzir. Tiranna, whose emanation Galattis sank beneath the Mountain as Queen of the Great Earth.

The Goddess opened Her mouth and spoke, and Her voice echoed like stars singing in Elsinore's dreams.

"The lords of the Old Ones filled the sea with poison and the granaries with mold and dust, burned forests and turned them into cemeteries and built border walls to justify filling the graves with the strangers they clamored to murder! They boiled the oceans and poured smoke in the air, till the children suffocated on their own breath and the ice thawed, and the world was fire and flood and wind all at once. The lords of the Old Ones ruined the world and had not even the will to restore it!

"The Old Ones themselves in their desperation had nothing but their lamentations to summon me to relieve them! They called me down from the moon, and I fell from the sky as a star that falls, as a stone image, as a radiant fragment of the Goddess whose body is the ALL. I destroyed the lords so that not even their spirits remained. I restored the world for a price. Not till I arrived

did the rivers run clean, and the cedars grow tall. I restored the world by drawing down the moon! The last of the Old Ones saw, and they feared my power, and with what little science they knew, they housed me here, in the heart of Eridu, beneath the Kur. But what is done cannot be undone. I drew down the moon! While long ago she fell away, she now draws closer, century by century, year by year, day by day, moment by moment. Some far day outside the range of human knowledge, the moon shall fall, and I shall be reunited and whole!

"My names are manifold, and I am part of many other names. Here in my Ganzir, I am Heqakigal. Welcome, my guests, my children, my siblings. Feast and die and live in death."

The fae stood silent, motionless while their queen spoke to them, intoning Her liturgy. She looked at none of them, peered off into the distance, to the far horizon of darkness, where water below met the night, the thin horizon that reflected the terrible light of Ganzir.

Then She turned, knowing where to look, and fixed Her gaze upon Elsinore. Her eyes were bright stars, not distant but very near, the steady light of the morning and evening stars.

"Who are you, child? Why do you come here, to the feast of the Eldest Daughter of the Moon? What is your name? Speak. I wish that you would."

Elsinore stepped forward, her body weak from the ecstatic rite, her mind weary from emotion. She looked around at the fae, but their golden eyes strayed not a little from the face of their queen.

"My name is behind my lips and in my heart," the young woman said. "I am called Elsinore. I believe . . . I believe I was traded for a human boy as a changeling, when I was a child. I have come to petition you, Far-

Reaching Queen of the Great Earth, for his release. His name . . ."

Elsinore hesitated and concentrated; it took all her will—all the emotional strength she had, more than it cost to cast her most potent spell—to call up and speak this name aloud.

"His name was Hamnen."

The Goddess raised both Her hands, and to Her side from inside the gate stepped two beasts, sphinxes, their braided manes framing their frowning, androgynous faces, the fur on their leonine bodies glistening, their wings flashing in the light. The fur of one was tawny, the other gold with black stripes. The latter was the same one, Elsinore was sure, that she sent through the magic door back in the Valley of the Mounds before the Mountain.

"The banquet is ended. The rest of you are to leave us," the Goddess commanded.

The two guardians rose and spread their wings, and with a motion Elsinore could not see, they swept the crowd away, leaving a trail of gold as they disappeared into the black distance. Elsinore thought she remained alone on the step of the palace, tiny and afraid before Heqakigal. But she felt someone hold her, and she turned to find Folia standing beside her with her arm around Elsinore's. Her black eyeshadow streaked down her cheeks in tears, and her once-golden eyes were red with weeping, looking not at the Goddess but at her lover.

"After you were taken from me, I wished for nothing more in earth and hell than to be with you again, always," Elsinore said, struggling to hold back tears.

She turned from Folia to the Goddess, cursing herself, fighting her every instinct to keep her eyes on her lover, looking at the Queen of Faerie with a defiance she never would have guessed she were capable of.

"But she is a galla, like me. A woman born in a body thought by her family to be that of a boy. By the law spoken by your gatekeeper, she may go. No woman born a girl nor man born a boy may enter here and return to the world above, and so Folia, who you call Delidua, a galla and one of your blessed daughters, should be free. That is the law of this place, and I call upon it for her safe return."

The Goddess lowered Her head, considering the young women before Her for a long time. Her mood was impossible for the sorceress to fathom.

"Your sister speaks the truth," the Goddess said at last, softly now, speaking to Folia. "You may go, my child; back to Eridu, if that is your wish. For though you are welcome here, you are welcome to return to the world above. Your life is your own, and you may do as you will."

Folia looked to Elsinore, her eyes welling again with tears. She held the rooster doll in her hands and caressed the comb and tail. She looked at the soft toy, felt the seams she had sewn, remembered how she had felt as she made it. The feelings passed over her again: the fear, the resolve, but most of all, her love for Elsinore.

"I have eaten from the drum," Folia said, her voice a gentle whisper, quiet but confident. "I have drunk from the cymbal. I have read the letters in the stars, and I have stolen into the inner chamber." She looked directly into Elsinore's eyes. "I am your sister."

Elsinore held her hands to her mouth, struggling hard to choke back a sob.

"I have eaten from the drum; I have drunk from the cymbal. I have read the letters in the stars, and I have stolen into the inner chamber," she repeated. She failed to hold back the tears that came to both their eyes, but she finished, breaking into a smile of melancholy joy and relief. "I am your sister."

Folia reached out and cradled Elsinore's cheeks in her hands and pulled her lover's face into hers. The two women kissed for a long time, tears mingling together like rain in the river, like the river pouring into the sea.

Great wings spread from Folia's back, with flashing yellow feathers like her dress, and she lifted into the air a little. Then she was gone, vanished into the light and darkness of the Ganzir. Elsinore hadn't even the time to call out to her before she was gone.

"Will she be all right?" Elsinore demanded, astonished at the presumption in her voice as she turned and addressed the entity before her. Astonished at all she had said. Her face was still wet with tears, and she childishly wiped her face dry on her sleeve.

"What is your true name, child?" The Goddess's voice echoed in the empty landing, and Her eyes shone steadily into Elsinore's thoughts.

"My name is Ensinurma," the sorceress said. "The Priestess of the Pomegranate Moon."

"You are a galla," the Goddess said, "a younger daughter of the moon. Come with me, child." The incredible being turned, going into the gate.

"I am not a child, my Goddess. I can remember twenty Seasons of Shadows, and there are more before that I cannot remember."

Elsinore stood firm, did not follow. The Goddess turned back and looked at the human woman, so small, standing beneath the dark sky.

"Come with me, younger sister," She said.

This time, Elsinore followed—the two of them, Goddess and galla, going into the Ganzir, in the heart of the Mountain.

✳ 17 ✳

THE GIRL AND THE BOY

Within the halls of the Ganzir, the way was lit dimly, but it was simple for Elsinore to follow the queen in the faint blue radiance of her body. The steps each of them took, the witch's boots and the queen's sharp talons, echoed widely through each room and passage. Through dining rooms of great size, for banquets like those they had just left; through narrow hallways lined with doors that stood closed, and not a hint of what lay behind them; through a shrine where a strange black stone was set in the surface of a gray altar; through a room of archaic broken marble statues and altarpieces, a room of dresser drawers, a room of paintings of unknowable faces, and a room empty, its walls, ceiling, and floor a polished, mirrored black.

They came to a library, a room with shelves, ladders, and balconies of more shelves, and Elsinore dawdled and looked at the spines of books and the caps of scrolls. Most she saw had titles and text in the nodiform script she had encountered in the library, unreadable and arcane, but she didn't want to look too closely and fall too far behind.

Quickly turning away, she nearly ran into the queen. The inscrutable being had stopped and come back to her. Stretching a long arm up to a shelf far above the girl's head, the queen selected a book and considered it for a moment. Opening it to the first page, She drew shapes upon the interior with Her finger, then gave it to Elsinore.

What the queen had written inside was short, maybe only one word, but its meaning was lost on Elsinore. At the edge of her mind, though, the witch thought there was something strangely familiar about the shape of the characters.

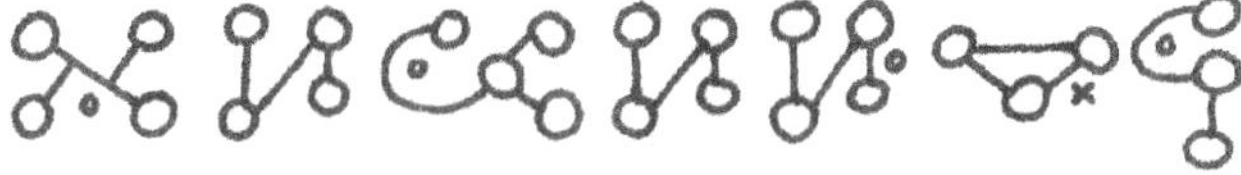

On the cover was an embossed picture of a turtle. The image was highly stylized, its extended neck and limbs like the heads of five serpents, the scutes on its shell like little mountains. The eyes in one of the dragon-like heads were turned out, gazing back at Elsinore conspiratorially.

She looked back up at the queen but could discern neither emotion nor expectation from the enigmatic skull visible through the face. She simply looked at the little witch and became, in comparison, larger and grander, not only in size but in knowledge, in history, in secrets.

What does she mean by giving me this?

Before Elsinore could give voice to the question or ask about the meaning of what the queen had written inside the cover, the great entity turned precisely and strode on past the shelves and out of the library. Putting the book in her bag, Elsinore hurried to catch up with the queen, out the door, down the hall, feeling very much as she had as a little girl in the marketplace with Milanda, losing herself in fascination at every stall and scrambling to catch up as her mother moved on.

Elsinore followed the queen around the periphery of a vast circular room, filled in the middle with a tremendous device, a mechanism that echoed with clockwork movements on gears and arms of brass that ended in orbs of various materials and sizes, many supporting subsystems of smaller orbs. In the heart was a huge globe, a transparent lamp burning with a yellow light that illuminated the room.

When Elsinore noticed one of the orbs was covered in a turquoise faience-like glaze, orbited itself by a silver ball, she realized what she was looking at: an orrery of marvelous scale, a model of the planetary system a person could practically wander through. A narrow circular bar divided the walk from the interior of the system, preventing an awestruck visitor from stumbling in and being caught in the inevitable mechanisms. However, her attention was drawn to a podium set into the dividing bar.

Elsinore approached and couldn't stop herself from reaching out to the smaller device set within. It was a network of gears, more like a small clock than the vast orrery before her. There were levers and switches, and a smaller two-dimensional rendition of the planetary system which moved in tandem with the massive device that dominated the room. Without thinking, or asking, Elsinore felt the urge to toy with the levers, and when she did, the planets whirred and moved at her touch. At the same time, the larger mechanism shifted as well; it was like turning the key of a clock, moving the hands and changing the time, and the sorceress felt an agency unlike any she had felt in as long as she could remember.

It was like the planets themselves moved at her whim, and the power was exhilarating. She felt so pleased that she hadn't noticed the queen standing behind her, peering over her head at her meddling. The Goddess gave no sign in Her face that She was disappointed or pleased or that She cared one way or the other. The great fae only reached over Elsinore's shoulder with Her far-reaching arms and deftly fiddled with the device, returning it to its previous state.

Elsinore felt a sense of shame and annoyance that she had almost broken the device, but she had the presence of mind to dismiss this as petulance on her part. When the queen moved on, Elsinore followed, with a final yearning look back at the ticking inevitable process of the device they left behind.

They came at last to a gallery, with marvelous items on stands and hung around the edges. In this room, the queen lingered, looking from piece to piece casually, deliberately, and Elsinore felt compelled to do the same. She was drawn to what seemed to be the centerpiece of the gallery. From long cords in an unseen ceiling hung a frame of black wood, in which was set a glass of murky crystal. Through the glass, whatever lay behind it was distorted, bent ever so slightly as if seen through water, and each object hung with an aura that made the scene difficult to see.

Or perhaps they make it all less difficult to see.

As she focused on each object through the glass, the auras of exaggerated color began to swirl ever so subtly, to flow in and out, at its deepest to flow into each other so she could no longer tell where one object began and another ended. She saw through the glass how the material of one thing—be it a table, floor, statue, hand, the very air itself—was of a piece and continuous with all other material around it, both physically and temporally. Through the glass, she could see, dimly and but for a moment, what had stood in that space before, and—most unsettlingly—what would stand there in the moments to come. She saw Heqakigal step into the space on the other side of the glass, but the Goddess did not yet stand there.

Elsinore drew back, her mind swimming and head aching, recovering from a sudden strong sense of nausea. Away from the glass, she realized it simulated or replicated the effects of the mushroom from the fairy ring she had taken to enter the Mountain. But unprepared as she had been then even with careful meditation, its effect in the mirror had nearly overwhelmed her with the feeling of having come unmoored in space and time.

Elsinore steadied herself on a pillar nearby, closing her eyes and breathing deeply, focusing on her inhalation and exhalation. When she opened her eyes, she found Heqakigal standing by the glass, looking at Elsinore from the other side contemplatively. She stood in the very spot the witch had seen Her through the glass, before the rush of nausea. The Goddess spoke.

"Through this, one may see all things as they really are. In daily life, one sees the surface. Through this glass, the surface is removed, the veil dropped. One sees uncovered the body of the Great Goddess, whose name is Tiranna, the Mother of the Mountain that is the earth, the Source of the Celestial River that is the galaxy. She is the mother of all things, for She is the source of all things, She whose body forms the ALL. It is not healthy for a mortal such as yourself to look upon the unveiled body of the Goddess for too long, though of course you see it veiled every moment, for the body of Tiranna is all matter, all phenomena, all motion, and all time. You are part of Her, and your mother is, but also every stranger, every blade of grass, every planet, every galaxy, the void of space. Every footfall, every failure, every want and need, every kiss, the moment you forget your grandmother's name or remember the face of a boy you once knew. The time it takes for light to reach you from the edge of the observable universe, and the unimaginable vistas beyond which you can never see. Everything you experience, and the folds of another dimension you can never touch. The cry of a child, the hush in the depths of the ocean, and the light of the moon. All are the body of the Goddess Tiranna, for She is the rainbow whose prismatic emanations create each level of observable and experiential reality.

"By looking upon Her form unveiled, the wise can see what is, what was, and what will be, for all are one in Her body. We are Her body, and we are Her dream. You have seen as much yourself, in a small way. I can see that you have recently consumed a substance that let you glimpse but distantly Her undisguised form. I know that is how you came into this place, through the veil. And I know what it is that you came here to find."

Heqakigal stepped out from behind the glass, put Her blue crystal hand, shadowed with black bone, on Elsinore's back, and led the young woman to the dimly lit rear of the gallery.

On the back wall stood a great dark coffin, larger than Elsinore, nearly the size of the queen. Its face wore a somber expression of deep mourning, and on its head, over a dome of stylized hair, rested a crown, simple and unadorned but crenelated. A mural crown, city walls surrounding the peak of a mountain.

The eyes beneath the crown were dark, empty, and hollow, and channels ran down the cheeks from the corners as if for rivulets of tears. Of a scale much larger than a human, it seemed less for burial than for torment.

It was, Elsinore realized, an iron maiden.

The queen took her hand from Elsinore's back and stepped away. **"Open it,"** She said, her voice echoing deep in the young woman's mind.

Without thinking, without hesitating, without knowing what she was doing, Elsinore obeyed. She took the edge of the lid with both hands, pulled with all her little strength, and it swung along its hinges and opened freely.

Inside, chained to the back and motionless with agony, Elsinore saw him.

He was herself.

His face was so like hers but for the manhood his body embraced. Like a brother, like her father, his was the face she would have had were she not who she was, had she not been who she made herself.

Elsinore was repulsed by him. She was repulsed not only by his suffering: his hollow cheeks and cavernous belly; his wide ribs, which she could count through his starved flesh; the sunken nipples in a flat chest torn by the hooks of the iron maiden; the blue veins visibly snaking along his hairy arms, hands, and legs. She was repulsed not only by the look of resigned mourning on his face, the want in his hollow cheeks.

She was repulsed by what she saw beneath his suffering: his strong jaw, dark with beard stubble; his proudly questioning brow; his broad, powerful shoulders that could have withstood so much weight; the arms that, in better health, could have been so strongly muscled, could have torn out the chains that held him in this dungeon. She was repulsed by the masculinity still so clearly visible beneath his suffering. He looked at her, and she could hardly stand to return his gaze, though she had no choice but to do so.

His expression was dark, and she could not decipher it, though the face was a parody of her own. Was it a look of pleading? Of supplication? Of apology? Of hate?

"Unchain and release him," the Queen of Faerie whispered from the dark, Her voice less reverberating, now a quiet promise in the hush of Elsinore's doubt. "And he may go free. Of course, you will, by necessity, stay here in his place. The even trade of my changelings. Not in this tomb, certainly not. But in the court of Faerie, where you shall celebrate in the waters at the aquifer of life, beneath the stars, and you shall never die.

"Or you may choose to let him remain here, for me to do with as I please, and in exchange for leaving his life with me, you shall return to rule as my regent in Eridu above. I shall bestow upon you whatever gifts you wish. Jewels, glittering stars from under the Mountain. Dominion over the currents of the Great River Gallas, over the fields of golden wheat that bow before the winds falling across the valley and grow tall in the light of the sun. You shall live among mortals as the Princess of the Pomegranate Moon, a great queen adorned with gold. Your death on some far-off morning shall break the hearts of entire nations, and you shall be remembered as a goddess."

Elsinore stood still, unable to look away. She barely heard what the queen had said. All she knew was the look of mystery on the man's impossible face. She knew not what to do. She longed to shut the iron lid, shut the face away, and leave, return home to her mothers and live the rest of her life as if she had never been to this place. But she knew if she did, she would see that face—the face on the coffin lid, eyes weeping bloody tears, the questioning eyes in the face of that man—she would see that face whenever she shut her own eyes. She would see him in every mirror she gazed into, matching her every motion. She would see him plead with her the moment she died.

She suddenly felt a weight in her hand as she gripped something solid and cold. It was Moonstar. When had she drawn the sword? She realized then it would be a simple matter to end the boy's suffering. To silence the endless questions from his bloodshot eyes by merely sliding the short white blade softly between his ribs. His questions would be answered, his fate known. His face wiped away, clear from Elsinore's mind. She wanted so badly to destroy him, this face of everything she never wanted, that she had worked so hard her whole life to banish.

She wanted so badly not to drop Moonstar, even as she let it clatter to the stone floor. She wanted so badly not to undo the chains, even as her nimble fingers released the locks. She wanted so badly not to touch him, even as she took his bony arm over her shoulder and let him down gently from the coffin, even as she released Hamnen from his tomb.

She wanted to see him look at her again, to smile, to thank her, but she saw his face no more as he turned away from her, fell over, and vanished. Looking around, she turned to the Goddess.

"Where is he?" Elsinore asked in a panic. "Has he gone? Is he returned to earth? Where is he?"

A terrible thought crept into her mind and took hold of her entirely. She looked at her hands in disbelief, felt her chest and her breasts, felt the curves and contours and skin of her face with her fingers. She looked at the Goddess desperately. What if . . . ?

Standing tall, the Goddess betrayed no expression on Her enigmatic face, only the shadow of a skull beneath blue crystal flesh. She turned and took something—a dark, wide object—from a table beside Her. She stepped closer to Elsinore, Her long stride covering at least two of Elsinore's, and held the object up before the girl.

It was a mirror, a tall, heavy thing of black obsidian but shining like silver, focusing the dim light of the chamber in a flash that stabbed Elsinore's eyes like a knife before settling into something visible. As her eyes grew used to the dimness after the flash, Elsinore gazed into the mirror, and at last, her sight resolved.

She saw, simply, herself.

Elsinore saw herself as she was, just as she always had been; as she had made herself, by the grace of . . . what, exactly? Of the Goddess, the entity before her? In the mirror, her face looked as it ever had since she had grown up, smooth and lovely, the face of a woman who had broken the hearts of men and women alike. Her hair was darkly teal in the black surface, shaved on the side, showing her ears slightly pointed—or had they ever been at all? Had she only liked to think that, when really they were no more unnatural than anyone else's? Her breasts curved lightly below the neck of her dress and jacket.

The fear that had taken her when the man vanished was eased, if not totally gone.

She looked like herself.

She looked, she realized, like any woman who by arts had made her body match her heart.

As the Goddess replaced the mirror on the table, a black cat emerged from behind its stand to curl around Her foot—Risky.

How in earth and hell did they get in here?

The Goddess reached down, picked them up, and stroked them. They seemed to scale up in the cradle of the Goddess's titan arms, to appear the same size relative to Her as they had to Elsinore before. She continued to stroke the cat as She spoke.

"I see now that you were strong enough, after all, to face your fear. Strong enough to face the *fear gorta*, the Man of Hunger. You were strong enough to show mercy to the man you could have been." The Goddess stepped back to the glass of Tiranna and looked through it again at Elsinore—at the Great Goddess behind and around and within her. She considered the girl for a long time before describing what She saw.

"There was no boy," the Goddess said. "No Hamnen. That was, I perceive, only the name your parents called you. You are no changeling; there are no changelings, except for children who are beat, burned, or abandoned by their mothers and fathers because they cannot support the child materially or emotionally. Like all the restless dead, they come here. To my palace. To the Ganzir.

"Twenty summers before you entered the Kur, you were left by your mother and father; that summer, in the bright heat and baleful light of the sun, there was a famine, a great hunger. They left their home to pursue promise of food elsewhere; they left you because they felt a child to be a burden to them as they fled. They left you with a grand story to ease your suffering. To give you a reason as they exposed you in the wood and left you to die.

"For days, you stayed in place in the forest, where your mother put you. You were starving, tired, fearful, and sick, and so close to death that my emissaries came for you, sent to bring you in death to the very gate of my Ganzir. They gave you a name of passage, the name you were to use to pass through the doors: EN.SIN.NU.-UR.MA. What you heard in your delirium as Elsinore, which became your true name in your heart.

"But before you could follow my emissaries, Glamis and Milanda of Nin found you and you lived. The man and woman you were born to scavenged and starved and died. What you do not remember of your first years with them is best left unremembered."

Elsinore fell to her knees as the Goddess spoke, put her head in her hands, her hair hanging over her face. She breathed deeply, heavily, but did not weep, though the weight of it all was almost more than she could bear. The weight of this knowledge of her life. The weight of that boy's face, which even now fled her memory forever, like the word of a spell cast with a whisper to change the very world around her.

She felt soft fur rub against her body and sat up to see Risky looking at her, eyes wide. She took the cat in her arms and scratched behind their ears, and they squinted their eyes slowly. Then they leaped from her hands and curled away, and Elsinore looked back at the Goddess.

"Then what?" she asked. "What of me? What am I? Where do I belong?"

"Be all that as it may," the Goddess continued, "you are a changeling as any are changelings: those who were abandoned, who came here, who were brought here. And you are welcome here, for you are a gala—a woman of transition, who made her body match her heart. A kurgarra, a banshee—a woman of the mounds. Like the pili, the men of transition, he who makes his body match his heart. But you, younger sister—you are also EN.BI, a high priestess of speaking fate, through prophecy and lamentation, who is outside the boundaries of male and female. Something else, neither man nor woman . . . else and nor. You are Fay-erie—one of the speakers of fate who are outside the bounds of day and night, of summer and autumn. Reed-marsh woman, twilight woman, crescent-moon woman, woman of crossing. You belong here, in the twilight, at Summer's End, under the hill. Else and nor; Elsinore. Ensinurma, Priestess of the Pomegranate Moon. You belong here, invited to my banquet, one of my children.

"There have always been people like you—enbi, gallae, pilli, banshee, farshee—from long ages before the rise of the Old Ones, from the very first days in the valley of the dawn, from the emergence of life in the unmeasured depth of the sea. Those who transition like the moon, who cross over like the star that marks the equinox; those who partake in all natures, or in none, or who pass in between. There will always be people like you in the world, until the moon falls. You belong there, in Eridu, your earth. You belong, little sister, wherever your heart leads you. And only your own heart can tell you where. For your fate, your spirit, your body is your own."

Elsinore studied the Goddess's face. Though it was hard to tell, it seemed to the witch that the great fae smiled. But Elsinore herself didn't know how to feel, or how to express it if she did. Neither to herself nor to anyone else, much less to so great a being as She who stood before her.

Elsinore sighed inwardly to herself, breathed evenly, held her arms crossed closely over her breasts. She felt the chill of this place, the cold wind from across the face of the shallow water outside the palace, creeping in through the halls and into the depth of the gallery. She had not felt the cold until now, had been too occupied to stop and feel the air around her. She shivered. Then she retrieved Moonstar and held it weakly in her hand as she bowed her head.

"I thank You, Queen of the Great Earth," Elsinore

said. "I thank You for the truth about my world and about myself. But as an enbi and a galla, I think I am free of the ban of entrance—that no man born a boy nor woman born a girl may enter the Kur and return. I was thought to be a boy when I was born, though I was really a girl. In transitioning to become a woman, I think I have grown to be more than a woman or a man. Or less. Or simply neither. Like my Goddess says, a woman of the reed marsh, of the twilight, of Summer's End.

"I wish to return to Eridu," Elsinore said at last. "To my real mothers, to my community. To follow Folia, my love, if that is where she has gone. I wish to return to my home."

Tears welled in her eyes as she spoke, not tears of lamentation but tears of gratitude and weariness. The Goddess held out Her mysterious hand, flesh like glass and bone like the night. Elsinore realized She gestured at the sword the young witch held at her side. She handed it to the Goddess, who took it and turned it over, only a dagger in Her great hand, its blade flashing in the dim light.

"SIN.UL you call it. The Moon Star. It is a simple sword, very pretty for a xiphos but otherwise not so different from many of those secreted around the halls beneath the Mountain." Heqakigal held it by the blade, the grip out to Elsinore, who took and sheathed it. "I bless it for you, galla, as a sign of your office. You are one of my representatives in the world above, in Eridu, like all gallae, all pilli, all enbi."

She looked down at Elsinore's feet, where Risky curled around them, tail up, ears cocked and curious. The cat meowed.

"And do you wish to stay with her, my guardian?" the Goddess asked. "Very well. I give my leave for you to do so, if you will. May you be safe. I bless you both, my children."

She led them to the door, another towering gate through which they found the open air on another side of the pyramid. The steps of gold led down to a walkway, which led to the endless waters of the aquifer.

"See to my galla's return, Puzur, my guardian."

Risky—Puzur—stepped forward. At the sound of their true name, their black fur unfurled like a scroll, spreading into black stripes on a majestic creature, the gaps between the stripes becoming the gold of a massive lion's body with wings outstretched, the tail ending in the sting of a scorpion. The creature turned to look at Elsinore with enigmatic eyes shining from a humanoid face ringed by a braided mane and crowned with curved horns.

They were the sphinx Elsinore had met outside the Mountain.

They lowered their head and neck, allowing Elsinore to climb on, which she did carefully, though only after overcoming her initial amazement at the creature's form. When she was safely on the sphinx's back, they dashed off the steps and, in an instant, met the horizon as the waters fell away behind them and the Ganzir became one of the host of distant stars in the sky.

* 18 *

THE LETTER, THE BOOK, AND THE DOLL

The two stood outside, the Mountain behind them, at the far edge of the forest. Elsinore fell to the ground in thanks, feeling the grass in her hands, and she looked up at the night as Risky sat beside her. They were once again a cat, with no indication they had ever been anything else, or could be, or ever would be again.

Elsinore looked around. The sky was clear, the moon silver and bright, shining down upon the woman and the cat as they stood in the open air within a wide circle of tall standing stones. A cool wind rustled the broad leaves of the trees of the Forest by the edge of the Valley of the Mounds.

She was where she had begun, at the stone circle outside Tudur, the ritual entrance to the forest. But there was something strange; when she had been shown the ring by Astra, and when she entered the forest, the grass within the circle had been sparse. Now it grew tall with herbs up to her knee, plants like fennel with yellow-green stalks and bright-yellow flowers.

Growing uneasy, she set off in the direction of the

town. From the look of the stars, it was very early, before dawn, and she thought if she hurried, she could make it before daybreak and surprise Vedon when he woke. His mother might already be awake, as Elsinore had gathered she sometimes rose early to prepare the library for the day and get ready for the patrons.

Elsinore thought of how much she missed her own mothers, in the months since she had left on her journey to Tudur and the Mountain.

Hurrying over the crest of some high ground before the arched bridge into town, she stopped suddenly. Risky caught up and looked up at her, rubbing against her leg. The moonlight was so strong and clear that the fields around the stream were almost as bright as day. But the stream itself was gone, the once-running bed empty.

Elsinore ran down to the edge, looked all over. It was surely the bridge over the stream into town, built of huge, firm, weighty stones. But as far as she could see in either direction, the creek bed was dry and looked to have been for a long time.

The stones of the bridge stood vigil as if in judgment, harshly shadowed by the moonlight, and there was no sign of water, nor of the vibrant life that once teemed in the river. There had been shrubs and growth, the vines around the large trees that grew isolated from the forest, but now the plant life was sparse and wan, unwatered and barely worth noticing.

Had it dried up in scarce span of a day or two that she had been gone? It couldn't have done; the bed would still be muddy and wet, and the plants would still be vi-brant and full-grown.

But there was nothing like that at all.

Elsinore sat on a stone and considered the moon above. A few nights ago, it had been the Pomegranate

Moon, a rainbow halo in a cloud-streaked purple sky. Tonight, the moon was silvery white, the sky clear and dark blue. The moon had likewise hung behind the mountain a few hours after midnight; tonight, not much later, it was on the other side of the sky, over the town nearby. Elsinore's worry rose and began to solidify into a cankerous dread. She set out at a jog, hurrying for Tudur. She would visit Vedon. He would surely have some idea of what had happened.

When she arrived in the town, it was shortly after dawn, and the villagers were beginning their morning activities. The town was the same as it had been when she had arrived days before; the same as it had been twenty years ago, when she had been found by Milanda and Glamis that terrible night. She knew the streets from walking with Vedon and easily found the library, where he lived with his mother.

She thought back to when chance had brought her in here that first night; it had only been a few days since, but it felt like an eternity. There were lights inside, those within no doubt preparing for a day of work. Elsinore approached, knocked on the door, and waited.

A woman answered. Her age was somehow imperceptible; there was a palpable glow about her face, a youthful vigor of some secret kind, but in truth she could have been as old, Elsinore estimated, as eighty or more. She was very pretty but had a tired look in her eyes, not from lack of sleep but from life. Elsinore thought her face looked familiar. She was dressed simply in a blue-and-yellow-gold dress, her dark-gray hair tied in a bun.

She had been smiling in welcome when she opened the door, but her smile faded when she saw Elsinore, a traveler come at so strange a time, her hair blue green and wild and half-shorn, her clothes black and purple, bearing on her back a traveler's bag and over her shoulder the flashing star in the pommel of her sword. The woman put her hands to her mouth, stifling a gasp.

"Good morning," Elsinore said gently. Vedon lived here with only his mother, the old librarian, but this woman did not look at all like the rude and demanding crone she had met in the library that first night. Who could she be? "I apologize for intruding, but is Vedon here? I've had a . . . strange few nights, and I'm a little confused, so—"

"It's you," the woman whispered through her fingers. "I can't believe it's really you."

Elsinore's sense of urgency grew. "Where is Vedon?"

The woman did not answer the question directly but gave her a look of pained discomfort and another expression Elsinore couldn't understand. Turning, she walked into the house, her pace betraying her great age, beckoning Elsinore to follow. She retrieved from a drawer a sealed letter, its paper aged and yellowed, and handed it to her visitor.

For: Elsinore

The witch looked at the woman, asking a question with her eyes, but the woman just nodded at the letter.

"It's for you," the old woman said. "They came and waited, but . . . please read it."

Elsinore gave up asking questions of the woman and sat on a little wooden chair by the fire. Opening the letter, she began to read:

To our dear daughter, Elsinore,

The night you left Nin, I buried my fear in the depths of my heart and stifled my worry that I would never see you again. Glamis gave little voice to her fear, as is her way. But I could tell she felt the same as I, though she was always quick to reassure me of your return. As I write this, it has been a year and a day since the night my little girl slipped off to venture into the Mountain. Some in town, as I suspect you are aware, insist you have returned home, a change-ling arrived again in Faerie. Others more level-headed and pessimistic say you must have been killed by something in the Mountain. But I know in my heart you are alive.

Glamis and I tried to go after you once you had been gone for enough time. After many months of waiting, of waking breathless wishing for your return, we packed traveling supplies and set out together on the Southern Road to Tudur. The region in the shadow of the woods was mysterious and foreboding, even in daylight, but we found the strength to go on in the hope of discovering what had become of you. We inquired in town as to whether you had been seen and learned you had passed through some months before. After meeting your friend, the librarian, Glamis and I agreed to follow your path into the woods, however dangerous it may be. A team from the town came after us, less concerned with rescue, I fear, than with pre-venting us from causing any disturbance to the place of the People, to the mysterious balance in which their lives have rested for generations.

By the time the townsfolk caught up, I had glimpsed the mounds that precede the Moun-tain, saw the terrible spires that strike from the earth, that try to scare intruders away. Glamis had provided encouragement through the dark of the wood, and though I have faith she would have repelled our would-be rescuers so we could push on after you, she collapsed under a wave of mourning when she saw those towers, dark and awful, though the sunlight reflected off them with deadly intensity. She was led back through the forest by the safest path, and I followed, unable to conceive of anything to do if my lover, stronger herself than any mountain, was broken as I had never seen her. All her worry, all her grief over your loss came out when she looked across the terrible valley, and I lost my way and had nothing I could do but follow her.

Your friend, Vedon, says you made it past the place of the mounds and spires. He speaks little of what he saw there when he found you, only that you saved him, that you yourself were safe, and that you pushed forward to the Mountain after sending him home. Those I asked in the tavern claim he seems different now, but I admit I knew him not at all before. He talked mostly to Glamis, who as you know is quick to build rapport with new people in the places we visit. I trust him when he says you were safe, and it bolsters my confidence that even now, you still live, though I wondered for a long time why you have not returned to us. Though we would have moved on to return home months ago, Glamis and I remained here, staying at the inn.

There is one story that gives me hope, and it is why I've waited until now to follow the road home directly to Nin. I waited a year and a day from the night Vedon says you disappeared into the Mountain. Some stories of Faerie relate that visitors to that country, who venture under the hills, spend only a day of their time with the People, while in the world above, time passes more quickly. I cannot imagine time moving more slowly than it has for Glamis and myself in this past year, where every moment of every day is drawn out with grief, but it may be that the gods portion out lengths of their thread of time differently at various moments of our lives.

Those who tell these tales of Faerie say that when the traveler in that land returns to earth, they may find that a hundred years or more have flown by, and if that is true, then I have no hope of ever seeing my daughter again. But others say—and here is where I fixed my hope—that the traveler's night may take only a year and a day of mortal time. I see today that this was not the case, and it is why Glamis and I finally follow the west wind and move on. But I do not give up hope. Not truly. For I know well from experience that anything might be possible—not in the limited rule-bound magic of Faerie but with the limitless possibilities of love.

I have left this message with Vedon to give you, while Glamis and I have returned to Nin, where I will continue to hope we will meet you, someday, when you return.

My beautiful little girl, please remember your mothers love you more than anything in this world and in whatever world you are in now.

With faith we will meet somehow again,

Your mothers,
Milanda and Glamis

Elsinore studied the letter over and over. At last, she folded it and put it in her bag within the cover of the book the Goddess had given her in the palace library. She considered the image on the cover for a moment, the turtle with the glaring eye. Unable to read the strange underworld script, Elsinore wondered oddly, incongruously, what the book would tell her if she could. Did it hold further answers? Had the Goddess given it to her for a reason? Had She known, whether looking through the glass or in some other fashion, what would become of Elsinore? The girl continued to sit in silence for some moments.

At last, she spoke to the old woman, who sat in a chair across the room, reading a book.

"How long has it been?" she asked, even though she dreaded the answer. The woman laid aside her book with a sigh and closed her eyes as if to remember.

"Sixty years," she said simply.

Sixty years, Elsinore thought. *Sixty years, for only the scant six seeds.* She closed her eyes and cursed herself as a tear stole down her cheek.

"The barkeep, Rosario, and his wife, Astra. What happened to them?"

"They passed some time ago. He sooner, she sometime later, but both died a long time ago."

"What about Vedon?"

The old woman sighed once more, looking uncertain and sad. "Vedon . . . isn't here anymore."

"What happened to him?" Elsinore asked, growing frustrated, but the woman said nothing.

This person is maddening.

It was not only her manner, either. Elsinore was not sure she didn't recognize her. Was she Vedon's widow or someone left behind when he took Elsinore's advice and left to explore, to live? She stared into the woman's eyes, and they sat in silence for a long moment more.

The woman finally stood with a sigh, ignoring Elsinore's last question. "I have something else for you." She stepped out of the room, leaving Elsinore alone with her thoughts.

Looking around, Elsinore's eye was drawn to the red cover of the book the woman had been reading. She walked over and picked it up. The title was *Love Poems and Songs of Intimacy*. She opened the cover and flipped through it, as if to prove to herself that that was really what it was.

She was so absorbed that she didn't notice the old woman return, and she jumped with a start and began to apologize. But when she saw what the woman held, she fell silent and dropped the book, too stunned to notice.

It was Elsinore's rooster doll.

"H-how . . . ?" Elsinore stuttered in disbelief as the woman handed it to her. "How did you get this?"

"Quite a few years after your mothers left—I can't remember how long exactly, but it was not very long ago; not nearly as long ago as when you left for the Mountain—someone else came to town looking for you. She asked around and found her way here. She was a tall, striking young woman.

"When you couldn't be found, she seemed a little sad but smiled strangely. I'll always remember that smile, and the way her bright eyes flashed in the sun. I can still picture how she walked away down the lane—just there, do you see? Where those yellow flowers grow? Later, when the seasons changed and the Season of Light came, they sprang up in the very earth where she had walked. Nothing had ever grown in that spot before, and I'd never seen any herbs or flowers like these ones, even in the books of my library. There was something special about that woman. She left this doll, and . . . she wanted it kept safe for you. And she told me to tell you: she will meet you one day in Sanisa."

Elsinore looked into the doll's button eyes. Some of its cloth was a little faded, but it was barely worn; it was uncertain how much time must have passed for it in the world. She hugged the soft plush to her chest and remembered; she tried to feel what had been lost. She thought of Folia, who she had left behind so long ago. She had left so many people behind.

"Thank you," Elsinore said, her anger melting away. "For everything." She put the doll gently in her bag, then took up her sword and swung it onto her back. She went to the door and looked out into the morning.

"If you . . ." Elsinore trailed off, looking at the woman again. She seemed so much older than Elsinore, but would she really be, after all the time that was lost?

"I hope you're glad here," she concluded. "I hope you've found something that makes you happy. Please . . . may the Goddess bless you. I hope She already has. Goodbye."

Outside in the street, Elsinore looked at the flowers the old woman had told her about. They were the same as the ones she had seen in the stone circle outside the forest. The stalks were about as tall as her forearm and hand, and they bore feathery yellow-green leaves topped with golden flowers. Little clusters of seeds fruited on some of the stalks, and Elsinore picked a few and shook them lightly into her hand. They were shaped like hearts.

Beneath the flowers, Risky sat cleaning themself with their tongue. The cat looked up at her curiously.

"Maow?"

"I dunno, babe, I couldn't tell you."

Elsinore pocketed the seeds, rubbed her head, and laughed a little. Adjusting her bag and sword, she walked on, to explore, to experience what had become of the living world in her absence. To learn the fate of her mothers, of her sisters and brothers at the temple, of her lover Folia. She knew, at last, that death was not the end. But she felt a gap in the depth of her heart, in a place that had once been full of love since the night she had been found in the woods, when Milanda comforted her, when Glamis listened to her name and Elsinore voiced who she was. She didn't know where to go, what to do, or how to fill that gap again.

She didn't know if she ever could.

But she knew she belonged here in the world. Elsinore was part of the world, one tiny part of the body of the Goddess, as her mothers had been, as Folia had been, as all life was.

She breathed the dewy air of the morning, squinted as the rising sun stung her eyes, and felt the soft furry tail of her companion against her leg. The weight of the past, the future, and life itself seemed bearable for even a brief moment, so she felt she could hold its incredible heaviness in her hand.

Smiling, and with Risky by her side, Elsinore set off into the morning.

Despite everything, she didn't cry.

Acknowledgments

Thanks first of all to Leo Otherland, Charlene Templeman, Theodore Niretac Tinker, and everyone at Balance of Seven for their support, for championing queer literature, and specifically for giving me the chance to share Elsinore's story with the world. Thanks to Ynes Freeman for help with marketing and promotional planning, and thanks to my friend and editor Dr. Nyri A. Bakkalian, whose encouragement and line editing helped prepare this book for publication.

Thanks to the incredible artist Rue Sparks for their striking and original cover, which is a better visual representation of the story and theme of *Princess of the Pomegranate Moon* than I could have imagined.

Special thanks to May Peterson for her invaluable early developmental editing work, which made this book so much stronger. Thanks also to my close friends: Michelle Kiker for giving me a home while I worked on the manuscript and for so long otherwise, Meg Eubank for her reading and feedback, and JP for providing valuable insight I was able to use in chapter six. Thanks to author friends Sarahlyn Bruck and Imogen Binnie for their valuable advice regarding writing and publishing, and to Kathryn Marshall for always cheering me on and being my oldest friend.

Thanks to Elizabeth Coffey Williams, Kendall Stephens, and everyone at Transway and the William Way LGBT Community Center in Philadelphia, who welcomed me into a community when I first came out and made my transition so welcome and safe. Without them, I would never have gotten as far as writing this book—both for their friendship and due to Elizabeth and Kendall's trailblazing work in film and activism.

Respect and kindness to my first cat friend, Ricardo Otto Potato, real name Otto Vo, the best friend I ever had, for showing me how Risky behaves.

More thanks than I can say, always, to Vera for your love, our life, and everything we have, share, and do together. I will love you forever, babe.

Finally, thanks to my brother, who has always stood by me, and to my parents, the most incredible and loving I could imagine having. Dad taught me everything about kindness, selflessness, and love. Mom—whether or not she was always aware of it—raised me to be the woman I am, and taught me to be curious and honest and to question authority and the power structures surrounding us. Everything I know about being a woman I learned from her, and all the best things I know about being a person in general I learned from them both. I love you and thank you for always being with me.

Appendix

Sources and Influences

The Gallae

A *Galla* was a member of a class of trans and third-gender mendicant priestesses who lived in the Mediterranean region until the fall of the western Roman empire (Roller 1999 and Lucker 2005). They spread with the worship of the mother goddess Cybele from Anatolia into Greece and Rome, where contemporary historians were for centuries at a loss to explain their queer gender identities and expressions.

Though assigned male at birth, the Gallae lived and presented as women, though Greek and Roman establishment writers fluctuated between describing them with masculine and feminine grammatical structures, and variously tried to define them (without their recorded input) as deficiently male, newly female, or something else entirely, a *tertium sexus*, as they were classified in Rome. Though often self-castrated, they were considered highly sexual, usually just in ways the patriarchal establishment struggled to understand.

One of the most famous literary depictions of the

Gallae, as well as one of the most well-known to use the feminine grammatical construct Gallae instead of the masculine *Galli*, was Catullus's poem 63, which retells the myth of the transition of Attis.

The Gallae were associated with a number of symbols and ideas, including worship of the Great Mother Cybele; the Goddess's home in the Phrygian sacred mountain, Mount Ida; taming or dispelling the wild cats or lions associated with the Goddess; playing the tympanum, or hand drum; and blessing important life events, such as births, marriages, and funerals, at the last of which they were known for professional lamenting. Their rites included ritually eating bread from the tympanum and drinking from the cymbal as part of a sacred gesture of recognition and initiation. They were also the priestesses in attendance at sacred sites such as the Ploutonion at Hierapolis.

The Ploutonion

A *Ploutonion*, or a *Plutonium* in Latin, was a Classical sanctuary to Hades or Pluto, typically built over a crevice or cave that emitted toxic carbon dioxide gas, which made the site's connection to the god of death obvious to ancient observers. One particular Ploutonion at Hierapolis was known for the Gallae attendants who would allow visitors to send birds and livestock into the gas's range as a sacrifice to the gods in exchange for a donation. The Gallae priestesses themselves would display their divine favor by entering the cave itself, and either by holding their breath, taking advantage of pockets of oxygen, or perhaps calling on the power of the Goddess, they would return to the surface unharmed, to the amazement of worshippers (Strabo 1924, 13.4.14, and Pliny the Elder

1855, 2.95). This association with the underworld, and the power to enter it and return unharmed, was attributed to gender-variant religious figures in humanity's oldest written records.

The Gala, Kurgarra, and Pilipili

The Romans speculated inconclusively about the origin of the name *Galla*. The general consensus among most writers at the time was that the name for the priestesses who arrived with their goddess Cybele from Anatolia derived from the Galatian Celts of that region. They also became linked with the river Gallos, the name of which also derived from the Galatians. Romans frequently associated the Gallae (written by many but by no means all contemporary historians as the masculine form *Galli* or singular *Gallus*) with a pun on the Latin word for rooster, *gallus*, which was also often punned on the Galatians and the Gauls (as "the bird of Gaul"). In his hymn to Cybele and Attis, "The Oration to the Mother of the Gods," Emperor Julian associated them with stars, punning the river Gallos with the celestial river, the galaxy. But a few modern scholars think the name probably has a more ancient origin more closely connected to transgender priestesses of another fertility goddess (see Lucker 2005 for more discussion of this etymology).

The Sumerian goddess Inanna was served by multiple related classes of temple priests and priestesses, including those called *gala*, *kurgarra*, and *pilipili* (Meador 2000). Gala shared a number of similarities with the Gallae beyond just their name: they were trans women temple priestesses of a great goddess and known for their role as ecstatic lamentation singers. The Sumerian gala or *galatur* ("junior gala") also featured in the myth of

Inanna's descent into Kur, the underworld, in which they and the kurgarra are created and dispatched by Enki, the god of life, to rescue the goddess when she has been killed and imprisoned by her sister Ereshkigal, the ruler of the Kur. Their ability to descend into and return from the underworld parallels the ability boasted by the Gallae in later centuries at the Ploutonion to enter the underworld cave and return unharmed.

According to Meador's interpretation, pilipili take more of what we would now call a transmasculine role, as another player in the "head-overturning" ritual by which Inanna is said to have the power to "turn men into women, and women into men." On the theory that the Mediterranean Gallae take their name ultimately from the gala, I posited a group of trans men, the *Pilli* (singular *Pillus*) who take their name from the pilipili. Gallae and Pilli then became the names I used in the story for trans women and trans men respectively.

Kurgarra was another name for transfeminine, or perhaps nonbinary or third-gender, figures in the temple of Inanna, who wielded swords in an ecstatic dance. Their name is linked to the Kur, which is literally "the mountain," within which is the passage to the underworld. Kurgarra means "little mountain" or "mound," probably child's talk for piles of feces, in reference to their supposed role as sexual bottoms. (See Meador 2000 and Wolkstein and Kramer 1983 for more about the gala, kurgarra, pilipili, and their roles and names).

The Sidhe

The literal meaning of the name *kurgarra* as "mounds," and its relation to the name of the otherworld, was really hard for me to get past, considering it was almost identical in meaning to part of the Irish name for the fairies, and the entrance to Faerie itself. These were the *aos sidhe*, the people of the fairy mounds, or *sidhe*—Neolithic pre-Celtic burial mounds that were the entrances to the otherworld of Faerie or the afterlife. This was the source of the name of the weeping fairy spirit, the *bean sidhe*, or banshee—literally "woman of the fairy mounds"—whose role as one who predicts death by lamenting recalls, to me at least, the role of the Sumerian gala and Cybeline Gallae as priestesses of the goddess known for lamenting at funerals. The word for a hypothetical male banshee would be *fear sidhe*, or farshee—a "man of the fairy mounds"—as the *fear gorta* translates to the "man of hunger." The *fear gorta* is a skeletal spirit of famine associated with the Great Hunger, or Irish Potato Famine, which was caused and exacerbated in large part by mismanagement, deliberate or otherwise, by English colonial landlords.

Fae

Most older scholarly work on the history of fairies and fairy belief uses the spellings *fairy* or *fay* for individual entities (Briggs 1976). The word fairy derives from Late Latin *fata*—"fate"—as in the three Fates, the MoiraI or Parcae. Fairies were conceived of much like those in Sleeping Beauty—Fate-like goddesses who would appear at births, weddings, and funerals to prophesy the mortal's fate (a role that, curiously, was also commonly performed historically by the Gallae in Rome and some other so-called "third-gender" peoples in other cultures).

Fata gradually came into English as *fay* via French *fée* and referred to the individual entities. The English suffix

-ry or *-ery*, as in bakery or harlotry, was appended to the word, and a state of enchantment or the involvement of the fay became *fay-ery*, or *fairy*.

Fairy, or Faerie, then became the term used for the world the fay dwelt in, a subterranean otherworld accessible beneath the Neolithic burial mounds called the sidhe, where time passes out of sync with the mortal world and where mortals who had been exchanged for changelings—fairies or effigies enchanted to take the mortal's form—may be encountered at the fairies' banquets and dances. Such stories show strong parallels with many tales about the world of the dead, especially the myths of Hades and Persephone; of Orpheus and Eurydice; and of Inanna, the galatur and kurgarra, and Inanna's consort Dumuzid. Indeed, some stories about Faerie make it explicit that the attendees encountered at the banquets are local people who died during the previous year.

English orthography was not standardized until the last few centuries and spellings for many words varied, so although the most common spellings are *fay* and *fairy*, some others proliferated. In recent years, the spelling *fae* has become popular on social media. The earliest draft of this story used the spelling *fay*, until in a later draft, I realized that if I spelled it *fae* I could introduce a visual parallel not just to the word *Gallae* but also to *faeces*, as in the hag's angry joke in the lost city (kurgarra / mound (of shit), sidhe/mound, fae/faeces). The unnecessary poop joke that unites the kurgarra to the sidhe to the fae was my primary motivation for using the spelling *fae* instead of *fay*. Also, paradoxically, I decided it just looks prettier than *fay*.

On the Anathema of Iron

For speculative but compelling discussion of the relationship between queer and trans folk, the fairies' fear of iron, and iron as a symbol for industrialization, capitalism, and oppression, see Leslie Feinberg's *Transgender Warriors*. Of particular interest are the chapters on Joan of Arc, and the Welsh anti-tollgate and anti-enclosure rebellions, the leaders of which were workers assigned male at birth but who nonetheless, for one reason or another, wore dresses and wigs and took women's names and titles.

Enby

Elsinore is transparently a self-insert Mary Sue, so like me, she is not just a trans woman but also nonbinary. I usually identify myself as an enby, a pronunciation of the initials *NB*. I particularly like the term *enby* because it sounds like a vaguely magical, mysterious old forgotten word like *Galla* or *Faerie*, instead of a dry descriptor like *nonbinary*. It also has the benefit of obscuring that *nonbinary* is saying what I'm not (not binary), rather than what I actually am (a mysterious, ancient, meaningless entity with no real origin or etymology).

Enby also makes me think of certain terms in Sumerian. The name of the god of life, Enki, who created the galatur and kurgarra, has a similar sound and means "Lord of the Earth (or of the Kur)." *En* meant "lord" or "priest" and was the gender-neutral title of the high priest or priestess of a temple. It was most famously the title in the first part of the name of Enheduanna—perhaps the earliest known named writer whose works have survived to the present day—who was the en priestess of the temple of the moon god Nanna in the city of Ur (Meador 2000).

I searched Sumerian dictionaries for a potential

meaning for *bi* or *by* and came up with a root that meant "to speak," which was perfect to me for describing people known for lamentation rituals. It also ties in once again to "fairy," which comes from the Latin *fata*, the Fates, ultimately from the Latin root *fari*, "to speak." I'm pretty sure translating *enbi* as "high priest/ess of speaking" isn't remotely grammatically correct in actual Sumerian, but I decided it's close enough for a far-off future when language would have drifted quite a bit.

I poetically conflated Sumerian and Classical Anatolian/Greek/Roman trans goddess priest/ess roles with fairies / aos sidhe to create the gallae, pilli, and enbi of this story.

Hair

The Sumerian kurgarra and *sagursag* eunuch priests were known for ritually donning a unique mode of dress where one side of their body was dressed in masculine attire and the other in feminine. This involved wearing their hair long on one side and shaved on the other. When Elsinore and Ardena shave the sides of their hair in the story, it's a reference both to the kurgarra and sagursag, as well as the modern fashion of undercuts and sideshaves, something that is anecdotally particularly popular among many nonbinary folks. Obviously, people follow whatever fashion trends for their own reasons, and I don't mean at all to imply that nonbinary folks are "half" one binary gender and half another; Elsinore is not, nor am I. But a fashionable hair style is a fashionable hair style, and ancient Sumerian third-gender ritual garb is ancient Sumerian third-gender ritual garb.

Cutting a lock of hair and leaving it as an offering also recalled to me the folktale of the Galla and the Lion.

The Galla and the Lion

One recurrent story featuring the Gallae is a story of one who, wandering the wilderness, encounters a lion in the mountains. The lion approaches, threatening to attack, and the priestess raises a commotion in the form of her usual ecstatic dance to the Great Mother Cybele, or Rhea, loudly banging on her tympanum, until the lion is frightened away and leaves her alone. In thanks to the Goddess for sparing her life, the Galla then cuts a lock of her hair and leaves it as an offering (Nisbet 2020).

This wasn't consciously the origin of the episode featuring the sphinx who eventually reveals themself to be one and the same as Elsinore's cat familiar, Risky, but when I noticed the parallel, I added the detail regarding the use of the tympanum to cast the spell. Cybele and Her Gallae's association with lions was, however, the basis for my decision to give Elsinore a cat as a familiar.

That, and my love of my late cat, Otto, who left us shortly after I completed major revisions of this novel in December 2021.

Colors

The traditional color associated with the Gallae in Rome was yellow, in their saffron robes and dyed, if not natural, blonde hair (which Roman writers would have associated with the blonde Celtic Galatians they insisted were the origin of the Gallae). I have no idea why that is, but in my personal experience, modern trans women often seem to like purple and turquoise. Like real-late eighties / early nineties kind of magenta/teal combos, so it is probably just one feature of my cohort's nineties nostalgia aesthetic. At least, this has always been my favorite color scheme, so maybe I'm reading into it too much. If I really push it,

I could argue that turquoise and purple are just saturated variations of the light blue and pink of the trans pride flag. I don't know that I'm going to argue that, but I *could*. I justified this color scheme in the story as a religious thing, but really, I just like it.

I do want to note that Attis, the castrated transfeminine consort of Cybele who is the prototype of the Gallae, is associate with pine trees, transformed into one after their death in Ovid and born out of a pinecone from a pine tree in their origin myth. The blue-green needle leaves of the pines that grow at the foot of the Mountain is echoed in Elsinore's dyed hair.

Dies Sanguinis

The name Sanisa, the city where the Goddess Tiranna's temple is located, was derived from Dies Sanguinis, the Day of Blood, a Roman holiday held near the spring equinox. This was characterized by frenzied self-cutting and castration rituals performed by the Gallae in honor of the death and castration of Attis, followed a few days later by the Hilaria festival of Cybele, which included celebration of Attis's resurrection / gender transition. Other celebrants (possibly a different name for the same participants?) were the *Bellonarii* of Bellona, a goddess of war who, in Rome and Anatolia, was conflated with Cybele and other equivalent mother goddesses.

The Goddess

The goddess Heqakigal is a syncretism of Hecate, Greek goddess of witchcraft and the underworld, and Ereshkigal, Sumerian goddess of the underworld and Inanna's sister, who figures in the myth of the latter's descent into the underworld and whose pregnancy-like bodily pains are soothed by the sympathetic lamentations of the gala and kurgarra. *Tiranna* is Sumerian for "rainbow," as well as the name of a minor goddess of the rainbow. The word literally means "forest of the sky" (though this may have been due to the Sumerian words for "bow" and "forest" being homophones), which for me was evocative of the rainbow halo around the moon that I named the Pomegranate Moon, as well as the modern rainbow flag of queer pride. The name is also somewhat similar in my eyes to Inanna, whose myths and rituals I combined with aspects of Cybele to create Tiranna.

The conception of the Goddess that we and everything around us are part of the living body of the Earth, and furthermore that the Earth Herself is part of a greater system of existence through the entire universe, is a common one in modern neopaganism. Cybele was commonly thought of as the goddess whose body is everything, as a sort of ancient neo-Platonic pantheism. It's also something I found really easy to visualize when tripping.

Language

Elsinore, the people of the river valley, and the dwellers under the Mountain do not actually speak Latin or Sumerian (much less English, for that matter), but I used some Latin- and Sumerian-inspired words and sounds for many of the words and names in the book. My Sumerian language research was mostly done using John Halloran's Sumerian Lexicon at www.sumerian.org. However, I do not understand Sumerian in any way, so the many errors and poetic licenses taken in word meanings and translations in this story are my fault entirely.

A Warning

The proposed long-term nuclear waste disposal warning is from the Human Interference Task Force and Sandia National Laboratories. They are well-known for the lines "This place is a message . . . and part of a system of messages" and "This place is not a place of honor," as well as for the proposal to incorporate a massive field of enormous blocks or spikes making the landscape around a containment site forbidding and unsuitable for farming and habitation. I liked the idea of combining it with the warning "Abandon all hope, ye who enter here" at the entrance of Dante's Inferno, and with the toxic Ploutonion entrance to the underworld described above (especially since the Latin spelling of a Ploutonion temple would be *Plutonium*).

The proposed long-term nuclear waste disposal warning is widely used in popular culture, though my knowledge of that isn't comprehensive. My favorite use of the warning in media is in the song "There's Nothing Here Worth Dying For" by Ada Rook and Devi McCallion of Black Dresses, which I privately like to imagine plays together with their song "Look Away" over the ending credits of the imaginary movie adaptation of *Princess of the Pomegranate Moon* that exists in my head.

Pregnant Mare's Urine

Until the late nineties, the most common estrogen medication used in hormone replacement therapy (HRT) for menopausal cis women and for trans women transitioning was Premarin, a coagulated estrogen made with pregnant mare's urine (hence the brand name *Premarin*). It was eventually mostly phased out with the introduction of bio-identical synthesized estradiol, which has much lower risk of blood clots and other side effects, as well as being easier and much more ethical to produce.

A very highly speculative theory was put forward by Timothy Taylor in his book *The Prehistory of Sex* that pregnant mare urine was drunk to induce feminizing effects by transfeminine shamans like the Scythian Enarei in ancient times. This theory appears to be based on a misreading of Ovid's descriptions of the use of mare's urine in cosmetics, as well as a tenuous understanding of shamanistic practices of drinking reindeer urine containing traces of hallucinogenic mushrooms, but acceptance of the theory has become very widespread regardless. I am extremely doubtful about the accuracy of this theory, but:

- this is a fantasy novel, and I don't see anybody questioning the historicity of invisibility and fireball magic and,

- it takes place in the far future, and Elsinore's use of pregnant mare urine as the basis for her hormone potions could easily be descended from knowledge of the Old Ones' use of Premarin, or it could be newly discovered by the Gallae after the renewal of the earth.

Either way, this book is not meant to indicate my stance on the speculation regarding the use of horse piss HRT by historical Enarei or Gallae.

Magic and the Dying Earth

Elsinore's world of Eridu is one that feels like it is dying, where the moon is broken and falling and the seasons are confused and uneven. It felt appropriate that the magic should be evocative of that world—the spells the gallae and pilli learn must be memorized with careful study, only a few at a time, and upon being cast, they will flee the magician's memory. This magic system is inspired by that in Jack Vance's Dying Earth series, which features a world so far in the future that the last vestiges of humanity cling to life while the sun burns out as a red giant and the laws of nature break down. If it seems familiar, Vance's stories are also the inspiration for the magic system in Dungeons and Dragons.

Other fiction that influenced the book is too varied to recount here, but particular points of reference besides Vance include Lord Dunsany's *The Gods of Pegana*, Ursula K. Le Guin's Earthsea Cycle, Michael Moorcock's Elric Saga, Stephen King's *The Gunslinger*, Jessica Amanda Salmonson's *The Swordswoman*, and Hayao Miyazaki's *Nausicaä of the Valley of the Wind*, both the film and the manga.

Shakespeare

As for the characters' names, whenever I had trouble coming up with a character name while playing D&D, I would fall back on lifting a place name from Shakespeare. Also, if you don't think at least some gay men and trans women were taking advantage of the Elizabethan/Jacobean ban of women onstage by playing women so they could wear dresses, then you're out of your mind. From the other direction, I don't have a print of Alphonse Mucha's portrait of Sarah Bernhardt as Hamlet above my altar for nothing.

If I'm really being honest, though, my habit of naming characters after random things from Shakespeare probably came from the Disney Afternoon cartoon *Gargoyles*.

The Dream

Taking very few liberties to fit it into the setting of the story, Folia's dream is an adaptation of recurring dreams I experienced throughout my life from the time I was a teenager.

In some of these dreams, I am lost in a maze-like public women's restroom, pursued by a dread that I don't belong there. (What common transgender anxiety could that possibly represent?) Frequently, in these dreams, I would finally find myself alone in the darkness, staring into a black mirror. In the years before I came out of the closet and transitioned, I would look into this mirror and see myself as a woman in the reflection. After years or decades of recurrence, this dream finally ceased once I began to transition.

BIBLIOGRAPHY

Briggs, Katharine. 1976. *An Encyclopedia of Fairies: Hobgoblins, Brownies, Bogies, and Other Supernatural Creatures.* New York: Pantheon Books.

———. 1978. *The Vanishing People: Fairy Lore and Legends.* New York: Pantheon Books.

Catullus, Gaius Valerius. 2005. "Poem 63." *The Poems of Catullus.* Translated by Peter Green. Berkeley: University of California Press.

Feinberg, Leslie. 1996. *Transgender Warriors.* Boston: Beacon Press.

Lucker, K. A. 2005. *The Gallae: Transgender Priests of Ancient Greece, Rome, and the Near East.* Sarasota: New College of Florida.

Meador, Betty de Shong. 2000. *Inanna, Lady of Largest Heart: Poems of the Sumerian High Priestess Enheduanna.* Austin: University of Texas Press.

Nisbet, Gideon. 2020. *Epigrams from the Greek Anthology.* Oxford: Oxford University Press.

Pliny the Elder. 1855. *The Natural History.* Translated by John Bostock and H. T. Riley. London: Taylor and Francis. http://data.perseus.org/citations/urn:cts:latinLit:phi0978.phi001.perseus-eng1:2.95.

Roller, Lynn. 1999. *In Search of God the Mother: The Cult of Anatolian Cybele.* Berkeley: University of California Press.

Strabo. 1924. *The Geography of Strabo.* Edited by H. L. Jones. Cambridge, MA: Harvard University Press.

O'Hartigan, Margaret Deirdre. "The Rites of Cybele and Attis." *TransSisters: The Journal of Transsexual Feminism* 4 (spring): 28–29. https://archive.org /details/transsistersjou1994unse_0.

Wolkstein, Diane, and Samuel Noah Kramer. 1983. *Inanna, Queen of Heaven and Earth.* New York: HarperCollins.

ABOUT THE AUTHOR

Emily Wynne is a devoted pantheist neopagan who tries to express her reverence for the earth and the stars in her writing. Her shelves are cluttered with books, toys, and wargaming minifigures, including a sorceress painted to look like Elsinore. Her favorite holidays are the Spring Equinox and Halloween.

Emily currently resides in a lovely city in Lenapehoking. She lives with her girlfriend, who is her star and her heart, and their family of stuffed animals called Bear Gang.

Princess of the Pomegranate Moon is her first novel, and she is presently writing further adventures for Elsinore, which she hopes to share very soon. Her poetry and essays can be found at emilywynne.net.

www.ingramcontent.com/pod-product-compliance
Lightning Source LLC
Chambersburg PA
CBHW060859210726
48293CB00006B/1880